Lottie Brook is the bestselling author of six previous novels under the name Anna Mansell. She's an alumna of BBC Writersroom (Cornish Voices), an emerging playwright and a New Associate of New Perspectives Theatre Company. Originally from the Peak District, she recently returned to live there full-time with her husband, two children and rescue Romanian Shepherd dog, Henry.

The CHEAP DATES Club

LOTTIE BROOK

Harper North

HarperNorth
Windmill Green
24 Mount Street
Manchester M2 3NX

A division of
HarperCollins*Publishers*
1 London Bridge Street
London SE1 9GF

www.harpercollins.co.uk

HarperCollinsPublishers
Macken House
39/40 Mayor Street Upper
Dublin 1
D01 C9W8

First published by HarperNorth in 2023

1 3 5 7 9 10 8 6 4 2

A catalogue record for this book
is available from the British Library

ISBN 978-0-00-862357-9

Printed and bound in Great Britain by
CPI Group (UK) Ltd, Croydon

For Daisy, with untold gratitude!

1

Isla perched on a coral, velvet barstool and peeked out from beneath her new heavy fringe. On reflection, she wished she hadn't let the hairdresser persuade her into having it because she did not look like either Claudia Winkleman or Dawn O'Porter and now she had to endure the months and months it would take for it to grow out, or attempt regular home trims to keep it at peak length, when everybody knows that no good can ever come of wielding nail clippers to one's own hair.

'Isla?' said a voice from behind her. She excitedly spun around on her chair, ever the optimist, as a be tweeded, ruddy-cheeked man lunged at her, planting wet lips on her carefully contoured cheek. She wasn't really a fan of contouring but the assistant on the counter in Boots had been all over a new product range that would bring out Isla's best features – by painting on ones that didn't really exist. She'd been prepared to try anything that might give her some dating luck on account of the fact that this was her third date this week, her fifth this month, and it was only June the sixteenth.

Date Number Five pulled up a stool beside her, his sweaty hand finding its way to suffocate hers as he studied her face. 'Sorry I'm late, got stuck behind a Toyota Yaris on my way in. Don't want to be sexist but it was a woman driver and you know what they say, hey? Wow, though, you're even better in real life.' He studied her from various angles as he sat down. 'I wasn't sure about your photos, the one in the bar looked a bit poncy, if you don't mind me saying. What was it you were drinking?'

'Erm . . . probably just a gin and tonic.'

'Ooh, lah-di-dah! Could have been worse. Thought it was one of them cocktails.' He gazed around the bar as if it was the first time he'd ever been in such a place. 'Nice to see someone who actually looks like their photo, mind.'

'Right . . . ' she said, smiling, wondering just how many years ago his own profile photo had been taken. What she'd thought were boyish good looks on a man kissing his thirties, was clearly, boyish good looks on a man who likes to lie about his age.

'So bored of turning up to a date to find they've just not made an effort. Or worse, they've sent their mum.' He paused, thought about what he'd said, then laughed so hard that Isla worried he might pull a muscle. 'If you're a woman still dating when you hit thirty, there's got to be summat up with you, am I right?'

'Well, I—'

'But you . . . ' He licked his lips lasciviously. 'We'd make quite the handsome couple, wouldn't we.'

This wasn't a question, he barely paused for breath. Not that Isla knew what she'd say anyway.

'*And* you look like you could handle a bit of muck.'

'Sorry?'

He howled again, grazing her ankle with a not-entirely-clean boot. It left a streak of mud on the only unladdered pair of tights she had.

He narrowed his eyes at her. 'Cow!'

'Pardon?'

'You know that thing where you try and match a face to an animal.'

'No?'

'I'm a bear. Apparently. No, you, you're a cow. And that's not a bad thing, some of our milkers are absolute beauties. It's the eyelashes. And the fringe. Look, here,' he whipped his phone out and pulled up a photo of a cow that did have a particularly spectacular fringe. Isla self-consciously touched her own. He'd mentioned on his profile that he worked on a farm up Loxley way, north Sheffield. She'd imagined that would mean he'd be hard working, fit and connected to nature somehow. She had not imagined being likened to a cow.

'Right, let's get this party started.' He clicked his fingers in the direction of a waitress who death-stared him before painting on a smile and weaving her way through the tables, pad and pen charged to take their order. Date Number Five, having shifted his stool so close Isla could smell the faint aroma of manure, scanned the drinks menu. He ran his finger down the whites, reds and prosecco, landing on the champagne. 'Ever tried this stuff? I'm more of a pint man me sen, John Smith's'll do me generally speaking. Still, you look like a goer so let's get a bottle.'

Isla stared.

'I'm kidding. Or am I? I am. Or am I?' Date Number Five bellowed a laugh: head back, mouth wide. He had two fillings and a bit of spit that connected his upper and lower teeth. His gullet glistened in the brasserie half-light and Isla wondered if this was going to be a new record for the shortest date she'd ever been on. And the most expensive if they were going Dutch on champagne.

'No, I *am* kidding. Costs a fortune, tastes rank. What'll you drink?'

'Right. A . . . gin and tonic, please.'

He raised his eyebrows at her as if he really did think gin and tonic was a cut above. She wished she could afford a double.

'And I'll take a pint of bitter, thanks.'

Date Number Five then proceeded to tell Isla all about himself: dairy farmer, though they're starting to dabble in beef too. Forever knee-deep in cow shit or out in a field on his tractor. On the rare occasion he wasn't head to toe in overalls, usually when his mum was cooking up a Sunday roast, he tinkered with an old Massey Ferguson that his grandad used to run. It was stored out in one of the barns that one day he was going to turn into a place to live, but for now he was fine at home with his mum, dad, three sisters, four dogs, two cats and the occasional calf if the mum had rejected it.

Ten solid minutes later, the drinks arrived. 'And are you ready to order?'

Date Number Five fixed stern eyes on the waitress. 'Your meat, the steak. Where does it come from?'

She smiled sweetly, earning every penny of a future tip. 'Dale Farm, out near—'

'Oh, yes. Brincliffe, James, I knew his son George from Young Farmers. James taught us both a thing or two about animal husbandry, if you get my drift.' He nudged Isla's knee, winking. Isla wasn't sure she wanted to guess.

'They rear a pretty effective Dexter. Succulent. Ha! Just how I like my women.'

He turned back to the waitress. If this had been the 1970s Isla was fairly sure he'd have smacked her on the arse. Surely men like this didn't really exist? 'We'll have one each. Well done, please. I hear enough mooing day-to-day. Don't wanna hear it off me plate too.'

Isla must have looked horrified because he swiftly added, 'Not veggie are you? Or worse, vegan?'

'Erm, no.' She was too shocked to defend the idea of not eating meat or his assumptions that she wanted steak, and for this date to continue. 'I quite fancied the salmon, though.'

'Salmon? Christ! On a diet? Hey, I've met women like you before. You order salmon and veg then proceed to steal all my chips. Well, not on my watch. She'll have the same as me.'

The waitress looked at Isla, perhaps waiting for her to offer up what she actually wanted to eat, but Isla's optimism had fast depleted and now she was tired. At the start of her dating journey, she would have made her excuses and left, but something about the last few months, and the last few dates, had all but sucked away any hutzpah she once had.

'The same as him, thanks.'

The waitress went away with their order. Date Number Five knocked back his pint, slamming the empty glass down. 'So, what else do you want to know? What can I tell you? I've got my own hair, my own bank account and no children. Well, none that I know about, eh!'

'That's, er, great. Erm, would you excuse me for just a moment,' Isla stood. 'I just . . . I must . . . I'll be back in a minute.'

'Come on, come on!' She was hiding in the bathroom, crossing everything that housemate Sophie would pick up. Sophie had promised she'd call Isla mid-date if she needed an excuse to leave. All Isla had to do was let her know and she would feign an emergency, then the pair could entertain a post-date debrief at the rickety dining table in the kitchen of their Walkley house share.

'Hi, this is Sophie, I can't take your call right now, but if you'd like to leave a message—'

Isla hung up. Instead she tapped out an SOS WhatsApp to the group 'Christmas Girls', so named because that was pretty much the only time any of her oldest friends from school actually got together anymore. Ella, Poppy and Molly.

Ella was trying for a baby with new husband Greg. Poppy was blissfully in love with her childhood sweetheart, Steve, the one they all thought had got away but reappeared last Christmas and the pair were now inseparable, and Molly was in a brand-new relationship with some bloke, Matt, who she met on a train. Who meets someone on a train and then gets to date them!? Despite this, one of them must be available to help her out . . .

> Terrible date. Send help in the form of a phone call. PLEASE!
>
> Anyone?
>
> HELP!

She dropped her phone back into her pocket, looked herself dead in the eye, adjusting the fringe. Maybe she should just dig deep for the strength to walk away. Maybe she was done with dating. Maybe she shouldn't have left her coat at the table. Did she really look like a cow?

'Wondered where you'd got to!' boomed Date Number Five as she reluctantly sat back down, closely followed by the equally brave-faced waitress. He winked, leaning back for his plate of desecrated cow to be placed before him. 'Now then, you're going to enjoy that. You can thank me later!'

Isla endured her steak, certain now more than ever that she really did prefer it medium rare. She also endured the subsequent hour and a half as Date Number Five 'impressed' her with stories of his days cutting school to work the land, his previous disastrous dates, and his ex-girlfriend, who actually sounded entirely lovely. His apathy for Jeremy Clarkson and Diddly Squat Farm was the only thing they agreed on.

There was no rescue phone call from Sophie or the Christmas Girls. And no pause in his charm offensive for Isla to make her excuses to leave. With one final click of his fingers, for which Isla was pretty sure the waitress had put a hex on him, the bill arrived.

'You strike me as a modern woman, am I right? Sometimes even feminism has its place,' he said, picking food out of a molar with his index finger. He inspected it. Raised his eyebrows in approval before enjoying the last morsel of his dinner direct from his fingernail.

Paid up, sick at the amount of money she'd just wasted on a man who said the waitress didn't need a tip because they were all getting paid a salary, Isla escaped Date Number Five's clutches, leaving him to stagger towards Wetherspoons. But not before he'd stated, 'To be honest with you, love, you're not really my type. Great face, but I prefer a girl with a bit more . . . up top.' He'd waved his arms in the general direction of her boobs as if that was reason enough to reject her, despite the fact she'd already rejected him. Isla snatched her coat into her chest in dismay.

She pulled out her phone to check her bank balance through half-closed, post yet-another-expensive date, eyes. £7.15. And still a week until pay day. She dialled Sophie. It went straight to voicemail. She tried Ella and Poppy, it just rang out. She tried Molly, relief washing over her as she picked up.

'Hey you.'

'Hey, did you not see my message?'

'Oh, yeah, sorry . . . I did and then . . . ' Molly started giggling.

A voice in the background told Isla all she needed to know. 'Intercity 125 Matt's round then?'

There was a rustling of the phone. 'Stop it, just a second,' said Molly in muffled tones. 'Intercity? What you on about?'

'It's a train. Dad used to collect them. Never mind.'

'Sorry, are you OK? Do you need anything?'

'I'm fine. Just wanted to complain about yet another hideous date. Honestly, I am so over it. They're all—'

'Oh, Isla, I definitely want to have this chat, it's just that, now's not . . . could we . . . ' Giggles. Muffled words. Neck kisses. There may not have been neck kisses but judging by the state of the love bites on Molly's neck on the last Insta story she posted, Isla imagined there were neck kisses.

'Don't worry. It's fine,' she said. Surely love bites were the reserve of lusty teens?

'I'm sorry, Isla. I really am.'

Not women in their mid-twenties who knew better. 'It's fine. I'll call you soon.'

'I love you. Another time! I promise.'

Isla hung up, trying to ignore the jealousy that surged through her veins.

This was unsustainable.

Expensive dates in bougie bars with douchebag men who seemed only to want the version of a woman Isla wasn't: more of a career woman, more of a family woman, quieter, louder, bigger, smaller, bottle blonde, or pillar-box red, because who really wants a brunette if she doesn't look like Megan Fox?

Or worse, expensive dates in bougie bars with men who made out they had liked her (and her malty brown hair), then ghosted her, time and time again.

And now she was stranded in Sheffield City Centre. Having to get home, the cheapest way possible, to save the last of her monthly wages.

Looking up at the night sky, a drop of rain landed right on the end of her heavily contoured nose. She pulled her jacket up over her head before the heavens opened and, keys through fingers in one hand, phone ready to call someone, anyone, in the other, she made the slow, hilly walk home. Alone.

2

Isla heavy-breathed her way through her front door, having run the last bit up the hill because no matter how safe she generally felt when she was in her little bedsit, there was something less than appealing about being a lone female wandering the streets of Walkley.

'Breathe!' she told herself, hands on knees, trying to recalibrate her lung capacity.

She flung her wet coat off onto the banister of a staircase that didn't go anywhere. The house had been split into three flats with a shared kitchen and bathroom, and the landlord had just blocked off her staircase with a bit of plasterboard. When Samia, a student at Sheffield Uni, used to live there, they'd often tap out Morse code to agree on whose room they were going to watch the *Eastenders* omnibus in. She missed Samia. Jay, the new housemate in Samia's room, didn't like *Eastenders.*

She reached for the last dregs of a bottle of red she'd been treating herself to a thimble-full of each night since last Monday, grabbed two glasses and tiptoed across the hallway to Sophie's door. She knocked. Then waited. Knocked again. Just as she was about to give up, the door creaked open a tiny slit.

'Isla!'

Isla held up the glasses. 'Hair's breadth of shit wine while I tell you how awful my date was?'

'Um . . . '

'Oh, interrupting, am I?'

Sophie was a big fan of one-night stands, though usually when she had a Tinder date round, she placed the Do Not Disturb sign she'd liberated from a Premier Inn on the door handle so Isla knew to stay well clear.

'Yes, and no.'

Isla glanced down at the duvet Sophie was rolled within and tried to peek through the door gap. 'OK, yes, and yes, but actually, you may as well come in. Mark's been round. Hang on though.'

Mark. The landlord. He rarely phoned never mind came round and Sophie's tone did not bode well. Isla waited with the door closed. Muffled voices. The squeaking of floorboards. At the point Isla began to feel a bit awkward, Sophie's door opened fully and Isla was invited in . . . to see new housemate Jay in a pair of joggers and a T-shirt, snuggled up under the duvet Sophie had been wearing. She was now dressed in shorts and an Oodie, hopping into bed beside him.

'Oh!' Isla could feel her chest and neck flush. The room had a certain energy though neither looked particularly sheepish, not that they had to, consenting adults and all that. They weren't especially pink-cheeked or mid/post-sex haired either, but still, as they sat there snuggled up together in their comfies, it was clear that this definitely was not just a chilled evening in, watching telly with a housemate.

Isla readjusted her top, wishing she'd got changed out of date-night clothes before venturing over the hallway, or at least taken her date-night bra off. It had been digging into her shoulders all night and clearly hadn't been doing a particularly efficient job of boosting what she had, given Date Number Five's less than glowing review.

'Sit down,' said Sophie, nodding over to the chair by a desk in front of the window. Isla did as instructed and now faced the two of them. Their heads were cocked to the same side and their little fingers touched above the (synthetic) duck down. 'So yeah,' Sophie's hand waved between herself and Jay. 'This kind of happened,' she grinned.

'I can see that.'

'I mean, this wasn't the first time.'

'I don't think I need any detail.'

'No. Sure. I just mean, we've been . . . '

Isla raised her eyebrows.

'It all happened so fast.'

Jay nudged Sophie with a familiarity that picked at Isla's vulnerability. 'She deleted Tinder tonight,' he said. His little finger entwined Sophie's properly then their hands clasped fully. There was a tone of gentle teasing to his voice but Sophie flushed with the kind of look that people falling in love have; his teasing received with the gentleness it was given. 'Pretty big deal, apparently.'

Isla swallowed. 'Very big,' she agreed.

Sophie sat up a bit, putting a cigarette paper's distance between the two of them as if sensing Isla's mood. 'I mean, it's early days. Obvs. But . . . he's all right. I suppose.'

Isla cleared her throat. 'That's lovely. I'm really happy for you. For you both.' She knew it was important to be supportive and grown up about this new development, and she really did want Sophie to be happy, of course she did. But she couldn't entirely ignore the stab in her heart. And groin, to be fair – she'd had more than a passing thought about Jay since he moved in, four-ish weeks ago, arriving on their doorstep with a Fjällräven backpack and a box of well-thumbed books. Isla had always fancied dating someone who actually read. That's probably why she'd said yes to Date Number Two, Peter from the charity bookshop up Devonshire Street. Turned out he only volunteered there because it was good for getting dates, and the last book he claimed to have read was *Lord of the Flies* in Year Nine. He'd said that not much happened but the swearing was good.

'So, Mark then.' Isla smiled as broadly as she possibly could. 'He came round? That's not good.'

'No . . . ' Sophie and Jay exchanged looks.

The stab in Isla's heart (groin) was fast replaced with a sense of foreboding.

There was a pause.

Sophie screwed up her nose then said, 'The rent's going up.'

Isla's heart sank.

'Cost-of-living stuff, or something. Says his mortgages have gone up.'

Isla groaned unsympathetically. 'His mortgages. Plural. My heart bleeds.'

'He was really nice about it, to be fair,' said Jay. 'Very apologetic. Left us a bottle of Claret in the kitchen.'

'A bottle of Claret won't pay my rent,' spat Isla. 'And *you've* only just moved in, how is that even fair? To put your rent up this soon!'

'Everyone's in the same boat, aren't they?' said Jay, rubbing Sophie's thumb with his.

She covered his hand with her free one as if hiding the reassuring gesture. Isla looked at them both and just about managed to hold back from saying, *Are we? Really!* She'd read something about being in the same boat on Instagram but couldn't quite bring it to mind when needed. Something about same storm, different boats. Whatever. This was bad.

The three of them sat in silence before Isla shook her head, grabbed for her glasses and the last bit of wine she'd been prepared to share. She tucked the chair beneath the desk with her foot. "I'll leave you to it. Looks like I've got a spreadsheet to cry over in the vain hope I can make more cutbacks.'

'You OK?' asked Sophie, climbing out of her love-filled duvet cocoon.

'How much?'

'Pardon?'

'How much is it going up by? What do I need to try and find?'

'£60 for rent.'

'Each?!'

'And . . . '

Sophie and Jay shared a knowing glance.

'Come the autumn, he's going to have to increase the bills too. £100 for gas and electric.'

Isla's legs turned jelly-like. '£100, so, £160 a month? Where are we supposed to find £160 a month from?'

'He really was sorry.'

'Yeah? Wonder if the bank manager will take my landlord's regret as a down payment for the extension to my overdraft?'

'Do we have bank managers anymore?' said Sophie, trying for light-hearted.

'You know what I mean!' The wobble on Isla's bottom lip was giving away her position.

'Isla.' Sophie reached out for Isla's elbow.

She stepped back. 'Sorry. I'm going.'

'Isla. Come and sit down.'

'Yeah, let's get the wine he left,' said Jay, making as if to get up.

Isla couldn't bear it. 'No. Thanks. You two have it. I've had a belly full after tonight anyway. Top tip. Steak should never ever be cooked well done. And if your date tells you that you look like a cow, however much they might think that they're flirting, you should absolutely, one hundred per cent, leave.' She held up the remnants of wine she'd been cradling. 'I'm going to finish this then spend the rest of my days indulging in corporation pop.' Jay looked confused. 'Tap water! Corporation pop is tap water, Jay. On account of it coming out of the taps and the corporation being the ones to provide it to us. Or something. Back in the day. I don't know, it's what me mum used to call it. Look, I'll . . . I'll see you tomorrow. Probably.' She fumbled with the door. 'Thanks for the update and yay for you two. Lovely news. Couldn't be happier for you both. Really.'

The door slammed a bit harder than she intended and she almost turned back around to apologise before tears spilled onto her cheeks so she rushed into her room, relieved herself of the wine and dropped onto the sofa. She'd already cancelled Netflix. She couldn't get a slower, less effective internet connection. Her phone had been pay-as-you-go for months and she hadn't added to her savings tin that was supposed to get her a flight to wherever her mum and dad happened to be this autumn but could probably only get her as far as Barnsley. She loved that they were enjoying their retirement, seeing the world – or Europe at least – but she missed them. She wanted one of her dad's big hugs and to sit and watch rubbish telly with her mum.

She also missed having someone to sit under a duvet with. Someone she could tell about her rent going up and have a little cry on their shoulder. It's not that she couldn't cope alone, but stuff like this made it extra tiring to have to.

She looked around her bedsit: small, dark, stuffy in the summer, freezing in winter . . . and lonely. She buried her head into the I Heart Malaga pillow her mum and dad brought back from their last trip. That would have to do.

estranged since a somewhat fiery holiday in the South of France, so for Leigh, her passion for the parrot came as something of a shock. Not one to disrespect her grief, however, he relented. It was also a surprise, therefore, that when Serena walked out on their marriage, a year ago practically to the day, she absolutely could not take Tarquin with her on account of the fact that her new boyfriend, celebrity personal trainer, Simon, was allergic to birds. 'He has allergic alveolitis,' she had said, with a self-righteousness she'd normally reserved for coffee-shop employees when they didn't have the appropriate milk for her chai lattes.

Leigh later googled allergic alveolitis and was mildly amused to learn that it was also known as pigeon fancier's lung, but resisted making any unnecessarily easy gags about his ex's new beau. She'd met him when she set up some PR events for a client that liked to use celeb faces to endorse average products on social media. One of them had turned up with Simon in tow and Serena decided in that moment that she absolutely needed someone to help her work on her abs. At least, that's what she called it at the time. Leigh hadn't thought twice about it on the basis that she'd always gone for the best of anything: the six-bed executive home, the 4x4 Porsche, the personal trainer added to her personal shopper and, on occasion, personal chef. He'd have been happy with a two-up two-down, his old, leaky Golf Cabriolet and the weight bench he kept out in the garden and, on that basis, things hadn't been great between them. Given that Leigh worked for her, it was getting tricky. They were right to split, but staying in every night consuming TV dinners for one was not how Leigh imagined his life would pan out.

Where was the nice home and career and two-point-four children? Where was the red fox Labrador called Floyd? The wife that would make him laugh, that he could cook for, the one who snuggled cold feet behind his knees which he would pretend he'd hate but would actually love, because then he could rest his hand on her leg and there'd be that frisson of temptation because they'd also have fantastic chemistry, and their sex life would never end up in disengaged missionary, twice monthly. Not that there was anything wrong with missionary, per se, Leigh quite enjoyed the closeness, but the disengaged bit ... that had definitely been the thing that changed pretty quickly after he and Serena got married. She'd stopped running her hands down his back and she hated whenever he wanted to do anything that made her feel good. Like, anything.

'This isn't the kind of Saturday night I favour, to be honest, Tarquin.'

'Sad face.'

He rubbed the back of his neck. 'And I'm talking to a parrot!'

Leigh made himself a tea and poured the rest of the water into a flask for later. It was a Fortnum & Mason one that he'd bought for Serena when trying to persuade her that picnics were lovely, and watching the sun go down was just as romantic as a fifteen-course taster meal in Soho. Turns out flasks and picnics weren't enough for her, nor were the further training sessions she'd booked, claiming the flat stomach Simon had helped her to achieve was now a vital part of her happiness. That much was clear when Leigh returned home one night to find her writhing around in their marital bed with Simon.

Funny how missionary went out the window when she was shagging 'Magic Mike'.

'And you never said a thing, eh, Tarquin. Piss-poor wingman, you are.' He lifted his T-shirt up and glanced at his stomach, satisfying himself that while they may not be abs of steel, for thirty-two, he wasn't doing too badly, thank you very much.

He switched the telly on. *The Wheel.* Not really his favourite, but he'd got into the habit of watching it when it took forever for his internet to be connected in the new flat last year, and all his android telly could pick up was BBC One.

His flat. That was pushing it a bit. Internet connection or not, it was very definitely a bedsit. One room with kitchen at one end, bed and sofa at another, and a shonky wall that the landlord had put up to create what they'd laughingly described as a wet room. Tarquin lived in the corner of this lounge-cum-bedroom-cum-kitchen-cum-diner, Leigh slept opposite. Thirty-two, working for his ex-wife and living in a bedsit. 'I suppose it could've been worse, eh Tarquin.'

'Could've been worse.'

'Positively palatial.'

A pile of newspaper awaited him on the small dining table for one that he'd been able to upcycle after skip-diving on Psalter Lane. If upcycling included half-inching an Ikea special from the top of an ex-student house clearance, then wiping it down with a spray of the Zoflora that his sister, Rachel, gave him when he moved in. She mentioned something about him following a 'Mrs Hinch' on Instagram because she'd give all the tips on how to use it, but Leigh figured he could pretty much work out the dilute, spray and wipe method and didn't need additional support from a woman on 'the gram'. Besides, he'd deleted all his socials when Serena started posting her engagement to them and people kept messaging to check if he was OK. He was, he didn't love her anymore, hadn't for a long time, but the size of her diamond engagement ring made him squirm. She'd tried to get him to buy one like that when they got engaged but he just couldn't afford it. Plus, it all seemed a bit ostentatious. He should have seen the warning signs when she rejected the vintage cushion cut he bought in favour of a giant emerald her mum passed down.

'What do you reckon, did Simon buy that ring or did she buy it for herself?' He opened Tarquin's cage. 'Come on, out you come. Make the most of the freedom.'

Honestly, if he didn't think the bird would freeze or starve to death within days, he'd open the window and let him fly out. He was sure it wasn't right to keep him locked up in a cage.

Tarquin hopped out onto Leigh's arm, then proceeded to spin around it while shouting 'Woohoo' repeatedly for the next five minutes as Leigh stared glassy-eyed at Michael McIntyre and his selection of celebrity guests. Fleur East was on. He was fairly sure she was one of Simon's clients.

'Right, that's enough. Go on. Over there. I need to change your paper.'

'Sad face,' said Tarquin, hopping onto the top of the rickety wardrobe that a previous tenant left behind.

Leigh collected the old paper, scooping bits of dried-up food, and goodness knows what else, into a pile that he thrust into the kitchenette bin that was nestled between the microwave and the only door in and out of the bedsit. Then he took scissors to the new newspaper that would soon line the bottom of the cage, cutting it into shape.

'Hey, look at that Tarquin, a missing cat has returned to its owner, seven years after it ran away.' Leigh held up the paper to show Tarquin the headline and photo of a happy cat and owner, reunited, then rolled his eyes. He needed to get out the house more. 'Maybe Rachel is right. Maybe I should get on Tinder.'

'Tinder! Tinder! Let's play!'

'Yeah . . . that's the worry. I'm too old for games. Where does one find a decent, funny, sexy, smart and honest woman these days?'

'Sad face.'

Not only that, but a woman who could get on with an African Grey parrot and wasn't turned off by Leigh's jumper collection. If the winter fuel rates were going to rise as much as people feared, he would not be having the heating on. He stopped, stared at Tarquin, then down to the piles of newspaper and around his room. He pulled out his phone, scrolled his call list. (Which was basically the office, Serena, Rachel and Rachel's husband, Jim.)

'Jim. Pint? No, come off it. I was watching it too but look,' Leigh reached for the remote control. 'I've just switched it off. You've got fifteen minutes. The time it'll take me to get Tarquin back into his cage. Yes, I still have Tarquin. No, she's not coming back for him. Never mind that, I'll meet you down the club. Yes, it's your round.'

'Pint, please,' ordered Tarquin.

Peering through lasers and dry ice, Leigh gingerly made his way into the packed-out Crookes working men's club. On the stage, a soft rock tribute band was belting out 'Hysteria' by Def Leppard as Leigh spotted Jim in the corner, nodding his head in time to the music. Jim nudged a pint in his direction.

'Didn't realise there was a gig on tonight!' said Leigh, apologetically, before knocking back half the pint in one go. 'Bit loud.'

'Nah, they're ace! And careful! Drink that too quick you might have to put your hand in your pocket. It's your round next.'

'Not sure I'd make it to the bar. I don't think I've seen this place so busy.'

'I'm not sure you'd make it either, that hen do lot were giving you the right eye when you walked in.'

Leigh looked over to a group of women dressed in sashes and pink T-shirts with 'Team Bride' written across their chests. 'If only I'd brought my hunky fireman costume.'

'Tell me you really have a hunky fireman costume!'

'Course not!' Leigh shook his head. 'Lost it in the divorce.'

Leigh and Jim chuckled to themselves, sipping at their pints.

'Rachel says they pack the place out every month.'

'Hen nights?'

'The band – Thor: Gods of Rock. I hadn't heard them before but the guy on lead guitar can really play!' Leigh nodded with approval. 'Though, I think the group next to the hen lot are pissed off. Tonight's set is interrupting the bingo.' Leigh glanced over to a group of four older women with dabbers who sat motionless among the throng of soft rock fans, seemingly unmoved by the drum solo. 'It'll be on in the interval apparently, but they're still not impressed. Hey, I could get us a couple of lines. See if we can beat them.'

'What are the prizes?'

'A gammon joint and a beer voucher for twenty-five pounds.'

'Worth it!'

'Exactly! Can you imagine your sister's face if I rocked up with the winnings?'

'We'd have to share it. You'd get the gammon. You can pop it in your air fryer. I'll take the vouchers cos you earn more than me.'

The pair cheersed. As they enjoyed the music, a woman they'd never met before passed them sandwiches leftover from her party's buffet and a little kid – the lead singer's child by the look of the ear defenders and cardboard guitar – followed the lead singer as he left the stage and paraded around the room. It might have been the cheap-yet-perfectly-drinkable beer, but while Leigh surveyed the room full of people having an honest, affordable night out, nostalgia nipped at his mood.

'What's up with you?' shouted Jim, leaning across the table to be heard.

'Oh, nothing.'

'Sure.' Jim side-eyed him.

'Nothing that's not the usual, and I'm bored of talking about it.'

'Of course you are. Because to fix it, you've got to pull your finger out and do something. I don't know why you don't just leave you know.'

'What?'

'Work. Hand your notice in. Break all ties.'

'I love my job.'

'You can do it anywhere. There are loads of ad agencies that need great designers.'

'There are *some*, not loads. Not in Sheffield. Besides, I love the team. I've worked hard to train some of them up. We work well together, we know each other's strengths and weaknesses. I like the travel, just enough, not too much. And there's the career progression—'

'She is never going to give you that directorship carrot she kept dangling. Not now you've split up.'

Leigh gulped at his pint.

'In fact, I don't even know why you came back. You could benefit from a fresh start. Manchester. Edinburgh. New York!'

Leigh looked at him, shaking his head. 'Sheffield is my home city. I bloody love being back here,' he said, ducking beneath the arm of a bridesmaid who vigorously shimmied past their table. 'New York is great, but it's too much for me.'

'What's too much for you is still being at the beck and call of your ex-wife. And that bloody parrot. In fact, I bet I could air fry that too!'

'You're not air frying Tarquin.'

'Point is—'

The music stopped. The crowd stood up, cheering. Then the lights came up in the hall revealing that a number of older bingo players had nodded off during their seemingly interminable wait.

'Point is,' continued Jim, blinking in the unfamiliar strip lighting but no longer having to shout. 'You are stuck. Here. With her. With that bloody bird. You need to take some risks.'

'I can't afford to take any risks.'

'You can't afford not to.'

Leigh had not come out for one of Jim's talks. A talk he will have one hundred per cent been put up to by Rachel.

'Life is too short to sit around being mournful.'

'If I was sitting around being mournful, I wouldn't be here with you, would I? And this was my idea, so . . . there.'

'Great. Proof then. You're the most proactive man I've ever met.' Jim shook his head, finishing his pint off. 'It's your round. Get us on the bingo too. You need a bit of luck and I reckon this is the night for it. And worst-case scenario, that woman over there, the one with the tight perm, she's taken a bit of a fancy to you.'

'Mother of the bride?'

'What happens on a hen night, stays on a hen night.'

Leigh stared at Jim, suspiciously. 'So I've heard.'

4

'You all right, love?' asked Doris, Isla's favourite resident at the home where she worked as the entertainment coordinator. She wasn't supposed to have favourites – if her boss ever asked her, she would flat out deny it – but Doris was the resident with a glint in her eye, a passion for gossip, and an unwavering commitment to Isla's weekly sing-a-long-a-whatever musical she could find the DVD for, and she couldn't help but love her. Last week it was *The Rocky Horror Picture Show* which, on reflection, may have been an ill-advised choice. Some of the residents felt the stockings, suspenders and implied oral sex were a little too racy for a rainy Wednesday morning, and Isla wanted the floor to open up and swallow her when Janet started singing 'Touch-a-Touch-a-Touch-a-Touch Me'. Doris joining in had taken the edge off the embarrassment, but Isla vowed to make sure she'd actually watched all future films before sharing them with the mostly octogenarian residents of Nether Edge Residential Care Home.

Doris adjusted her walking frame to steady herself for a better look at Isla. 'You look a little peaky.'

'Me?' Isla feigned innocence. 'No, no, just got a lot on my mind. With work. You know.' This wasn't entirely a lie. There'd been lots of hushed conversations happening among the higher-ups, and a few visits from regional management which up until now, Isla had rarely seen. She wasn't worried about her job necessarily, but if money was getting tight for her at home, it had to be here, too. 'I'm fine. Honestly.'

'You're pale. And them eyes.' She narrowed her own. 'You've been crying.'

Isla's phone pinged in her hand and she glanced down to read.

> Isla, I've been thinking, since our date. Maybe I was a bit quick to judge, how do you fancy another go?

She shuddered and deleted the message from Date Number Five. 'Honestly,' she said, absentmindedly. 'What the hell is wrong with men?'

'Well, normally I'd suggest that was a sweeping generalisation, but you rather look like you need me to just agree?'

'Oh, ignore me. I'm being grumpy. It's probably the time of the month.'

'Hey! Don't undermine a woman's entirely legitimate hormone cycle just to put me off the scent. Now, I could do with a hand in my room. Do you have a moment?'

'I am supposed to be setting up our Guess Who? tournament in the day room.'

'Oh, Ged mentioned something about that when we were playing Boggle the other night.'

'Boggle?'

'Yes. You know, letters, words, a bit of . . . stimulation, shall we say.'

'Oh, "Boggle", you say. Right.' Isla raised her eyebrows. 'I'll have to check my urban dictionary on that one.'

'I don't know what you mean.' Doris held Isla's gaze but there was a definite smirk to the edges of her mouth.

'Well, anyway, I think he has designs on becoming the new champion. He's seen that there's a prize, though I've not yet worked out what it is. Might try and get a few carvery tickets for The Moorlands at Owler Bar.' Isla scrawled a reminder on her hand.

Doris's eyes narrowed. 'Look, it'll not take a minute. Just . . . could you just . . . ' She hooked her arm into Isla's, leading her down the paisley carpeted hallway. 'Do you know, I can't fathom why they didn't go for plain beige,' she said, pointing at the floor. 'People our age, all them swirls, you can have a funny do just trying to navigate the fleur-de-lis.'

'Move upstairs,' Isla said. 'It's sage green on the landing for rooms nine through fourteen. Eleven's free now . . . '

'Nobody makes it past six months in room eleven. Cursed. I'd rather grab a handrail and take my chances. Now come on in.'

'What is it? Is everything OK?'

'No. I don't think it is.'

'Go on?'

'I mean you.'

Isla's phone pinged again.

`If not a date, then maybe just a hook up? It's been a while for me` `and I reckon we'd be a pretty good fit, if you know what I mean.'`

Isla wasn't sure if it was the additional message or the spurting aubergine emojis that tipped her over the edge, but after deleting the message she blocked Date Number Five's number too. She'd been ghosted enough times, now it was her turn. 'Why is it so hard to find a man who actually wants to get to know someone. They're either showing off, or they can't be arsed to but are quite happy to ask you to sleep with them. Or worse, both.'

'Well . . . there's a time and a place for passion, love.'

'I know that. And . . . I've had my moments. But passion isn't everything when you just want to . . . '

'Netflix and chill?'

'No. No. That's not what . . . never mind.'

Isla wandered to the bay window overlooking the street outside. Doris did have the best room for people watching, gazing out as life pottered on around her. A middle-aged woman with a giant white dog walked by. The dog popped his paws on the wall, head cocked to one side as if staring right at them.

Doris tapped and waved. 'That's Henry. Romanian Rescue. Gorgeous but a giant. Should have been border collie sized, apparently.'

'I see.'

Doris kept watch for a moment longer, her face breaking into a broad grin as she waved again. Isla peered out the window to see Ged, a gentle-looking man with highly polished boots, standing below Doris's window, saluting.

'Why is Ged saluting you, Doris?'

Doris raised her eyebrows in Ged's direction. 'I was an officer in the Air Force. He only ever made Corporal.'

When Doris stepped away from the window, Ged seemed to wait until he couldn't see her anymore (though she could still see him). Then he stood down and wandered off, glancing back just the once before disappearing round the corner of the building. Doris adjusted her cardigan. 'Anyway, never mind that, come on. What is it? You've not been right for weeks and I just don't like to see you this way.'

'I'm fine, Doris. Honestly.'

She motioned for Isla to sit down on a chair by her small wooden coffee table. 'You're functioning. You're turning up to work, doing an excellent job as always, but there's no sparkle in your eye.'

'Well. There's nobody to put one there, is there?'

Doris studied Isla for a moment then sat herself down in the wingback chair that was perfectly positioned to spy on the garden next to the care home. 'They've got a pizza oven now. To add to the barbecue. He's out there all weather, cooking up a feast.' She paused. A brief sadness washed over her. 'My George used to love cooking. Was unusual in them days, but he was always better at it than me. Nothing fancy, mind. A pork chop. A cottage pie. We'd do a roast dinner together, though I was always the sous chef.'

'Sounds lovely.'

'It was. We'd have the radio on. Bit of music. I'd peel and chop, he'd make it all delicious. We'd sit at our Formica dinner table, a wedding present from mother and father, and we'd share a bottle of Mackeson.'

'With roast dinner?'

'Iron's important.'

'Right.'

'Point is, it was simple. A simple life. Forty-five years of happy, simple life.'

Isla nodded.

'When he wasn't getting on me nerves, mind. I don't want to paint no picture of perfection here. If we had a dip, as anyone does, we got through it. Together. We were always better, together.'

'Mum and Dad always say that. They don't need much so long as they've got each other.'

'Exactly.'

'They've been away for months now. I miss them.'

'Course you do, pet.' Doris gave her hand a little pat then pulled the head off a China dog-biscuit barrel. 'Here.' She passed her a Werther's Original. The original Original, not the chewy ones. 'Simple. Sweet. Lifts the mood.'

'Are you really giving me a Werther's Original? Are you taking the mick?'

'Only a little bit. My niece bought them for me. Been in that pot for about eighteen months. Can't stand 'em.'

Isla unwrapped the Werther's Original, popping it into her mouth. 'They are good, though. Ever so creamy.'

'Whatever floats your boat.'

Isla fell silent.

'Your time will come, love. You're too special for it not to.'

'I know. I do, really. I just don't know how, or when. You have to be so out there these days, just to get noticed. Nobody goes out to bars to meet anyone anymore; it's all done online. You meet online, you get taken on big dates, expensive restaurants. You go halves because—'

'Because it's not the 1980s anymore.'

'Or worse, you're invited on cheap dates in cheap bars, followed by the promise of what I can only assume would be cheap, unsatisfying sex. And you know what, Doris, even cheap is unaffordable when your rent is going up and the bills are getting higher. Basically, before you know it, you find you're single, broke and thoroughly depressed.'

'Are you really?'

'Single and broke, yes. No, I'm not depressed, I'm just a bit fed up. Sophie, my housemate, she's shacked up with Jay, our other housemate. They can share the pain of increased bills. If not financially then emotionally. All my mates have settled or are settling and I love this job, I do. I love you lot, but . . . '

'I don't imagine it pays that well.'

Isla nodded. 'Come this winter, I'll basically be coming here to get warm!'

'We might all be doubling up the Aran knits later this year.' Doris smiled. 'Look, love, you just need to bide your time. I can't speak about the job, but I can speak about love. It's not about big grand gestures—'

'It's not about text invitations for average sex either, is it, surely?'

'Oh, I don't know about that. A bit of sexting can do wonders!'

'Doris!'

On cue, Doris's phone pinged. She raised her eyebrows, winked, read her message then gazed out the window a second before furiously tapping away on her phone. Isla waited. Doris chuckled to herself. Isla waited a bit longer until eventually, Doris seemed satisfied with her response, clicked send and placed her phone face down on the table. 'Isla, online dating sounds hideous.'

'It's brutal.'

'If that's how things go these days, then maybe you need a bit of a break from it all so you can buckle up again before round two, you know? Get some strength back.'

'And money. Oh, shit. Look, I'd better get this tournament sorted. If it interrupts afternoon tea, Geraldine's going to go mad.'

'Geraldine needs to chill out. A ten-minute delay on lukewarm, stewed PG Tips is not going to finish us all off. Though I really do prefer a Yorkshire Tea, if I'm honest.'

'I'll pass the message on,' said Isla, making for the bedroom door. She paused on a photo of Doris and George. They must have been in their forties. Sat on a grassy bank with a flask of tea and big grins across their faces.

'There's no beauty in perfection,' said Doris, gently. 'Marriage, people, or otherwise. Just remember that one.'

'No beauty in perfection. Nice.'

Doris's phone pinged again and she leapt on it as fast as anyone with slightly arthritic fingers could. She allowed herself a wry smile before tapping out another response at the same time as saying, 'Hey, put an extra Guess Who? table out, will you? I think I'm feeling lucky.'

5

Isla shut Doris's door behind her, padding down the hallway. Her phone pinged again and she checked it without thinking.

```
Sorry we all missed your SOS! You
OK? How bad was it?
```

Isla laughed to herself. 'Well, he was—' but before she could finish her message back to the Christmas Girls, a notification popped up.

You've got a new match!

Her dating app. The last few times it had gone off she'd been reluctant to even look. Date Number Five had definitely put her off meeting anyone new and last night's post-cry spreadsheet poring had left her in no doubt that she could not sustain a lifestyle of paying rent *and* having a life. One or the other was going to have to give by next month or she'd be in big trouble. Her mum and dad had both said she could jack in her job and head out to spend some time with them in the camper van, but third wheel on four wheels was not at all appealing – however many times her dad said he'd make her bacon sandwiches in bed every morning.

She resisted temptation to look at the match until after she'd set up Guess Who? Five tables, ten guessing trays. A whiteboard to keep the score – a job for Betty who always used to keep the cricket scores for her local team before they folded and she moved into the home. The tea urn was bubbling away for mid-match break time, and the little CD player in the corner of the day room was charged with a compilation of music from the 1950s. Isla couldn't really name any of the singers, and to be fair, neither could many of the residents, but the sixties were a bit upbeat for a Guess Who? tournament and the seventies always ended in a Carpenters marathon. While her little chat with Doris had helped, Isla wasn't sure she was emotionally robust enough for songs like 'Goodbye To Love' and 'I Won't Last A Day Without You'.

Half an hour later, Doris was on a winning streak, and Ged – inexplicably wearing his war medals – was furious about a questionable beard/moustache confusion leading him to lose his second game. Betty had fallen asleep.

Deciding they could fend for themselves for a bit, Isla nipped off to her office. She liked describing it as an office because it made her feel grand, like she'd succeeded at something. And she did have a photo of her mum and dad on the wall, and a motivational quote that Ella had bought her last Christmas – although the quote had to be half obscured because Ella had a potty mouth and so did all her gifts. In truth, however, her office was really more of a cupboard near the main entrance that still contained a mop, bucket and stash of blue roll alongside her very small desk. So small that if she wanted to make notes in her pad and research anything on her decrepit work laptop, she had to sit back and have one of them on her knees. *No beauty in perfection*, she said to herself. *No beauty in perfection.*

Maybe she just had too high expectations. Maybe she should stop expecting thunderbolt love from online dating. She grappled with her phone. Maybe she should delete the app and just look up once in a while. But . . . what if today's message was the one? What if that chat about relationships with Doris was a moment's synchronicity and whoever had messaged was in fact the beauty without perfection. She glanced over her shoulder then opened the app.

New message. Rupert. Location: two miles away.

A posh name, not one Isla ever imagined herself crying out in the throes of passion, but then she had read Jilly Cooper's *Riders* and Rupert Campbell-Black was hot, so she wasn't going to discount it.

Hi. I saw your photo and you have nice eyes. Sparkly. I don't really know what else to say by way of introduction, I've only just joined the apps and they're just a bit weird, aren't they? Like, what can I tell you? I think you're very attractive and I'd like to take you for dinner? I should probably delete this and write something witty, entertaining, and mildly flirtatious but it turns out that I'm not much cop at messaging random women on the internet. Not that I'm saying you're random.

> See, I'm really terrible at this! But we are where we are and they say women like authenticity. So here I am. I'd love to buy you dinner, if you'd let me?

Isla read the message a few times, checking if her first response of laughing and feeling a warm sensation in her belly was her real response or just relief that there was an entire message from a male stranger that did not imply that sex would follow their date. The third time of reading it she wondered if yes, Rupert should have deleted and started again but her fifth time of reading it made her think that, actually, his ability to own the fact that he's not as smooth as he'd like to be was quite endearing. And the floppy haired photos helped. Isla wasn't sure when she'd grown a soft spot for floppy hair, probably her Justin Bieber fangirl days, though the less said about that the better. Whatever it was, floppy hair still did it for her. As did a nice smile and a well put together outfit that suggested if he was offering to take her out for a meal, he could actually afford to pay for it.

Her belly growled. She'd been hoping to have some lunch leftovers at work so that she could save the £7.15 in her bank account for topping up on knock-off baked beans, farfalle pasta (because it was cheaper than fusilli) and the cup-a-soup that had croutons. But it was sausage and mash day and all she could scramble together was half a Lincolnshire and a teaspoon of gravy. She couldn't blame the residents – sausage and mash was always good at the home, and Cook did say that they were going to have to stop buying extras for the staff.

She tapped out a response.

Hi. Nice to get your message. And yes, this is quite weird and yes, maybe you should have deleted your message and tried again, but as you've offered to pay for dinner and I'm down to my last tin of baked beans, I say I'll think about it. This sounds like I'm a money grabber, I'm not. Just really hungry and my landlord put the rent up so I'm also feeling quite sad. And cross. Not that I will be on our date, if we go on one. No, I'll be sweetness and light. I'll bring the sparkly eyes . . . they're not in a jar, they're in my face.

She paused, reading her message back, and feeling pretty confident with her witty repartee, added:

Also, you don't look like a serial killer in your photos and coming from a Yorkshirewoman, I'll tell you that's a compliment.

See, you're not the only one that should probably delete their messages.

Feeling a bit spicy, she threw her phone on her desk. But a message came back straight away.

If it was cool to write ROFL I would. You're funny. Go on, let me buy you

```
dinner. You can complain about your
landlord and leave full up on deli-
cious food. What have you got to lose?
```

Isla shuffled in her seat. Her heart was a bit fluttery but her cynicism still lingered. She closed the app and opened Instagram instead. Stacey Solomon was pegging out crisps in a cupboard and one of the home interior accounts she liked had new curtains. They were nice. Vintage-esque. But with a thermal backing to keep the warm in and the cold out. There was an affiliate link but Isla resisted because £7.15 was not going to buy Instagram curtains and maybe she should save it in case she needed to at least show willing and buy this Rupert chap a drink.

If she went on the date.

Which she had not definitely decided upon.

She scrolled. She 'liked'. She skipped past ads for Oodies, Too Good To Go boxes, and second-hand clothing sales. She responded to a comment from an Insta friend she'd never met and pressed her finger onto the screen of a photo of her mum and dad with the hashtag #TravelsWithTheLoveOfMyLife. Not exactly catchy, but Isla liked the sentiment. They'd had a holiday romance, meeting in Bude when they were seventeen. Everybody said it wouldn't last and look at them now.

Was it too much to ask for something at least a little bit like that?

Did Rupert like Bude?

Then another ad. One that made her pause, then snort with laughter.

'The Cheap Dates Club!?' Isla read out loud, aghast. '"Find love for free!" Yeah, righto. That's how love works.' She carried on scrolling, flicking past stories from Sophie of her and Jay on a tandem on the Monsal Trail. How was everyone always having such a bloody brilliant time!? Was this it? Was this her? Alone in her cupboard office, avoiding the inevitable fall out of Doris snatching a tournament victory from right beneath Ged's beard/moustache? While trying to decide whether to go on a date with a man who was offering to buy her dinner.

She scrolled back to the Cheap Dates Club ad. *Are you a Sheffield single looking for love but dating's getting spenny?*

Then forward, shaking her head. Rupert sounded nice enough but maybe she just needed to focus on herself for a while. Live vicariously through Sophie or the Christmas girls. Or Ged and Doris, by the looks of it.

She peered out of her cupboard office door, chair on two legs to see if things were still pottering along in the day room.

She placed all four chair legs back on the floor and scrolled forward.

Pause.

'I don't need a man.' She said out loud, which might have been problematic were she working anywhere with residents blessed with fully functioning hearing.

'I've never needed a man.'

Scroll back. *Then you might want to hear more about our brand-new club. Let our experts match you with your perfect date and help out in your local community to boot. Find love for free!*

'The Cheap Dates Club,' she scoffed.

Scrolled.

'Find love for free,' she tutted.

Scrolled.

Rupert didn't want her to pay. So that was a free date. Technically, she supposed.

```
Rupert, tell me more about this food
you're offering. Then I can think
about it. ;)
```

Insta. Scrolling. Searching.

'The Cheap Dates Club.'

She looked at the advert. Rupert responded with a list of possible restaurants that slightly terrified Isla because he might be paying but these were not the kind of places that she could just rock up to in any of her regular clothes. She'd wasted enough money on outfits for dates that went nowhere and certainly couldn't compete with someone who ate out in places like that.

'Find love for free . . . '

She clicked the weblink. Read the details. And in a moment that caught her by surprise, emailed hello@imacheapdate.com.

6

'Cuppa?' asked Leigh, moving a pile of folded washing off the sofa so his sister, Rachel, could sit down.

'Go on then, just a quick one.' She rearranged the messy bun that sat on top of her head, hoiking up her knock off Sweaty Betty leggings as she sat down, cross-legged on the sofa.

Six o'clock. Normally one to happily work into the night, Leigh turned his phone on silent and slapped his laptop shut, closing the latest design for a longstanding client that Serena had been messaging him about all afternoon.

'I've left Jim clearing the office out. I'm sick to death of the sight of all that bloody paperwork everywhere.'

'So you thought you'd bring it here,' Leigh said, dropping seven weeks of the *Sheffield Gazette* on the kitchen side.

'It's for Tarquin.'

'I know.'

'Though why I'm bothering bringing you newspapers for an animal you should have got rid of months ago is anybody's guess.'

'Because you're an excellent human and I love you for that.' Leigh grinned at her as he reached into the fridge for the milk, pulling out a large gammon at the same time. 'We can swap.'

'Eh?'

'Newspapers for gammon. Jim said he was taking it and I'd get the vouchers but somehow it ended up in my fridge and the vouchers are nowhere to be seen.'

'They're obviously in Jim's wallet. Incredible sleight of hand when it comes to owt for nowt, that man. Anyway, as you and Jim only ever go out drinking with each other, it doesn't matter whose wallet they're stored in.'

'Dunno if we'll be allowed back, to be honest. You should have seen the face on some of the regulars when Jim jumped up with his full house.'

'Yeah, well, new club members aren't supposed to win the bingo. You've got a good few more visits to make there before you're considered locals.'

Leigh passed Rachel her tea and dropped onto the sofa beside her. 'Where there's a will. So other than a messy office and your disdain for my parrot, how's life with you?'

'Yeah, it's all right. It's good.' She blew across her tea for a moment, avoiding eye contact. 'Aside from worrying about you, life's not bad at all.'

'What you worrying about me for?' he gestured around the room. 'I'm clearly fine, couldn't be better, I'm in my prime. Success is my middle name.'

'Mhm.' She paused. Leigh could feel it coming. 'There are job pages in those papers too.'

'Oh yeah? How about that. Handy given a lack of the internet for that kind of thing.'

'Don't be facetious.'

'Bet you can't spell it.'

'Shush. Some good jobs, too. I had a look.'

'You're about as subtle as that hammer dad used to lock the dodgy garage door with.'

'What do you mean!?'

'*And* you're no good at playing innocent either. Give over.'

Rachel feigned horror. 'Me!?' Then she sighed. 'You do need to find something, chuck.'

'I have a job.'

'Jobs that don't include you working for your ex-wife, and that might give you the means to escape this . . . ' Rachel resisted finishing the sentence.

'Hey, I will not have you speak ill of my home. I have always wanted to live in a wonky bedsit with ill-fitting windows and a damp problem from October through to March.'

'You just need a plan of action. Come to ours, I can help you make one. Like, I know you're a grown man and more than capable of working stuff out for yourself, but maybe you don't have to do it on your own?'

'I dunno. Maybe I shouldn't have a plan,' said Leigh, ruffling his hair. 'Maybe that's where I went wrong before. Serena and I, we always had a plan of sorts.'

'I'm not sure that was a joint plan . . . '

'Well, whatever. But maybe it's time to be a bit more . . . what's the word . . . free-spirited. That's it, maybe I should roll with the flow and let the universe decide.'

Rachel choked on her tea.

'That's karma,' he said, slapping her on the back.

'You are the least free-spirited man I've ever met. In fact, I'm surprised Tarquin didn't pipe up to point that out before me.'

'He's asleep.'

Rachel got up to go peer beneath the cover of Tarquin's cage. 'I bet the girls love him. Is that why you're keeping him? It's normally puppies or babies isn't it, but I bet there's something intriguing about a man with a parrot.'

'What girls?'

'The girls you bring round here.'

'Have we met? As if I bring girls round to my flat.'

'You're single! Why wouldn't you?'

He reached for the mugs and made for the kitchen. 'The dating scene's changed a bit since we were in it the first-time round. It's all a bit . . . I dunno. I feel like people basically just want sex these days.'

'Heaven forbid! Oh my god, why is that such a bad thing? Go, meet the women, have the sex. Get back out there!'

Leigh rolled his eyes at her. 'Look, I just . . . ' he groaned. 'Is it too lame to say that . . . I don't know that I'm ready? And when I am, I definitely want more than just that. It's not like it kept me and Serena together, is it?' He adjusted his posture. 'And let me tell you, Rach, towards the end it was—'

'Tell me nothing, I do not want detail.' Rachel moved to stand beside him. 'Honestly, you're such a total loser, but—'

'I'm hilarious, excellent at sex-ing and I can cook.'

Rachel shuddered. 'But I suppose someone will find it alluring that you don't want to be a massive dickhead to women.'

Leigh started flicking through the newspaper. 'I think I preferred it when you were laser focussed on me getting a new job.'

'Good. Hey, try flicking through it with your eyes closed and see what the universe decides.'

'You laughed at me for suggesting that.'

'Yeah well, a woman can change her mind. Look, I'd better go. Jim will either be sat in a heap of his own misery, or he'll have got so into shredding things, it'll take an entire roll of Sellotape to piece together our birth, marriage and GCSE certificates.'

'Why do you still have your GCSE certificates?'

'Because you never know when you might need them, brother. Mr Froggatt told us that on our last day and I believe him. He trusted the universe too.'

'Really.'

'Probably.'

'OK.'

'Keep your eyes peeled. For signs. That's what they say, isn't it.'

'Signs?'

'Exactly.'

'And what will these signs say?'

'God knows, but I reckon you'll know it when you see it. And when you do, tell me!'

'Or what?'

Rachel pulled him in for a hug which he reciprocated before pushing her playfully out the door. 'Go on. Go. Leave me alone. Oh, hang on!' He reached for the gammon, tossing it in her direction before closing the door.

Peace in his flat restored, Leigh turned on BBC 6 Music, opened a beer and sat on the sofa with a pile of the newspapers and some scissors. He checked each paper for jobs before cutting Tarquin-cage-shaped circles out and laying them neatly, one on top of the other, muscle memory dictating their size. Then he stopped and screwed his face up. Maybe Rachel was right. This was not a very free-spirited way to pass his time. He placed the scissors down and tried ripping a couple of circles instead, which was deeply dissatisfying, when something caught his eye. He studied it for a second, then laughed and went to screw it up and bin it. But as he got to the bin, he paused.

No. That would be laughable. Not now.

He unscrewed the paper and read it again. Now could be as good a time as any, he supposed . . . no. Maybe? No. That's daft. It's a job he should be looking for, not . . .

Grappling with phone and paper, Leigh paused, started an email, deleted it, put his phone down and chucked the paper in the bin, swigged his beer and shook his head. Then he grabbed the paper back out the bin, tapped out an email and clicked send, throwing his phone on the table as if it suddenly got too hot.

And he had zero intention of mentioning anything to Rachel.

7

Isla nibbled the top layer of an Aldi custard cream, scraping the cream off with her front teeth while she FaceTimed her mum and dad. 'Where are you again?'

'Barril de Alva,' said her dad in his best Portuguese accent.

'We just sort of ended up here, didn't we Peter.' Isla's mum looked over her shoulder to her dad who sat behind so the pair of them could both be seen on the screen.

'How do you "just sort of end up" in Portugal?'

'Took a wrong turn, probably. Your father was driving.'

'I think you'll find you had the map, Marion.'

She playfully batted him away; the screen froze on the action but the voices continued. 'There's this lovely river for swimming in. A fitness club that me and your dad have signed up to. And next month, there's a writers' retreat happening in the next village up. Côja.'

'You don't write.'

'But what if I could?'

The screen leapt back to life and Isla's mum was leaning into it with a mysterious grin plastered across her face. She'd always been something of a dreamer, like nothing was out of bounds, anything was possible. Isla had long wished she was more like her mum.

'Go on then, what would you write about?' she asked.

'Me and your dad: a love story.'

'No sex please,' said her dad. 'I don't want anybody knowing my secrets.'

'What secrets?' asked her mum, incredulous.

'Well,' her dad looked coy. 'You know . . . '

Isla shoved her fingers in her ears, 'Lalalalala, not listening, not listening.'

'Oh, Isla.' Her mum rolled her eyes at her. 'Sex is a perfectly healthy part of an adult relationship. And by the sounds of it, something you could do with a bit more of. Your dad and I were only saying so the other day—'

'Well, we weren't talking about that, Marion . . . !'

'Well no, not that specifically, Peter . . . we'd just love to see you happy, love.'

'I *am* happy!'

'Of course you are, but . . . it's always nice to have someone. To have your person.' She reached out for Isla's dad's hand, he kissed it gently.

Isla looked at the email she had been replying to when they had unexpectedly called.

From: The Cheap Dates Club. Subject line: Date 1. Tonight. Sheffield Botanical Gardens.

In her response, she'd written three sentences. One that said: Sorry to mess you about, I'm afraid I've changed my mind, one that said: Actually, I realise I'm not available tonight, maybe another time?, and one that said: Lovely. Thanks. I'll be there at 6.30 p.m. She kept highlighting different sentences to delete.

'Hey, Mum, Dad, here's a funny thing, do you remember when the newspapers used to help you find love. Singles ads and that?'

Isla's dad laughed. 'Crikey, do I. That's how your Uncle David met his wives.'

'Wives! How many's he had?'

'Oh, just the two. Did we never tell you that story?' Isla's mum shifted to the edge of her camper van seat. 'Yes, Elaine was his first wife's name. Circled each other in the newspaper, can't remember which, *Telegraph* maybe, anyway, they had a whirlwind romance and we all thought they'd be together forever.'

'What happened?' Isla highlighted the sentence accepting her date, preparing to delete it.

'Well, I think your Uncle David rather enjoyed the chase. Kept putting more ads in the paper. Even on their honeymoon in Blackpool.'

'No!'

'I can't say I approved of my brother's behaviour. And I told him.'

'Then Elaine found out that he'd met another woman—'

'Women, more like!' Isla's dad was shaking his head.

'And it all fell apart from there. Mind you, she went on to marry a butcher from the big Morrisons in Hillsborough so all's well that ends well.'

'Right.'

'Why do you ask?'

'No reason.'

Isla's mum and dad nudged each other in a way they thought she wouldn't notice. She always noticed.

'Look, I really should be getting back to work.'

'Isla.' Her mum folded her arms.

'I'm really very busy.'

'Come on. Out with it. You wouldn't have asked if you didn't want to talk about it.'

Isla scowled at the screen. 'I just sort of stumbled across this mad project. Online.'

'What sort of project?' asked her dad. 'I hope it's nothing dangerous. You have to be careful, love. Single women are—'

'Peter, she doesn't need a lecture about the risks of being a single woman. Especially not from a man.'

'I wasn't going to give her a lecture, Marion, I was simply going to say that—'.

'The Cheap Dates Club!' Isla interrupted the sound of their ultimately harmless bickering.

There was a pause.

'I saw this thing online, Instagram actually.' As if that made it all OK. 'And, on a mad whim, I signed up for it.'

Her mum and dad resisted looking at each other and didn't respond. This was a well-used tactic implemented when neither of them was clear as to what kind of response Isla was looking for; neither prepared to nail their sail to any particular mast until they understood Isla's direction of travel. It was annoying.

'I probably won't do it actually. In fact, I was just about to tell them that I'd made a mistake.'

Still nothing.

'And if Uncle David's singles ads caused the downfall of his marriage, I don't know if this is the sort of thing I should be signing up for.'

'Well, it caused the downfall of one marriage, but it's also how he met Aunty Jan and they've been married for thirty-five years so it can't be all bad. And what does a singles ad have to do with this project anyway?'

'The *Gazette* are running it.'

'That old free paper? I didn't realise that was still a thing, did you Marion?'

Isla gulped as her mum shook her head. 'No, me neither.'

'Right.' Still nothing. Poker faced.

She ploughed on. 'It's not singles ads, it's more . . . match-making. Combined with finding love in a cost-of-living crisis.'

'Mhm.'

She scrunched up her nose. 'You answer some questions about who you are and what you like and they match you with another candidate.'

'Candidate?'

'Well, single . . . person.'

'Mhm.'

'They match you, then send you out on a series of free, or really cheap dates. Then they interview you afterwards to see how it went.'

'They interview you?' said her mum.

'Yeah.'

'For the paper?' said her dad.

'Yeah . . . '

'What kind of dates?' Her dad sat forward now, still not entirely giving his position away but keen to make sure he fully understood what was going on. This was tactic two: he drew out the detail while her mum listened and formed the opinion.

Isla looked at the map that pinpointed the meet-up location. 'I'm not sure but the first one is at Sheffield Botanical

Gardens. I think sometimes the activities can be romantic, sometimes good for the community . . . ' her voice wavered.

'Good for the community how?' Her mum was beginning to thaw. She always approved of community investment in whatever form that took.

'Just helping people out. Maybe we'll be doing meals on wheels or helping out at a soup kitchen or something? They haven't specifically said.'

'And you do this as your date?'

'Yes.'

Her dad steepled his fingers, nodding gently.

'An interesting way to meet someone with similar morals, then,' said her mum.

'Could be, I guess. And because they interview us afterwards, there's none of that "are they interested or aren't they?", because we can read what each other has to say.'

'Well, why would anyone not be interested in you. You're positively brilliant,' said her dad.

'It sounds marvellous,' exclaimed her mum. 'What a smashing idea.'

Sail pinned to the mast, Isla's dad nodded enthusiastically. 'It absolutely is. So, what's your worry?'

'Well, whether to go.'

'To the Botanical Gardens?' said her mum. 'You used to love it there as a kid. What's the activity?'

'I don't know yet. What if—'

'You still there, love?'

'Yes, still here.'

The screen went blank. There were fumbling noises. Isla could picture them both, fussing over the phone trying to fix the connection, neither of them technically competent enough. The screen came back on and Isla had a close up view of her mum's ear.

'I think the signal's . . . ' Crackle. Screen freeze. 'One of them Winnebago things has just parked up next to us . . . We'll call you back.'

'No, mum, I should really get back to work. Sorry.'

' . . . line is going. Hello? OK, love . . . call you on the weekend then. We'll want to hear all about that date. Pardon, Peter? . . . Oh, your dad agrees. Go on, have some fun.' The line went fuzzy again and Isla couldn't make out what else was said before she hung up.

She stared at her laptop.

She bit the inside of her lip.

She remembered her mum always told her not to bite the inside of her lip.

She scratched at her left palm and ignored the old wives' tale about left for love and right for spite, she'd had that itch for days. Maybe she needed some cream for it. She deleted two of the three sentences, then reinstated one, then deleted another. Sat back. Leaned forward. Closed her eyes and clicked send.

8

Isla jumped off the bus at Hunters Bar so she could run-walk the last bit, trying to get rid of all the nervous energy that was fizzing through her bones. She fiddled with her fringe and pinched her cheeks because at the point she'd decided she wasn't going to show up to the date, she'd used an old hanky to wipe off her blusher and now she was regretting it. She ignored a new message from Rupert because as much as she was enjoying their to and fro, at the point she'd decided she *was* going to show up to the date, she knew she had to focus.

The roads glistened in the glow of the summer downpour that no longer fell, steam rising from the still warm concrete. Students and office workers walked, jogged, ran up and down the roads. Were any of these people her date?

As the columns at the park gates loomed into view, she tried not to look over her shoulder, or too far ahead in case her date saw her and had second thoughts. There was little more humiliating than being stood up on a blind date. She knew, it had happened before. More than once, though in fairness, she had also darted away from one date when she saw he was dressed like a magician: all shiny suit and pointy shoes. No cape, but a goatee. There was nothing wrong with a goatee on some people. Laurence Llewelyn-Bowen could really carry it off, but she didn't want to have sex with Laurence Llewelyn-Bowen and oh god, what if her cheap date had a goatee? Or was Laurence Llewelyn-Bowen.

A bus stopped up ahead, passengers spilling out on to the path, jogging over the road, up and away. Isla kept her head down. 'Please no goatee, please no goatee.' She neared ever closer to what may have been the worst decision she'd made that week. 'Please no goatee. Or an arsehole. Please not an arsehole!' She was aware that muttering like this may not give the best first impression and in the absence of any particular religious allegiance, she wasn't even sure who she was talking to. But she couldn't help herself, if this was another disastrous date with someone who had no intention of finding out anything about her, but couldn't wait to tell her all about how brilliant he was, and why they absolutely should be dating, she was going to absolutely—

'Look out!'

Footsteps.

Arms reached out to grab her. 'Step back!'

'What are you doing?' she shrieked, jumping.

Arms lurched forward towards her again, trying to spin her around. 'You're going to—'

And that's when the 218 to Bakewell ploughed through a giant puddle. The kind of puddle a wild swimmer would definitely have satiated their need for an open-water fix in. The kind of puddle that covered Isla in a fountain of muddy yet weirdly warm, rainwater. Head to foot. Like a comedy drenching that you'd see in a film. Only this wasn't a film.

And it wasn't funny. And when Isla opened her eyes, the man with the arms that reached out, was also drenched, standing right beside her.

'I was trying to stop it,' said man-with-arms, looking disbelieving at the state of himself. 'Then I realised that rugby tackling a woman in the street isn't really the done thing but before I knew it, you were right in the firing line. And then so was I.'

Water dripped from Isla's fringe. A wet fringe was the worst kind of fringe. And her jeans, too; soaked. And maybe it didn't matter that she'd wiped most of her makeup off because she now looked like a drowned rat. A drowned rat with coral cheeks was not likely to be any more attractive than drowned rat without.

'Shit,' she said.

'Yeah . . . ' man-with-arms agreed. 'Shit.'

Isla ineffectually brushed herself off. She looked around to see if her cheap date was waiting, watching. He'd probably seen it all happen and scarpered. Who could blame him? Maybe it would be a blessing, really. She was very definitely not date ready now.

'God, I . . . ' man-with-arms began rooting through his pockets. 'I had a tissue. Somewhere. Clean!'

'It's fine. Honestly. Don't worry.'

He pushed his own hair back off his face. A slight curl like the kind you'd expect from an Irish movie star, bounced back down onto his forehead. Kind eyes pleaded a silent apology. A lesser-looking man might not have been quite so easy to forgive.

'Honestly. It doesn't matter. Look, I've got to . . . ' Isla looked at her watch, then up to the gates to the park. 'I've got to go . . . '

'Yeah, sorry, me too . . . '

'Right.'

Isla stepped forward.

So did the man. 'Sorry, I just, I'm going this way . . . '

'Course. OK. Bye then.'

She tried again. He did too. Had she still got a sense of humour she might have asked if he were dancing, and, were he single, he'd have probably said, are you asking? And then they'd have laughed and gone for a drink because that would be the way to actually meet someone in a romantic setting instead of a stupid cheap date, in an outfit that was very soon going to give her pneumonia.

'I'm supposed to be meeting someone,' he said, looking up and down the road.

'Oh right . . . me too . . . '

Then the penny dropped and Isla's heart sank.

The man's face fell and he looked at her fringe. Or was it *as* he looked at her fringe? She couldn't tell. He might not have looked at her fringe at all, but that's definitely what she thought he was looking at which was probably, on balance, better than looking at the rest of her because she was in an actual state and why did man-with-arms also have to be man-with-beautiful-face and lovely eyes and man who she was supposed to be meeting for a "cheap date" because this was not how she would ordinarily want to meet man-with-arms-and-beautiful-face.

'You two here for that *Gazette* dating thing?' said a gruff voice from behind them.

'Yes,' they both said, spinning round to see a groundsman carrying two litter pickers, two black bin bags, and a confused look on his face.

'Right. Well. These are for you.'

He handed them over. Isla took one, man-with-beautiful-face took the other. She forced a bright, wide, couldn't be happier to be litter picking on a first date smile, hoping it hid the actual, oh god, this is a nightmare, we're litter picking, feeling she had in the pit of her stomach. The groundsman reached inside his pocket for an envelope that he passed to man-with-beautiful-face, looked them both up and down then wandered off.

There was a pause.

Isla swallowed.

'I'm Leigh,' said man-with-beautiful-face. 'I'm really sorry about the puddle.'

'Oh, no. It's fine,' she said, trying to style it all out. 'Who doesn't want to get wet on a first date?' As soon as the words came out of her mouth did she wish she'd stopped talking at *oh no it's fine* because she'd been on enough dates with enough men to know that this was a line bound to illicit some kind of *I wouldn't mind getting you wet* response. She braced herself.

9

Leigh looked at her for a moment, his beautiful face broke out into a grin. 'You wish you hadn't just said that don't you?'

She grinned back. 'You have no idea how much!'

'If it's any consolation, I was about to say that I generally preferred getting wet when I'm naked so I think we can both agree there have been better ways to kick off a first date.'

Isla flushed, trying to push away the image her brain was desperately trying to conjure up. He laughed again. So did she. Then she wondered if it was too soon to text the Christmas Girls and tell them that she had definitely met the one. Or if not the one, *a* one that she would happily—

'And sorry, what's your name?' he asked.

Yeah, too soon. 'Sorry. It's Isla. Like Isle o' paradise . . . not Isla, as in Bonita. Sorry. That only really works if you see it written down. In fact, I don't even know if it works then? Was Isla Bonita spelled I S L A?'

'Um.'

'Sorry. Ignore me. God, anyone would think I don't date! I do. Been on loads. I was on one earlier this week, in fact.'

He cocked his head to one side. 'Oh god, that makes me sound . . . he was terrible. Awful. It might have been the worst date I've ever been on. I probably shouldn't be talking about other dates, should I? Or slagging off men. I'm sure he's lovely really, just not the man for me. And I probably wasn't the woman for him, to be fair. I mean he basically said as much. Said my boo—never mind.' Isla screwed her face up and wondered, however good looking he was, if it was too late to pretend she wasn't here for the date but when she opened her eyes, man-with-beautiful-face . . . Leigh . . . was looking at her, smiling. His eyes sparkled, maybe they always did. Was that a look that said he was entirely charmed by her or was he wondering if she was out on day release? Either way, he made her knees go a bit wobbly.

'Hey, don't worry,' he said, 'I'm nervous too.'

'You are?'

'Totally!' He looked around. 'Nearly didn't come, actually.'

'Oh.' Isla realised that in that moment, she understood what crestfallen felt like. 'I mean, you can go . . . if I'm, you're, this isn't . . . '

'No, no. I'd like to stay.' He reached for her hand, his fingertips grazing hers just briefly. 'If you want to stay, that is?'

She shivered. 'I'd like to stay.'

They smiled at one another. Coy. She now also felt coy. Had she ever felt coy before? It was hard to say. It made her want to twist her fingers, the fingers he'd just touched, and bite her lip, the lips she would like to crush his with, which she realised was in fact anything but coy so she pushed through the weird lusty coy ridiculous version of herself that he drew out and just tried to be her version of normal; whatever that was. 'So what does it say?' she asked, nodding down to the envelope.

Leigh looked at his hands in surprise, as if he'd forgotten the groundsman had given him anything. 'Oh! Right, yes.' He fumbled with the black bin bag and litter picker before offering them to Isla to hold for a second. 'OK.' The paper shook slightly in his hand. Or maybe it was the breeze. 'Dear Leigh and Isla, you have been selected by our experienced team of matchmakers, based on the answers you gave to our questions, and new physical profiling technology.'

'So they looked at both our photos and tried to decide if they could imagine us as a couple,' she said.

'I reckon.'

Isla's cheeks flushed. It felt pretty good to have been paired up with someone that looked like Leigh. She was definitely punching, but if the 'matchmakers' believed it . . .

'Welcome to the Cheap Dates Club. Today's date is litter picking. You have all the tools you need to clear and tidy the beautiful Sheffield Botanical Gardens. Keep an eye out near the benches for a flask of tea left especially for your break. We hope the conversation flows naturally, but to get you started, here's a question you can ask each other: what is your first memory?'

Leigh folded up the letter, stuffing it into his pocket. He took the litter picker and bin bag back from Isla and the pair stood, staring at one another.

'I'll go first,' Isla volunteered, then paused to cast her mind back. 'I was baking a cake with my grandma. Dad took a photo, and I don't know if it's really my first memory or a memory triggered by the photo, but I remember when we cut the cake afterwards, Grandma's hand on mine, pushing down the knife, I remember thinking that I had to smile for the photo, and look pretty, but my hand was hurting against the knife handle.'

Leigh held her gaze, listening. He had the kind of eyes that softened when she talked but maybe they just did that for everybody. Nice eyes were like that.

'So yeah, that's my first memory. I think. Or maybe it was the time I insisted on kissing a stone frog at the garden centre. I must have been about three?'

'Three and looking for a frog prince?'

'It was my favourite book. I'm generally less desperate now.'

'And have the garden centre let you back in since or . . . ?'

'No. I'm banned for life.'

'Fair.'

'Go on then, what's yours?'

He screwed his eyes tight and started walking. 'I can't think of one quickly enough.'

'Everyone has a first memory, don't they?'

'Yeah, but my actual first memory is really embarrassing so I'm trying to think of something else, but my mind has gone blank.'

'Tell me.'

'No.'

'Go on!' She jumped in front of him, stopping him in his tracks. 'Tell me!' He locked eyes with her as she grinned, making her breath catch in her throat. 'I told you mine, so you have to.'

'OK.' He laughed to himself. 'But *first* memories, so no judgement.'

'The smallest of judgement.'

His eyes widened.

'I'm kidding. No judgement.' He stared, a flicker of a smile touching the corners of his mouth now. She held her hands up. 'No judgement.'

'OK. We were on holiday. In the Lake District.' He groaned then rubbed his eyes. 'I can't believe I'm about to tell you this.' He paused, then rushed through his admission, 'I peed in the hotel pool and my sister who's older than me, dobbed me in to Mum and Dad.'

'Haha!'

'By shouting it across the pool for everyone to hear.'

Isla's hands shot up to her mouth. 'No!'

'Yeah. In fact, bringing up this memory makes me want to crawl inside of myself until I disappear. If you wanted to leave, I would totally understand.' A beat. 'Though I can tell you with complete confidence that I don't pee in pools anymore.'

Isla head-back cackled, then wished she hadn't because an ex once told her it wasn't very ladylike. 'Oh god, that's . . . no, I believe you.'

Leigh burst out laughing himself, before lifting up his bin bag. 'I think we're supposed to be picking up litter.'

'We are.' Isla began searching the ground, adding, 'And I'm obviously definitely judging you.'

He litter-picked her binbag, 'Oi!'

Was that a fizz of chemistry between them?

Leigh, the first to find some rubbish, scrabbled to collect an empty packet of Monster Munch – pickled onion – wrestling it into the bin bag with Isla's help. Isla tried to think of something else to say, but for some reason now they were multi-tasking, her mind was literally empty.

'Thanks,' he said. 'I mean, I'm normally much better with bin bags.'

'Sure . . . Ooh, Smarties!' She grabbed at an empty packet on the ground. 'I used to love those.'

'The orange ones were always my favourite.'

'Did they taste any different?'

'Absolutely. They were the only ones that did. They had orange chocolate in them.'

'Oh. Right.' She shook her head. 'I don't remember that.'

They carried on walking.

'Dog-poo bag.' He dropped it in his bag.

'Yeah, it's not really the most glamorous of first dates, eh?' Pause. 'Sandwich box,' she lifted it, dropped it, lifted it again.

'What sort?' he asked.

'Chicken, Bacon and Mayo.'

'Nice.'

'What's your favourite?'

'What?'

'Sandwich . . . ' Isla lost faith in the question as soon as she had said it. She was so wrapped up in fancying Leigh, wondering if he liked her back, she was only retrospectively aware that questions about sandwiches were unlikely to seal the deal.

'I like a cheese, or a ham.' He smiled at her and even if he didn't like her, she appreciated that he was kind enough to humour her. 'I'm pretty basic like that.'

They pushed on. Each focussing on the ground before them, announcing their finds before dropping them into the bag. Why was she finding it so hard to think of interesting, fun things to talk about? The flirty vibe between them was fading, if there had been one in the first place. Plus, Isla was now cold from the bus-puddle drenching, and with every piece of rubbish they picked up, every rubbish conversation opener she attempted, she was feeling less and less confident in her abilities to charm him. Also her mouth was dry, and the rubbish bag kept clinging awkwardly to the damp leg of her jeans. Why was she being so socially inept? Would she have been on better form were they sat in a swanky restaurant? She screwed her face up then said, 'What was your favourite subject at school?'

'Science.'

'Oh, nice.' Great, this would open things up. 'Do you do something in science now?'

'No. I'm a designer. For an ad agency.'

Or maybe not. 'Oh, cool.'

'Mm. You?'

'I work at an old people's home. Oh look, the flask!'

Leigh went over to the bench, wiping it dry with his arm as best he could – a sweet if futile gesture, given that both their clothes were still soggy – then offering it to Isla to sit down. She poured the drink and they both watched as steam twisted between them, their half-filled rubbish bags trapped beneath the litter pickers. She sipped the hot tea gratefully – her shivering subsided. Maybe it would calm her nerves a bit too?

'So, the old people's home. What do you do there?'

'Entertainment. I organise games days, exercise sessions, stuff that keeps their bodies and brains working.'

'Do you love it?'

'Yeah . . . ' she thought about Doris. Ged. Betty. Her little cupboard office and the gentle aroma of hot pot that travelled through the corridors every Tuesday morning. 'I really do. I'd be no good at actual care work, I don't think. It takes someone really special to look after older people, but I love being able to create moments. I love watching the residents' eyes light up when a certain song gets played in a sing-a-long. Music triggers memories, doesn't it?'

'It does.'

They fell to silence again. Staring forwards while blowing across their tea.

'Why did you feel you had to look pretty?' asked Leigh.

'Pardon?'

'You said that you had to look pretty for the photo with your grandma. Why?'

'Oh.' Isla sat back. 'I don't know, really . . . '

Leigh nodded gently.

'What's your favourite biscuit?' She could have kicked herself. He was being profound. She was asking about biscuits.

'Digestive.'

Relieved he was playing the game, she pushed on. 'Strong choice. I'd go a Hobnob right now. If I could.'

'Chocolate covered?'

'No. I don't think so. I like a naked biscuit.'

Leigh's eyes flashed. She noticed they were creased slightly at the edges and he had really long eyelashes. When he said 'Me too', maintaining eye contact, Isla immediately found a bit of muck on her jeans pretty damn interesting and scuffed it away with her nail. 'This is kind of awkward, isn't it.' She darted her eyes up then away from his again.

'Yeah . . . it is a bit.' He shifted in his seat, pulling at his T-shirt which clung to his body.

Isla pretended not to notice. 'More so than a normal date?'

'Possibly. So far.'

'I'm not sure if the concept of a cheap date works?'

'You'd rather a really expensive one?'

She couldn't quite read him, was he judging her? 'God no, I mean, I'm broke but also not very sophisticated.' More things she wished she hadn't said.

'Talking's nice, though.'

'Yeah.' She smiled down at her cup, draining it before saying, 'Talking's nice.'

Leigh screwed both empty cups onto the flask, resting it against the arm of the bench where they found it.

'Where do you stand on a custard cream?'

Isla looked at him and saw the definite crinkle of mischief again. 'OK, now you're taking the piss out of my date chat but since you've asked, I think it's important to answer: you have to deconstruct them carefully and any other way of eating them is only done by masochists.'

'Oh really?'

'Really.' She plucked up the courage to hold his gaze, head to one side. 'Shall we carry on?'

It was another hour of a kind of silly small talk that seemed to get easier the more they just rolled with it. First pet, favourite pizza topping, team Ross or Rachel (she was relieved to hear that he was not really fussed about either Ross or Rachel and found a lot of *Friends* kind of problematic now.) *Star Wars*, yes or no? Yorkshire pudding on all roast dinners, or just with beef? (Regardless of how he ate a custard cream, this answer, she decided in the moment, could have been a deal breaker, no matter how beautiful he was. Thankfully, he was aghast that anyone would have a roast dinner without a Yorkshire pudding).

Before they knew it, they were back round to the main gates, both bags full, as footsteps came from behind them. 'Did you bring the flask back with you?' said the groundsman gruffly.

'Oh! No, sorry!' Isla turned to Leigh, guiltily.

'We didn't think, we were too busy . . . '

' . . . chatting.'

'We're really sorry. Would you like me to go and get it?' he offered.

'No. No,' tutted the groundsman. 'I'll go. I've got to lock up now, so . . . '

'Right. Yes.'

The groundsman stared at them both. Then about-turned in the direction of the flask, muttering to himself.

Leigh looked at his watch.

'What time is it?'

'Almost eight,' he said, sounding surprised.

'Wow. Where did that go?'

'Time flies when you're discussing biscuits and Yorkshire puddings.'

'Yeah . . . ' Not exactly the casual, but ultimately hot, date she had been hoping for when she had signed up.

The groundsman came jogging back, flask in hand. 'Give us your bags then,' he said, breathless. 'And the litter pickers.'

'Sorry, yes, here you go.' Isla handed hers over.

'Bye, then,' said the groundsman, stepping towards them, which in turn, made them start walking backwards towards the gate.

'Thanks for letting us . . . ' tried Isla.

'Sorry for keeping you . . . ' started Leigh, with a look of amused confusion.

Out the other side of the gates, the groundsman rattled large keys in the lock then huffed the rubbish bags on his shoulder, retreating into the dusk. Isla and Leigh both watched him for as far as they could see before eventually turning back to one another.

'I should probably—' began Leigh, pointing in one direction.

'Yeah, me too.' Isla nodded, pointing feebly in the other.

'You know, you don't have to make yourself pretty for anybody,' Leigh said suddenly, holding her gaze.

'Pardon?'

'In the photo, with your grandma, you said—'

'Oh, right. Yes, of course. Thanks.'

'No, I mean, I wasn't giving you permission. I was just—'

'No. Right.'

They both swallowed and looked around awkwardly. She suspected he liked her but couldn't tell if he fancied her too.

'It's been . . . '

'Yeah . . . lovely. Thank you.'

Leigh went as if to shake her hand, which Isla thought was weird but didn't want to leave him hanging so did the same only he didn't shake her hand at all, but placed his arm on her elbow, kissing her gently on the cheek – as her hand brushed against his groin.

'Shit. Sorry.'

He laughed. 'Don't worry. It was nice to meet you.'

'You too. Thanks. Lovely.'

'Bye, then.'

'Yeah . . . bye, then.'

Isla turned away first. Yeah, he wasn't fussed. If she hadn't been friend zoned with her bang average chat, she definitely had after accidentally touching him up. Whatever the journalists thought about their compatibility, Leigh was way out of her league. He'd have asked her out for a drink afterwards if he was bothered. And however much she fancied him, and she really did – how could she not, she had eyes – it didn't really feel like it was going to go anywhere. She walked at first, then began to jog, and eventually found herself running all the way home. And this time, not because she was frightened but because she was cold, and felt stupid for thinking the Cheap Dates Club could have remotely worked. At least through the newspaper, she couldn't actually get ghosted this time. Silver linings.

Once again out of breath, lungs gasping for air, Isla pushed through her front door, dropping her keys on the little table beside it. She saw there was a message on the dating app from Rupert and opted to make him wait. She flung her coat off, missing the banister, and brushed her hair off her face in the mirror.

And that's when she saw the state of her face. Mascara all down it. Like, not just a little bit smudged, but literally smeared down her face. And Leigh never said a thing; except that she didn't have to look pretty for anyone.

Lucky that, considering.

She sank down into her sofa. Her heart dropped with a teensy ache. She guessed some things just weren't meant to be.

10

Yoga morning at the home; a much needed bit of peace, given that Isla's head had been pretty noisy fending off a message from Rupert again, while deconstructing every last detail of yesterday's date. This post-date analysis, in and of itself, irritated her. The fact that she wasn't in direct contact with Leigh had prevented her obsessing about when was a good time to message him, and whether he'd message her back. But now that there were others acting as middlemen to their relationship – not that she could call it a relationship – she had no control, and that made her obsess even more, which was ridiculous. After all, it was only one date. One slightly disastrous, make-up-down-her-face, lame-chat date. Can you ghost someone via a third party? And why was she even stressing over it? Did she have nothing else to think about other than a man? Yes! Yes, she did. Her job. Yoga. Namaste.

She stopped, took a breath, then moved around the room again, adjusting residents' arm and leg positions, as she counted out their breaths, 'In, two, three, four. And release, two, three, four. And stretch, two, three. Gently, William, we don't want another episode like last week, do we?'

'How did it go?' whispered Doris as Isla repositioned her elbow.

'And release, two, three. Breathe in through your nose, and out through your mouth.'

Doris stared at her as she wandered around the room. 'Tell me everything,' she added, as Isla moved past her again. Isla shook her head. 'I'm eighty-three, I've got to get my kicks from somewhere. There's a lot to be said for vicarious living.'

'What, no "Boggle" last night?' said Isla, pointedly.

'He had a headache.'

She giggled. 'OK, everyone. That's brilliant. And release. How are we all feeling? Better? Me too. Just what we all needed, a moment to pause and breathe. Good for the soul and it smells like lunch is ready, too. Perfect appetite worked up. Oh, here you go,' Isla jumped over to one of the residents whose balance wobbled as she got up. 'Steady on.' She set her straight and smiled at the rest of them. 'And don't forget we've got book club in the library at four, for anyone who wants to join. It's our first session so we'll be choosing what we want to read from a new selection that the library sent over to us.'

Doris sidled up next to Isla. 'Books, schmooks. Come on! Spill the tea.'

'Spill the tea? Look at you all down with the kids!'

'Hey, don't be so ageist. And stop deflecting. How was your date?'

Isla started moving the chairs back into position, shaking her head at Doris. 'It was . . . well . . . ' She took a breath in, two, three, searching for the right words.

'Oh,' said Doris. 'That's not good.'

'No, no, it was . . . I mean, he's . . . it was just . . . ' There was a beat.

'You want to say nice, don't you.' Doris rubbed her nose with tissue retrieved from her sleeve.

'I don't know. I mean, maybe?'

'Who wants to go on "nice" dates,' she said, dropping said tissue into the bin.

'But it *was* nice. And he was . . . well, to be honest, after recent dates, the fact that he was utterly respectful, like, a really nice—'

'That word again—'

'Guy well, that's good. But . . . '

'But?'

She let out an audible sigh, 'I dunno, I guess I just don't think he was interested.'

'Were you?'

'Was I? Oh my god, Doris,' she checked over her shoulder then leaned in. 'He was hot! And funny. And he seemed kind.' Isla left the day room, heading back to her office, Doris giddily following.

'Kind is good. Especially when accompanied with hot.'

'Right!? And like I say, totally respectful. I can't remember the last time I went out with someone who was like that. Who didn't come across like a total moron/misogynist/dickhead, delete as appropriate.' She sighed again. She'd done a lot of sighing since last night. 'But I don't think we'll be seeing each other again.'

'Why ever not? Have you looked in a mirror lately, my girl? Your face, added to your lovely bonnie personality, I'd say you're a pretty good catch too.'

'Experience tells me otherwise, Doris, you know? I mean, I've got to answer some post-date questions in a bit. I guess he will too, but . . . I'm not hopeful.'

'Post-date questions? What on earth for? Is he doing research?'

'What? Oh, no. It was for the paper. The *Gazette*.'

At that exact moment, a man came into reception dropping a pile of *Gazettes* on the side and Isla remembered why she hadn't mentioned it. She turned to face Doris. 'You cannot tell anyone!'

'Tell anyone what? What are you talking about?'

She pulled Doris closer, lowering her voice. 'It was—is an experiment. For the paper.'

'For the paper!?'

'I mean it, Doris.' Isla put on her stoniest, sternest face.

'That paper?' Doris peered at the pile.

'Not. A. Word!'

'Me? No! Of course not.' Doris stood up as straight as her arthritic hips would let her and smiled benignly. 'My lips are sealed.'

Isla recognised the smile and knew for a fact that this was a massive lie. However much they shared confidence, Doris couldn't wait to get into the dining room and tell everyone whatever it was she thought she knew about Isla's date and the newspaper experiment. Doris was clearly itching to reach for a *Gazette*.

A rush of cold air came through the hall again. Not *more* copies?

Doris's eyes widened. 'Oh my.' She nudged Isla, newspaper briefly forgotten.

Isla turned to see a man: tall, full suit, a nice one, not shiny like a magician's or tweedy like Date Number Five's. It was sharp, and well-tailored, and was worn by a man who, it seemed to Isla on first glance, oozed a level of sex appeal few could compete with. Harry Styles. Stanley Tucci. A (well behaved) Hemsworth.

'Hi, sorry to bother you,' he said, confidently. His voice was the kind of silk reserved usually for Jeff Goldblum's wardrobe.

Isla flicked her hair.

'I was looking for Prudence Fairweather?'

'Ahh, lovely Prudence?' Prudence had moved to the home after her husband died, six months before. She was one of those elegant older women with expensive clothes, a sparkly diamond ring and immaculate hair coiffured by the mobile hairdresser every Tuesday and Friday morning. She came from a bit more than some of the other residents, like she'd once lived something of a lavish lifestyle though didn't appear to anymore. Despite this, she'd settled right in. 'And who might you be?'

'Her nephew, well, her great nephew. Rupert.'

'Oh,' said Isla, surprised. She let out a coquettish laugh and Doris smirked. 'I didn't realise she had a nephew.'

Rupert looked sad. 'Yeah . . . spent a lot of time with her growing up. Not that she remembered me the last time I saw her.'

Isla studied his face.

'And . . . well, it's been a while since I was last here. Life, work, I've been pretty busy.'

'I see. If you could just sign in for me then, please.'

As Isla ducked behind the reception desk to fetch the visitors' book, Doris shuffled closer to the man.

'Our Isla has an excellent memory for faces,' she said. 'I'm *very* surprised she doesn't remember yours.' Isla glanced over and saw through Doris's entirely straight face – mischief was radiating from every pore.

'You can check her file if you like?' he said as he scribbled his name in the book, apparently taken off guard by Doris's line of attack. 'To prove it's me. Erm, I know she's just moved rooms. She's in eleven now.'

Doris's eyes widened again and she mouthed 'Room eleven,' in horror.

'Oh wait,' he said, stepping back. He gave Isla the once over. 'Well, I never.'

'What?' Isla looked around.

'It's you, isn't it?'

She double checked behind her in case he meant somebody else but there was nobody there, when she looked back, he was still staring at her. It wasn't in a pervy way, as such. But he was clearly very happy for her to know that she was pleasing to his eye. The feminist in her was a teensy bit affronted but the single woman standing before a (very) handsome besuited man went a little bit quivery.

'We've been talking, the last few days. I've been trying to charm you enough that you'll eventually say yes to dinner with me.'

'Oh!' Isla's neck got hot.

'I'm Rupert.'

'From the app!'

'The app?' mouthed Doris, eyebrow impressively arched.

Isla took a moment to put the almost impossibly attractive man in front of her together with the photos she'd swiped right on. It *was* him: the floppy hair was true to life and if anything, it was even more gorgeous off camera. She'd enjoyed their banter, but had been so preoccupied with the

Leigh debacle she just hadn't got round to replying . . . which she could now see was incredibly remiss.

'I was kind of hoping you'd have said yes,' he said. 'And now I'm even more hoping you'll say yes. Sorry, is that a little bold?'

Doris had, by now, manoeuvred her walking frame round to behind where Rupert stood and was urging Isla on. Pointing at Rupert and generally acting like the embarrassing aunty at a Christmas get together when the person whose paddling pool you used to play naked in rocks up in a terrible Christmas jumper. Had she seen the *Bridget Jones* films? They could play those at film club next. Isla could try once again to work out which one of the love interests she preferred.

Except this wasn't a film and dear god what did a man like Rupert see in a woman like her. He was like one of those models that sold really expensive watches or exclusive after-shave worn only by men with the perfect amount of stubble and straight white teeth, and she was, she was . . . she was not answering his question.

'Maybe that *was* a little bold. I won't push my luck, but message me? This could be . . . serendipity,' said Rupert, smiling directly at Isla.

'Serendipity indeed,' said Doris, sounding a lot like she was about to launch into a Miss Marple-esque investigation. Isla was confused – did Doris approve or not? Not that it mattered. Rupert was the nephew of a resident. She couldn't possibly go on a date with him now. Even if she had been thinking about it, which she definitely hadn't. In fact, she'd just decided, she was swearing off men.

All men.

Even really, really handsome, confident, suave and sophisticated ones who wanted to pay for her to have a meal out in a restaurant.

A full meal.

In a restaurant.

Her belly grumbled. Did it say anything in her contract about not dating residents' family members? Was it morally ambiguous? Might dating a great nephew be more acceptable than dating a closer relative, like a son, or an ex-husband? She grasped for some sense of professionalism . . . 'Do you believe in serendipity then?' . . . failing.

'Do you?'

'I might.' She flipped the visitors' book shut in an action she hoped looked efficient, not officious. 'Well, it was nice to see you in person, anyway. Room eleven is up the stairs and down the corridor. The first door on your left after the defibrillator.'

'Right.' Rupert nodded. Isla stood her ground. Doris checked him out a final time. 'Thank you, and . . . See you soon, I hope.' he smiled an almost irresistible smile and Isla sort of hoped he might give her a wink or something else equally ick-able, But he didn't, he just strode off up the stairs being all effortlessly handsome.

'Great Aunt Prudence, eh. He has definitely *not* visited before,' whispered Doris when he was out of earshot. She paused, craning to watch him disappear up the stairs. 'Never mind you, Isla, *I'd* have bloody remembered.'

'Come off it, Doris, he's not *that* good looking.'

'Who said he was?' Doris reached for the *Gazette*, 'Oops, would you look at that, *two* copies.' She folded both papers under her arm with a wink.

'We won't be in it yet, I've not answered any post-date questions.'

'It'll not harm to just refamiliarize myself with the publication.'

'You don't need two of them.'

'Oh, you know how it is, Isla,' said Doris, pointedly. 'We all need a back-up plan. I mean, spare copy.' And with that, she pottered off down the hallway.

Giddy, in need of a sit down and a moment to think about what she could say to Rupert if she saw him before he left, Isla took to her cupboard.

11

Flicking through her phone, Isla hid in her office, reading back the few messages she and Rupert had exchanged. The last one had in fact been him suggesting that they could just go for a drink if she felt that food was too much of a commitment. (Though he had wondered if bar snacks would be allowed because if it was after he'd finished work, he'd be ravenous. She'd joked that she wasn't offended by a stuffed olive and resisted making a joke about nuts.)

She also swiped through his photos. Pretty restrained, she thought. Most blokes on dating sites chose photos that made them look one thousand times hotter (younger!) than they were in real life, the odd few using weird filters, and not few enough posting ab shots. This was the one occasion Isla would have welcomed an ab shot because if his face was anything to go by, she barely dared to imagine what the rest of him might look like. Not that it made a difference; abs, dad bod – whatever that was supposed to mean – she reminded herself that of course she was more interested in who he was than how he looked. She absolutely was not going to spend undue time objectifying him. Even though it was really hard not to objectify him. Each photo she saw looked like a version of him, but not quite the version she'd just stood in front of – basically, they didn't remotely do him justice.

Maybe his bio would knock a few points off. She read it again, Rupert. Thirty-three. Likes food, wine and walking.

Well it wasn't exactly sparkling but it also wasn't a collection of reviews from ex-girlfriends or a list of sexual preferences (read: demands).

Opening her laptop, she responded to a few work emails, then tried to find Rupert on Facebook. She'd tried looking for Leigh the other day and had no luck anywhere. Was Rupert less elusive? Nothing on Facebook, no Twitter either. She avoided LinkedIn, aware that they would send him an email rounding up who'd checked out his account, wincing at the memory of her search for a boy she'd had a holiday romance with when she was sixteen. Four years after meeting Ed who lived in Malaga, Ed, now from Milton Keynes, was a Project Manager for Specsavers. He had lots of 'connections', and the occasional photo of a new store he'd just done out. She'd wondered what he thought when he saw she'd checked him out, only mildly disappointed he hadn't returned the favour.

She tried Instagram. Bingo. That was definitely Rupert. Again with the slightly average photo but he took a lovely shot of a Peak District gate and seemed to have had a brilliant time on a recent trip to Barcelona. Isla had always wanted to go to Barcelona. She kept scrolling back to see if she could see any photos with previous girlfriends, careful not to accidentally like something. The only thing she found was the photo of a woman stood next to a car with a body con dress and legs that went on for days. No comment, only a few likes. Was she an ex? And if so, what the hell did he see in Isla? She took a sip of coffee and spilt some down her top as if proving how badly matched they were. She was sat in a cupboard office with dry shampooed hair and freeze-dried cappuccino down her top. She was the opposite of sophistication and even if that wasn't an ex on his Instagram feed, they just weren't a match.

Except, he had looked like he really liked her. Maybe even fancied her . . . ? And he still talked about them going on a date, even when he'd seen her in person, albeit minus the cappuccino stain.

She rolled her eyes at herself, shaking her head, and replied to another work email, setting up some painting workshops for the residents with a local artist. But she couldn't bring herself to focus. She wondered what Rupert's political allegiance was. Did he consider himself an ally of any of the causes she felt passionately about?

Did Leigh?

Before she could give it any more thought, an email landed in her inbox.

Subject line: Post-Date Questionnaire.

Dear Isla,

We hope you enjoyed your first cheap date. As agreed at the start of this experiment, we'd love you to answer the following simple questions.

1. What was your first impression of Leigh?

Isla sat and wondered. First impression. He'd grabbed her, she'd been terrified, then the reason became clear, and she'd been mortified. And that was before she'd realised he was her date. Should she be honest about how it went? Her feelings? It's not like she had anything to lose. She read on.

2. Did you feel any chemistry.

Had he received the same questions? Had he felt any chemistry? Was he even going to bother filling them in? She'd fancied him, one hundred per cent. But she'd talked a lot of rubbish, and owing to the mascara situation, bore an uncomfortable resemblance to Marilyn Manson. Was it even possible for a man to feel chemistry towards a woman with scarier eye makeup than someone who named himself after a psycho killer? Sometimes she felt like he was awkward, moving around her. But then, at other times, he'd been funny and warm and thoughtful.

She remembered him telling her she didn't have to be pretty for anyone.

A knock at the door made her slam her laptop shut. 'Hello? Yes? How may I help you?'

Rupert stood before her, holding out a business card. 'Now, I know this is a pretty cringeworthy way to give you my contact details, I'd like to think that it is not representative of the kind of person I am.'

Isla smiled. 'You're not the first, to be fair.'

'Worst business card moment?'

'Doctors surgery. Given to me by a tree surgeon called Stretch.'

'Stretch?'

'According to his business card.'

'Did you call him?'

She laughed. 'He joked about being there for the clap clinic, what do you think?'

Rupert gave a small smile and looked down at his very expensive leather brogues.

'Also, he wasn't my type,' she added.

'What is your type?' he asked, hopefully.

She paused, raising an eyebrow at him until he laughed. She definitely wasn't going to tell him about her weakness for floppy hair.

'Nice card,' she said, thumbing it. 'Thick, expensive.'

'Does business card paper stock matter?'

'I'd say to ask Stretch but it was the risk of an STD that put me off more than his twenty-four hour turnaround business cards – complete with clip art.' He laughed again, she was on a roll. She noticed he had an office up Ecclesall Road and his job title was Head of Acquisitions. She had no idea what that really meant but it sounded impressive. 'You know I can reach you via the app. If I want to.' She held out his card, impressed with how calm she thought she was sounding. Progress.

'I'm coming off it. Turns out it's hard to find what you're looking for using algorithms and corny one-liner biographies.'

'You don't have a corny one-liner.'

'No. I couldn't think of one. I don't perform well under pressure it turns out.'

She smiled wryly. He didn't take the card back. Should she keep holding it out for him? Or casually drop it on her desk in case she did, in fact, decide to call him. No, he was Prudence's great nephew. He was also, clearly, too good to be true. She shouldn't. She definitely shouldn't. No good could come of this, of him . . .

Did *he* think she had to make herself pretty for people?

He leaned against the doorframe. 'And even when you do find exactly what you're searching for, or so it seems,' he looked down briefly, then back up at her. 'The woman in question doesn't seem all that interested.'

Isla's cheeks flushed. She was not going to give in. She was absolutely going to stay strong.

He clenched his jaw, eyes flashing.

Must. Not. Buckle.

'So, I figured if I left you my number, and crossed my fingers, maybe you'd take a leap of faith and agree to a date.'

'You cross your fingers?'

'One dinner. I promise it's on me. Somewhere nice. I'm not a perv or a letch or someone who expects anything in return for buying you food. I'd just like to get to know you, that's all. No pressure.'

She nodded, studying his card. She was enjoying being a little bit in control of the moment, but when he finally reached over and took the card gently from her hand, the smell of his aftershave almost undid her. 'I mean, you can just throw it away, right?' he said, dropping it on her desk.

She picked it back up, looking from it to him, to her bin.

'Ooh, that's harsh.' He laughed.

'If you'd like to sign out before you leave, I really must get on. Very busy you know.' She crossed her arms, brushing his business card against her lips.

'Right. Of course. I wouldn't want to keep you any longer than is absolutely necessary.'

He took the pen, making a show of signing out. She watched him walk away, making sure that when he turned to give her a final glance, he saw her put his card in her pocket with a flirtatious smile. A smile he reciprocated.

Isla pretended not to keep watching him out of the corner of her eye as he climbed into his car. It was something clean and white and sporty, cars had never really been her thing but it was fit, whatever it was. When he'd gone out of the car park and her heart rate had begun to slow back down again, she opened up a reply to the *Gazette* and began typing out her answers.

12

The Cheap Dates Club: Date One, Isla and Leigh

We had an incredible response to our Cheap Date call out and with the help of our experts, whittled the entrants down to four couples who all agreed to take part in the experiment. And our first outing? Isla and Leigh.

Entertainment Coordinator Isla (28) and Designer Leigh (32) are both are Sheffield, born and bred. We sent them off on a litter-picking date at the botanical gardens and despite the fact that this date was free of charge, it got off to a splashy start. Before they'd introduced themselves, Leigh tried to wrestle an unsuspecting Isla out of the spray from a bus driving through a puddle. The unsuccessful rescue attempt left the pair drenched for the entirety of their date, but we get the impression this didn't put too much of a dampener on their evening. Leigh did say his lasting image of Isla was the puddle water dropping from her fringe – maybe not the lasting image she would have wanted to leave – but we reckon puddle or no puddle, she'd be hard for Leigh to forget.

So what about chemistry? The pair were pretty coy about this, both said they made each other laugh and thought the other was attractive, puddle water notwithstanding, but neither wanted to fully commit to the question, do you fancy each other?

A bit shy, or a mismatch? Only time will tell. What we do know is that both thought the other was easygoing with a great sense of humour. 'Lovely', being how Isla described Leigh, even though he wasn't her 'usual type'.

When asked, both Isla and Leigh said they left the date unsure if the other wanted to see them again, so it was up to us to find out. What we know for sure is that for Leigh, it was a definite yes.

Will our dates make it to a Cheap Date number two? You'll have to wait and see . . .

In the meantime, to continue the conversation, tag us on socials, #TCDCIslaAndLeigh

13

'Well, you're a dark horse!' said Jim, pushing past Leigh, phone in hand.

Leigh was having a spot of lunch in between meetings. He loved going into the office but those days of working from home had definite food-based perks. Not least because it was cheaper. 'Hello to you too. You want some cheese on toast?'

'Only if you've got Hendo's?'

Leigh pointed to a bottle of Henderson's Relish on the shelf above him with a look that said, of course I've got Sheffield's answer to Worcester sauce, only better. (This wasn't a scientific or legal deduction, simply Leigh's semi-professional cheese-on-toast-making opinion).'Perfect.'

'Why am I a dark horse?'

Jim brandished the phone at Leigh. It was the *Gazette* website.

'Oh . . . ' He turned away, taking a second to look up to the gods that were apparently not on his side. Leigh had spent the morning trying not to overthink their date, or the roundup in the paper, given that Isla seemed pretty indifferent to him but Jim was about to get insufferable. 'Right.'

'Never mentioned *that* did you?'

Leigh rattled the cheese on toast beneath the grill. 'I wonder why?'

Jim flicked through the page with relish. '*She had puddle water dropping from her fringe.* Your sister nearly imploded when she read that.'

Leigh cringed at how open he'd been in his answers. If he'd have known he wasn't her usual type, he might have been a bit more reserved.

'She said it was so romantic that you would mention a detail like that.'

Jim shook his head, laughing, and Leigh smiled at the memory of Isla's mascara running down her face and the occasional shiver she gave, because if she felt like he felt, she must have been bloody freezing.

'"*Will our dates make it to a Cheap Date number two? You'll have to wait and see . . .*"' He nudged Leigh's arm. 'Well, will you? Give us the inside scoop. Come on!'

'This, here, this is what I mean.' Leigh warned him with a stare.

Jim feigned innocence. 'I haven't said anything!' Leigh carried on staring. 'Leigh and . . . what's she called?' He checked his phone again. 'Isla. Nice name.' He nodded to himself, then wandered away from Leigh before bursting into, 'Leigh and Isla kissing in a tree.'

Leigh threw the dishcloth at him. 'Give over.'

'K, I, S, S—'

'You're thirty-five.'

'Yeah. And I've been married to your sister for seven years. Forgive me if I find a bit of excitement in somebody else's love life. I, N, G!'

'I'll tell her!'

'Don't you dare.' Jim threw the dishcloth back then tucked into his lunch.

Leigh tried to act nonchalant. 'Not exactly sizzling, is it?'

'Read to me like they thought you were both holding back.'

'I literally said I'd like to see her again. She on the other hand . . . '

'Not her usual type. Yeah . . . I mean . . . that's OK though. It doesn't mean you couldn't be her type. Was she *your* usual type?.'

'She was lovely,' said Leigh.

'Equally as sizzling. Was she not that great then?'

Leigh stuffed a large piece of his own, now congealed cheese on toast into his mouth. If he was going to save face, he wasn't going to be rushed into showing his full hand.

'Buying time,' said Jim, pointedly.

Leigh chewed. Then took a sip of a cold cup of tea he'd left on the coffee table, wincing. 'I mean, it was . . . weird.'

'Well, you were litter picking. It's not exactly sexy.'

'Exactly. Though, that didn't matter. I just—'

'Didn't fancy her?'

'I didn't say that. I just don't think, based on what she said, that she'll be interested.'

'Rachel's right. You're going to die alone.'

'Jim! It was just all so . . . set up. I didn't know if I should ask her for a drink afterwards, I didn't know if it would be breaking the rules of the whole cheap date thing. So I didn't, and now she's probably decided that I'm not man enough, or upfront enough and so I've probably ruined it all anyway.' He paused. 'But I am not going to die alone.'

Both Leigh and Jim caught each other shooting a look in Tarquin's direction.

'Rachel thinks she liked you.'

'How can she tell?'

'I dunno. But she's a woman. They know this stuff. She'd have been flat out negative if she wasn't interested, surely?'

Leigh got up, taking his plate to the sink. 'She was probably being polite. She doesn't seem like the type to embarrass someone in a national newspaper.'

'The *Sheffield Gazette* is hardly a national newspaper.' Jim shoved his last slice into his face and handed over his plate too.

'OK, no. But she doesn't seem the type to embarrass someone in a free local paper, either. Like I say, she was lovely.'

'Look in the mirror dude, you're not exactly rough. I would. If I was a girl. Or a boy who liked boys and you liked me back. Or a non-binary—'

'Jim.'

'OK, I'm just saying, if you liked her, and she liked you, you should probably see each other again.'

'See her again!' piped up Tarquin. 'See her again.'

'Whose side are you on?' said Leigh, scratching the back of his head, then he reached for a tea towel to dry off the plates and stacked them in the cupboard. He wasn't normally this tidy so soon after eating but he'd found for the last few days since the date that he just needed to keep himself busy. He hadn't been able to stop thinking about Isla since they met. She wasn't like any other date he'd met before and he was really (really) attracted to her; even with mascara smeared down her face and terrible small talk. But if she was interested, why didn't she look back at him when she walked away. Just a second glance, as he had her. She basically walked, then jogged, then ran away. Couldn't leave fast enough.

'So you liked her, but you didn't ask her for a drink afterwards because you didn't want to break any arbitrary rules of the Cheap Dates Club.'

'Jim.' Leigh gave a look that he hoped made it clear he'd had enough.

'No, no. I get it. No rule breaking. No seeing someone afterwards that you clearly like – because I know you, I can tell that you do. So can Rachel. You like her.'

'And?'

'It's good, mate. And hopefully, type or not, Rachel's right and she likes you too.' Jim got up, making himself a glass of water. 'It's about bloody time after all this Serena nonsense.'

'Serena nonsense? She was my wife, mate.'

'Yeah. But she's not anymore and you and I both know you weren't a match made in heaven. I don't know what happened to change things between you and her, but it was only ever going to end up one way.'

Leigh tried not to be irritated by Jim's wholly accurate, albeit hurtful, assessment of his marriage to a woman he pretty much had nothing in common with and yet had fallen for, once upon a time. She'd not always been the person he knew her to be now. He'd convinced himself that he knew a different version. One that only he had the privilege to know.

'Look,' Jim went on, 'I get that maybe it's scary after the last year or so, but you need to get out more.'

'See her again,' squawked Tarquin.

'Three against one.'

Leigh warning stared at Jim again. 'I've got work to do.'

Jim paused, presumably considering whether to continue, ultimately deciding to relent. 'Right you are.' Leigh was relieved they knew each other so well. 'I'd best get back too. Though I appreciate the cheese on toast. Cheers, mate.' He went to the door. 'Oh, and Rachel wanted me to invite you round for dinner, a week Sunday, by the way.'

'Will there be Yorkshire puddings?'

'Will it make a difference?'

'Of course it will. Sunday dinner isn't Sunday dinner if it doesn't have Yorkshire puddings.' Leigh smiled to himself, appreciating a little reminder of Isla.

'OK. Done. It'll have Yorkshire puddings.'

'Great, cheers. Probs see you before then, though eh?'

'More than likely.'

Presumably safe in the knowledge the door was closing behind him, Jim couldn't resist throwing a parting shot. 'And get that second date booked in!' The door slammed shut behind him. Leigh shook his head in good-natured despair.

He went to the sofa and lifted his laptop onto his knee. He tapped out the *Gazette* web address and pulled up the piece again . . . then an email notification from Serena grabbed his attention. If a bus had drenched *her* before a date she'd have kicked off; not picked up litter and talked nonsense with a stranger. Please could he make himself available for a meeting, a week on Monday, in London, to discuss a new account. He'd have to make his way to the new office in Soho and could he 'please make an effort'. He could hear her voice as he read it. The way she spoke. The inflection on please, the crisp *t* at the end of 'effort'. There'd been 'some complaints' about his casual way of dressing, apparently. He huffed to himself. 'Some complaints. Course there have been. Not just you, hating my clothes, as usual.' For years she'd hide his clothes and replace them with items she'd bought. Then she'd be offended if he didn't wear them or expressed any dislike of her choice of sharp suits and designer ties. And the kind of trousers that men with names like Hugo or Jeremy would wear with a slip-on shoe and no shame.

He looked down at his trainers, his hoodie. The jeans he'd had for years that were the single most comfortable pair he'd ever owned. He liked to make an effort, he liked to look nice, their tastes just differed – wildly.

Another email pinged. *From: The Cheap Dates Club. Subject line: Date Two . . .* His palms itched and he clenched his jaw. He tried to get a handle on why he was nervous to open the message. If there was a date number two email, that was good news, right? And maybe that was part of the problem, him not being her type gave him a get-out clause. But if Isla liked him back, this might be the start of something new. Was he ready?

14

Isla fished through her cupboards eenie, meenie, miney moe-ing between beans on toast, tomato soup, or tinned chilli for dinner. Such (own-brand) culinary delights. She thought about Rupert's business card, still in her back pocket. Was it too soon to call him? Because today would actually be the perfect day to be taken out for a slap-up meal. She permitted herself the brief fantasy of a creamy carbonara washed down with a New Zealand Sauvignon Blanc. Perhaps a chocolate mousse for dessert with a dash of flirtation on the side. In the imaginary conversations she'd been holding with Rupert since they met, they laughed, she was hilarious, erudite, he was clearly taken by her. Also, she decided to imagine, he thought she was really sexy. She wasn't sure if she was entirely comfortable with anyone thinking she was sexy, it felt like a lot of pressure. Sexy people always wore matching underwear, didn't dribble in their sleep and effortlessly moved through the world as if powered by magic. But she was going to have to try and lean into something if (*if*) they were going on a date together. She closed her eyes and imagined the version of herself that could project all of the above but this time, just as imaginary Rupert was leaning in to kiss her – the smell of his aftershave wrapping her up in a heady mix of satisfaction and longing – the sound of giggling interrupted her fantasy. She begrudgingly reached for the chilli con carne as the kitchen door burst open.

'Oh, hi!'

Jay bustled in first, followed quickly by Sophie who clung on to the back of his jeans as if they were doing a conga without the side kick.

'You want some chips? Jay got two large portions and I'm not being funny but there is no way I can eat a fish the size of a shark, a cob stuffed with chips, *and* that battered sausage we shared on the way home.'

'So many jokes, so little time,' said Jay, dropping a takeaway bag on the tabletop.

The smell of vinegar crept up Isla's nose and burrowed deep into her soul. 'Have I ever told you that I love you. The very bones of you. From the deepest part of me.'

'You've never said that, no. But then, we've not been housemates for long,' said Jay.

Sophie smacked him playfully. 'It's me she loves. Go on, Isla, fill your boots.'

They passed plates, knives and forks between each other. Salt. More vinegar. Isla dug out a slice of bread and made her own chip butty. For a moment, silence descended in the kitchen because: food and deliciousness, and why were chip shop chips so good when doused in vinegar and wrapped up in buttery bread?

'So, will there be a cheap date number two?' asked Sophie, interrupting Isla's fantasy for a second time.

'Probably not.'

'What do you mean?'

Isla savoured a particularly salty chip before answering. 'I just don't think he's interested. You didn't see my face when I got home. Honestly, mate, it was horrendous. And I just couldn't think of anything to talk about with him. He was so fit, and I was bloody freezing cos of the puddle, I just . . . I was not my best self, shall we say.'

'Soph said the newspaper sent you a load of questions?'

'Yeah, just a few follow up ones. So, I guess I'll find out eventually.'

'You've not heard owt yet then?' Jay reached over to wipe ketchup up from Sophie's face. She leaned over to kiss him a thank you. Weeks into a relationship and they were already sickening.

Isla's green-eyed monster reared. 'I've got options, anyway.'

'Options, you say,' said Sophie, tapping away on her phone as they talked.

Isla mentally face palmed herself because sometimes jealousy took over control of her mouth and as soon as the words came out, did she want to scoop them back up and pretend they never happened. After an embarrassing incident with an ex and his obscenely young-looking mother, who, it turned out, had not been outrageously flirting with her son, rather just buying him coffee because his bank card had been rejected, Isla named her green-eyed monster in an effort to tackle how noisy he could be. Brian. Because Brian felt like the kind of name for a monster that couldn't really do any damage. The kind of name for a monster that you could laugh at and ignore, because clearly *Brian* had nothing useful to tell her about her life.

Jay added another splash of vinegar to his chips. 'Speak more of these options. Soph and I require all of the details.'

Nice one, Brian.

'Go on?' said Sophie, still glaring at her phone screen.

'Yeah, this guy I met on the app. Rupert. We were chatting a bit, then – and how's this for mad – he came into work the other day. Couldn't believe it. His great aunt lives in the home and he came to visit her.'

'Wow!' said Sophie.

'Such a coincidence. Or serendipity, maybe?' said Isla, enjoying a moment to repeat Rupert's suggestion.

Sophie looked earnest. 'And you can't just ignore serendipity. So what's he like? Who recognised who first?'

Isla panicked. Brian went silent.

'Yeah, and was he fit?' added Jay.

Isla and Sophie stared at him as he rifled through his chips, picking out the best ones. 'Honestly, this is the best bit about house sharing and dating,' he said, barely looking up. 'Getting in on the girly chats. Why don't blokes talk like this? We are one hundred per cent missing out!'

Sophie patted his hand. 'You are, in this moment, an honorary girl. Come on then, Isla, have you got a photo?'

'Ooh, yes! Photo!' said Jay.

Isla, deciding she was just going to have to embrace the moment, she'd come this far, licked her fingers clean then picked up her phone. 'Have you got signal? The internet's being a right bag of, oh, hang on, right. Here.' In the absence of his dating app link, annoyed she hadn't saved a few pics . . . for research purposes . . . Isla pulled up Rupert's Instagram, flicking to find the single photo of him. Not a selfie, so who knows who took it, but a pretty beaut shot of him stood among a group of people, laughing, pint in hand, but looking direct to camera. The caption just read, 'Ride or die.'

Sophie took the phone from her and instantly whistled.

She showed Jay, he whistled too.

Isla took another look and couldn't help but agree with them. Rupert was extraordinarily good looking. And this time, she knew that's how he looked in actual real life too.

'So? When you seeing him?' asked Jay.

Sophie picked her phone back up.

'I don't know. I haven't called him yet.'

'Why the hell not!?' Sophie nearly choked on a chip. She pointed to Isla's phone, Rupert's face still grinning out of it. 'Exhibit A!'

'I know, but I just didn't want to rush into anything. I was keeping him on his toes.'

'Ah, bingo!' Sophie read out from her phone. 'The Cheap Dates Club, date number one, Isla and Leigh.'

'What?' Isla paused with a chip mid-air. Her heart flipped then all the blood drained from her face. 'Oh god . . . ' Now she felt a bit sick.

'Hang on, I'm just . . . ' Sophie kept on reading to herself, scrolling, nodding. She showed Jay, he scrolled and nodded too.

'What? What did he say?' Isla grabbed for her own phone and tried to open the web page. 'Gah! Do we need to reset the router?' Then her phone sprang into life and, breath held, she could read what the paper said. 'It's not very long.'

'It doesn't need to be.'

'I've blown it haven't I? I've actually blown it.'

'Just read it.'

'I didn't think he liked me, I didn't want to look a dick. I'm so used to being ignored after dates and I just didn't . . . Oh god.' Isla's eyes darted over the words, not really taking them in. Why had she said he wasn't her type? He was totally her type, he couldn't be more her type. If types were an Olympic sport he'd have won gold. (And probably silver too.)

'See, it's fine.'

'Yeah,' said Jay. 'More than fine.'

'He wants to see me again?' Isla's breath was shallow, her voice small. She knew she'd been carrying that panic in her belly since she left the date, that knowing in her gut that it would probably all go wrong. And she knew that saying he wasn't her type was just a moment to deflect so that she wouldn't look a dickhead if he wasn't interested, but to see it in print, followed by his frankly more mature response of yes he'd like to see her again. She stared at the page, disbelieving. 'But, did he not see my face?'

Jay smiled, kindly. 'Looks like he did.'

'And now he thinks he's not my type.' Isla bit down on her bottom lip, her hands shook a little. Then an email alert popped up on her phone.

From: The Cheap Dates Club.

Subject line: Date Two.

She opened it, a little bit giddy and a little bit sick. 'We've got to meet at the Millennium Gallery. Winter Garden entrance. Three o'clock on Saturday.'

'I knew he would like you!' Sophie dropped her fork and clapped her hands. 'What did I say to you, Jay!'

'You said you thought he would like her.'

'So that's two dates you've got!'

'Oh, I don't know about that.'

'Of course you do! You're free and single. You've got two people interested. Get yourself out there, get on it!'

'Yeah . . . get on it!' Jay's tone was different to Sophie's and the girls both looked at him, knowingly. 'Sorry, I didn't mean . . . I just meant—'

'We know what you meant, you dirty dawg!'

Sophie and Jay started play fighting.

'You two! Pack it in.'

'Look,' Sophie got up to stand behind Isla. She placed her hands on Isla's shoulders, crouching down. 'You're single. You're young. You're gorgeous, even Jay thinks so.'

'"Even" Jay,' said Jay. 'I'm not sure what that means? But yes, you're a very attractive woman.'

'See,' said Sophie.

Isla's cheeks flushed. And she was also a bit jealous that Jay and Sophie were now so comfortable with each other that Jay could compliment another woman without Sophie feeling threatened.

'I don't know. I feel like Rupert's a bit out of my league. Like I'd spend all my time worrying if he was dating me for a bet. Or a joke. It happens, doesn't it? People do that. Date someone clearly not as good looking as themselves, just for a laugh.'

'Why on earth would you think that was the case?' Sophie pulled out her phone, flipped the camera on and turned it to selfie mode, leaning in so the screen captured them both. 'Look at you, you're smoking. And smart. Any man would be lucky to have you.'

Jay, cleverly on this occasion, remained silent.

'Date them both, have a bit of fun, if you decide you like one more than the other, you can finish things and focus. Easy.'

Yeah. Easy. Not scary at all.

Isla caught sight of herself from the selfie angle nobody wants to see. She adjusted her position but even then, her face was not the face of a girl who kept multiple dates on the go. It felt like hard work, a bit deceitful, not to mention high risk. Getting to know two people, meant two chances of falling for someone and two chances of getting hurt. She knew only too well that *that* would be anything but easy.

15

Isla clasped her hands together, then around her bag strap, then stuffed them into her pockets before realising that her jeans were too tight to accommodate anything other than possibly a piece of wafer-thin ham. Although why she'd be pocketing a piece of wafer-thin ham was anybody's guess and maybe she should try focussing on the sculptural plants that towered above her in the Winter Garden, an urban glasshouse in the centre of town. She should try and enjoy the gentle, temperate heat – even though it was a little warm for someone who was basically a walking bag of nerves. She should look up, and around, try and enjoy the cathedral-esque, curved glass roof that connected the garden to the Millennium Gallery, quite a feat of architecture and ambition. It had always just been one of those spaces she'd nip through to get from one part of town to the next but today, she was embracing the distraction by really paying attention. Kids laughed and played. People passed through – some enjoying the space, others moving from A to B, heads down. She could smell something, a flower, she had no idea what species and . . . nope, actually, she couldn't distract herself at all. Her hands were a bit clammy and she couldn't quite catch a hold of her breath and she might need another wee and it was just a date; just a date! Or it would be, if he'd actually turn up. The Cheap Dates email said this was a chance for romance, a reward for picking litter. Their only rules for today were to enjoy time one on one, without spending any money.

A chance for romance though, did that put on some pressure?

Too much pressure?

Maybe he wasn't ready for romance. Maybe he was just curious about what she looked like without mascara down her face and whether she was capable of better chat.

Maybe he'd had second thoughts.

She should have known.

It was her own fault, she'd taken all that time to decide if she wanted to actually go on a second date, even resorting to a pad and pen to write down the pros and cons before realising that it was far too practical a way to decide whether you wanted to explore a romantic connection with someone or not. And also the cons read: *he only likes ham or cheese sandwiches.* She'd been known to enjoy both cheese and ham in a sandwich before now and using that as a reason not to date him seemed illogical.

The top she'd scraped money together to buy from the H&M summer sale was a bit itchy. She had remembered hiding a ten pound note in an old copy of *Pride and Prejudice* (She'd never read it, but liked the idea that one day, she might) and blew it all on the top to give her a bit of a confidence boost for the date, but now the itching was making her feel really hot under her armpits. She tried lifting her arms a little to generate some air movement around them, but not so much that she'd look mad. She'd assumed it was a cotton top but it definitely wasn't a cotton top and she kicked herself for spending the money. And she kicked herself for standing inside the doorway to the Winter Garden when she'd been told to wait outside by the water features. She was usually the kind of person who did as she was told but the sight of a grey cloud across the otherwise blue sky had panicked her. She did not want a repeat performance of date number one but what if he was standing outside as instructed? What if he was somewhere she couldn't see? What if he missed her and she missed him and the date didn't happen because they both thought they'd been stood up?

Maybe she *had* been stood up!?

She surreptitiously blew down her V-neck, trying to lower her core temperature. She should have just asked Sophie if she could borrow one of her tops but when she'd crossed the hallway to ask, the Premier Inn Do Not Disturb sign was placed on the door handle and Isla could hear Sophie's sexy-time Spotify playlist.

Doris, speaking on behalf of the book club who'd all read the *Gazette* and now had a vested interest in Isla's love life, had reminded her that love should be gentle, warm; safe, even. Yes, a bit spicy, lusty, especially to begin with, (Isla had wished the ground would open up when Doris said 'lusty'!) but mostly, love should feel like a kind of peace because it's where you belong. Maybe if she was this nervous, it wasn't meant to be? She didn't feel like she belonged right now as she stared out the Winter Garden doors, checking to see if he was about. A newly married couple walked by the fountains that leapt at varying heights, delighting kids who played among them. The couple's photographer, a long dark-haired woman with excellent tattoos, expertly snapped away as they made their way towards the tropical glasshouse. What a nice place to have photos. What a lovely wedding dress. Isla had never been one to obsess over weddings or getting married, not even as a kid, but they looked happy, the bride and groom. Did they look peaceful? Would Doris think they belonged together?

Isla checked her watch for the third time in as many minutes and when she looked up, Leigh had suddenly appeared. She jumped.

'Hi! Erm, I'm not late am I? Oh God, sorry if I am.' He took his phone out to check the time.

'No, you're not late. I was just . . . don't worry.'

'Oh good. Great.' He paused, fixing his eyes on her. 'Hi.'

'Hi.' There was that coy feeling again.

'Nice to see you again.'

'And you.'

He leaned in to kiss her cheek. She closed her eyes for a second and felt his hair brush the side of her face. The hair on the back of her neck stood to attention.

'Thank god I didn't grope you again, this time,' she said afterwards, immediately wishing she hadn't.

Leigh laughed. Mouth open, head back. There were no fillings, no stringy saliva and no glistening gullet. He was already winning.

'Thought I'd better wait inside so I didn't get totally drenched by a freak raincloud or fall in the fountain or some such. Didn't want to spend a second date with you looking like a background artist from some terrible action film. I'll be buying waterproof mascara when I next go to Boots.'

'Hey, you looked great last time.'

'Well . . . I didn't.'

'I came for a second date, didn't I? Can't have been that bad.' He grinned.

'I suppose.' Isla's belly flipped a bit. She flicked her hair and tried to act nonchalant. She'd never been nonchalant in her life. She couldn't even spell it without having to really think about it first. Was it nonch-a? Nonch-e?

'Shall we go in?'

'I'd love to.'

The wedding couple were now inside the Winter Garden too, posing in front of some giant bamboo. Leigh offered them a congratulations before opening the Millennium Gallery door for Isla. She waited for him on the other side, and they walked, in sync, towards the desk. His arm brushed hers and she felt a definite frisson of something. Had she felt this kind of frisson when she met Rupert? Well, yeah, obviously.

Must. Not. Compare.

In the first exhibition was a collection of Sheffield steel. Isla paused by a glass case packed full of spoons. 'Good old Sheffield, we love our cutlery, eh,' said Isla.

'Over eight hundred items on display,' said Leigh.

'Oh, wow. How do you know?'

He pointed to a board next to where they were stood. 'I read it.'

'Oh. Yeah.' *Don't be an idiot, Isla.*

'Shall we?' Leigh pointed in the direction of a different exhibition. 'I've been meaning to come and check out this one.' He placed his hand on the small of her back, leading her away from the spoons.

'Oh! A Hockney!' Isla exclaimed, excitedly, once inside the gallery space.

'You like Hockney?'

'I love him. Well, it's Mum really. She used to take me to Saltaire when I was a kid, that's where his gallery is.'

'Oh, I know it. I've been a few times too.'

'Yeah? Can you imagine if we'd been there at the same time?' mused Isla.

Leigh stopped and looked at her. 'I'd have noticed you.'

She swallowed. 'Course you would. In a room full of Hockneys and lilies.'

Leigh's eyes sparkled a bit. 'I'd have noticed you.'

They walked. Pausing at paintings, heads tilted in unison. Studied it, read the note, moved on. One of the pieces was a photo of some kids jumping into a river. 'Have you ever done that?' he asked.

'Not yet. Think I'd hate it, to be honest.'

'Me too. It's supposed to be good for you though.'

'So is snuggling up under a duvet and watching a film with a hot chocolate, and out of the two, I know which I'd prefer.'

'Sounds like a perfect Sunday.'

'Almost perfect,' said Isla, pointedly. But when he looked at her with eyebrows raised, she felt her skin tingle and her cheeks pink and why was she so rubbish at flirting?

'Are you Isla and Leigh?' a voice said from behind them.

Isla spun around. 'Erm, yes?'

A woman stood before them. 'I thought so. I loved your first interview. So cute! Made me feel a bit nostalgic for those early days of a new romance. I've been with my husband for twenty-one years now and let's just say the magic is a little harder to see.'

Both Isla and Leigh stood in front of the woman, uncertain of what to say. She didn't look old enough to have been married for twenty-one years. She must have been really young when they got together. Maybe they were childhood sweethearts, or a teen holiday romance like Isla's mum and dad.

'Enjoy that magic while you still have it. Which,' she eyed them both up and down, 'I assume you do, to look at you.'

Isla laughed nervously. Leigh coughed and ruffled the back of his hair. The woman smiled, apparently revelling in causing them a bit of embarrassment.

'I've left you a coffee each behind the café bar. Thought you can sit and chat, if you want to. They'll pass it on to someone else if not.'

'Oh, that's lovely. Thanks,' said Isla.

'Really kind, thank you. We've been given explicit instructions not to spend anything and if I'm honest, the coffee does smell good,' offered Leigh.

'Of course you have, it's the Cheap Dates Club, isn't it! Love the idea. Just enjoy it. And remember these moments.' She went as if to leave then, paused. 'If you're lucky enough to make it to twenty-one years, you'll need these memories for when he "forgets" to take the bins out, snores after too much Rioja, or forgets your anniversary because of the rugby or football or cricket.'

'Right . . . ' said Isla, not sure she wanted the reality of this woman's marriage to dampen the spirits of their date.

'Still,' the woman reached for Isla's arm. 'I'm sure I'm not perfect either. And where would I be if I wasn't with him, eh?'

The lady winked, patted Isla, then wandered off towards the museum shop.

Leigh and Isla stood stunned for just a second before Leigh shook it off, offered Isla his arm and said, 'Can I get you a free coffee?'

16

'Come on then,' Isla leaned her elbows on the table, resting her chin on one hand, spooning up coffee froth with the other. She was hoping it would look sexy and confident but as she put the spoon face down into her mouth, clashing her teeth first, she wasn't convinced she'd pulled it off.

'Come on, what?' Leigh asked, apparently not noticing her display of goofiness. Though how was anybody's guess. He'd been watching her intently since they sat down, his knees touching hers beneath the table. She'd never had fizzy knees before, but they were definitely fizzing now. She assumed this was physical attraction and not a medical episode. He leaned in. 'What do you want to know?'

He had a really beautifully shaped mouth. She wondered again what it would be like to kiss it. And . . . 'Well,' she cleared her throat. 'What's your situation?'

'My situation?'

She rolled her eyes. 'Do you always act so innocent?'

'Innocent? Not a word I'm often associated with . . . ' He took a sip of his coffee, the corners of his eyes crinkled.

'OK then, I'll just come out with it. Why is a man who appears to be as lovely as you are—'

'As "lovely" as I am?'

She really wanted to adjust her position but didn't want them to disconnect. 'Lovely, yes,' she pulled a face and he broke out into another smile. She loved it when she made him smile. 'And I stand by it.'

Narrowing his eyes at her, flirtatiously, he asked, 'Is "lovely" fanciable?'

She sat back, fanning herself for a second with a menu before realising what she was doing and shoving it back between the salt and pepper pot. 'Objection. "Is lovely fanciable" is a leading question and I refuse to be drawn.'

'Your honour.' Leigh laughed.

Isla was beginning to enjoy these moments. He wasn't cocky, he didn't seem to be arrogant at all, but the nerves they'd both seemed to have on their first date, and at the start of this one, had dissipated and he had a self-assuredness that she liked.

'The question still stands. How come a man like you—'

'Like what?'

'A man who clearly likes to fish for compliments. Maybe that's why you're single? Too high maintenance?' she teased. 'Come on. Spill it.' She was also now exuding a confidence that she quite enjoyed. 'Why are you single?'

Leigh scraped around the edge of his cup, eating froth from his spoon – managing not to smash his teeth with it.

The pause went on too long and Isla panicked. 'I mean, I was kidding. I don't think you're too high maintenance.' Confidence drained. Classic Isla. 'I just wondered. Sorry . . . '

'No, no, don't apologise.' He took a deep breath and sat up in his chair, their knees disconnected. 'It's . . . well . . . '

And that's when the penny dropped. He wasn't single!

She should have known.

Why didn't the paper check first? Why are all men absolute—

'I was married. I'm now divorced.'

Oh. 'Oh.'

He drank the last of his coffee. She wondered what to say.

'You've got . . . ' Isla motioned to his nose where a bit of chocolate sprinkle had come off the cup.

'Typical. Where?'

'There, no . . . there . . . ' She reached out to move his hand to where the froth was. 'That's it.'

He curled his fingers round hers briefly, now they fizzed too. 'Thanks. Gone?'

'Gone.'

'Cheers.'

'So . . . ' Isla wondered if she could ask this question in a casual, almost disinterested way, even though she was the most interested she'd ever been about anything before – apart from the time she was interested to find out if you really could make yourself sneeze by stuffing something really far up your nose until your eyes watered a bit. Turns out you can and then making yourself sneeze can get quite addictive but should not be tried at home. 'What happened? With you and your wife?' She studied a grain of sugar on her saucer.

Leigh stretched. He looked around the room. 'I don't really want to talk about it,' he said, for the first time in their date avoiding her eye.

He cheated on her.

He had an affair.

He broke her heart and she had the good sense and strength to leave him. Again, why are all men absolute—

'I guess we grew apart.'

There was a tone to his voice though. It was not the tone of a man who had an affair. Not that Isla was one hundred per cent certain what tone that was, but there was something in the way he looked that made her doubt the assumptions she was jumping to.

'Sorry, it's none of my—'

'No, I'm sorry. It's just—'

'It's fine. We barely know each other—'

'Yeah, but—'

'Honestly, it's fine. Hey, why don't we take another look at the Hockney?'

'Yeah? OK.'

As they got up to leave, he reached for her hand, his fingers gently taking hers. 'Thanks,' he said. This time, he didn't let go.

Hand in hand, they went all around the gallery again, pausing at paintings they'd overlooked the first time, pointing out things that they each liked. She told him all about her mum and dad, he regaled her with a story about the time he came off his BMX and ended up in A&E then apologised for telling her because he wasn't sure why he'd said it. She told him all about how she loved her job and he asked her all kinds of questions about the residents and the activities and suggested she show them *High Society*, one of his favourite films, despite having watched it every time he went to his grandma's because it was the only video she ever owned.

'It's the nostalgia, isn't it?' he said, staring at the same display of spoons where they started out.

'What? Spoons?'

He rolled his eyes. 'Films, or moments, that you connect to your past. To influential people. Also, can you imagine being able to dance like they did back then? I bet some of your residents know how to dance properly.'

'You wanna learn? I bet Doris would teach you.'

'I mean, don't get me wrong, I reckon I could pull out a few moves.'

'Yeah?' She fixed him with a look, 'Go on then.'

'Go on then what?'

'Show me.'

He placed his hand around her waist and pulled her into him, spun her out, then in, then leaned her back in his arms. They were connected at the hips and he held her gaze the entire time which made her swallow, hard. He looked mischievous, playful, but also really, really deeply into her eyes which meant that she realised his were the deepest greeny blue; eyes she could get entirely lost in. She was glad her old smart watch broke as it would definitely have done that alarm thingy it did when her heart rate peaked.

'Well, I didn't see that coming,' she said, still resting backwards, really hoping she wasn't too heavy to hold this way.

'Ha! No, me neither.' He stood her back up again. 'Watches one episode of *Strictly* and he thinks he's Giovanni Pernice. Who knew I was that smooth?' A gallery assistant walked past them, and Leigh loosened his hold. Isla looked down to the floor as she walked on, wishing they'd sealed the moment with a kiss, though she had to acknowledge that a family of five had also just come into the room and perhaps it wasn't the time or place.

'You like *Strictly*?' she asked, trying to cough her heart rate back down.

'I mean, I don't not like it.'

They ended up back in the Winter Gardens. Back under giant, exotic plants, Isla felt small. 'So, I guess, this is it, then.' She crossed her fingers behind her back hoping he'd suggest they go for a drink.

'I guess it is.' He took her by the hand. 'And look, I'm sorry if I made it weird earlier. About the marriage stuff.'

'Hey, that's OK. I'm sorry I asked.'

'No, you're allowed. It's all allowed. I don't have secrets as such, I guess I just hadn't realised I wasn't ready to talk about it.'

She threaded her fingers through his. Both hands. They stood face to face. 'It's fine,' she said. 'Honestly.' He nodded. She gave his hands a squeeze and was about to drop them when he held on. 'I should probably go . . . '

'Yeah.'

'Right.' Her mouth ran dry. She really wanted him to kiss her. Right then, right there. She wanted to know that even though they'd stumbled a bit, that he still really liked her. She wanted him to lean down and press his mouth against hers, leaving her in no doubt how he felt. And for a second, it looked like he might. He looked at her lips, she looked at his, her heart raced, he leaned in slowly, their eyes now locked. And as she closed hers, just in time for him to make contact, his lips brushed the corners of hers as he kissed her on the cheek.

The cheek.

He definitely didn't fancy her.

'I'd love to see you again,' he said.

'Really?!' She tried to regain control of her surprise. If he didn't fancy her, why would he want to see her again? And if he did, why did he not just kiss her full on, like she had so desperately wanted him to? I mean, sure, she could have kissed him. She could still kiss him. She could take his collar, right now, pull him into her and kiss him hard. Giving him zero reason to doubt what her intentions might be if they were ever lucky enough to spend a Sunday morning together, beneath a warm duvet with hot chocolate. OK, maybe not with hot chocolate, it would have gone cold by the time she'd managed to do what she really wanted to do. 'I mean, sure. Yes. It would be lovely to see you again.'

'Lovely?' He said, raising his eyebrows, that mischievous look back again.

'Yes,' she said, meeting his look with her own. 'I said what I said.'

'OK. But I guess we have to leave it to the Cheap Dates Club? You know, if we're going to play by the rules.'

'Sure. I mean, I guess we do. We definitely wouldn't want to break any rules.'

'Nope. Not at all.'

'Right.' Isla moved as if to leave, then changed her mind. Took back hold of his hand, stood on her tiptoes and leaned into him. Her lips on his, soft, gentle, then briefly firm. Short enough a kiss not to escalate, long enough for him to know what was on her mind. He stood back, then moved as if he might kiss her again. Heart (and groin) racing, Isla smiled, about-turned, and strutted away from the Winter Garden knowing full well he'd be watching until she was out of sight.

17

The Cheap Dates Club: Date Two, Isla and Leigh

Well, we don't want to get you all excited, but we think the matchmakers may have hit on something with our Isla and Leigh and their second date. Eyes on the ground tell us that a wander through the stunning Millennium Gallery led our pair to share their first kiss. 'Loved up, hand in hand, deep in conversation,' said another source.

Both were nervous before meeting. Isla said she'd been surprised Leigh even wanted to see her again, but as soon as she saw him she began to relax. Leigh, meanwhile, said Isla is 'lovely' and that they 'had a lovely time'. Isla told us that Leigh 'actually listens to the things she says', which makes us wonder what kind of dates she's been on before. Come on guys, do better!

Leigh likes how confident Isla appears to be, and how she's not afraid to be vulnerable. Both said the other made them laugh and were quick to confirm that, with absolute certainty, they wanted to see the other again. So, date number three? What will we have in store for that one?

Our dating team are just in the middle of making arrangements and it's time to send our pair back out into the community. Be the change they want to see. Don't forget to look out for an update, next week.

And as ever, to continue the conversation, tag us on socials, #TCDCIslaAndLeigh

18

Isla tidied up the bookshelves in the library, then organised the chairs and cushions, gazing out of the window from time to time. The window looked out onto the home's walled garden; the dahlias were beginning to bloom, the raised beds were bursting with colour and a couple of residents meandered with secateurs and trigs. Gardening club had been a success this year, with lots of the residents enjoying tending to the veg patch or clipping back the blooms for displays in the day room.

Not that Isla cared much about that right now.

Of course she did, she cared a lot, but at that particular moment she was too busy remembering how she took control of the situation with Leigh and kissed him. Just kissed him. She was too busy screwing her eyes tight shut to try and dial into the moment, the feeling, her lips on his. His on hers. The look on his face afterwards. How wobbly her legs felt as she attempted a confident sashay away, not that she'd ever admit it to him. He needed to completely believe that she was capable of being sexy, upfront, and unafraid to go after what she wanted, which is why she waited until she was out of sight before leaning against a wall and heavy breathing into the path of passersby.

She'd got home. Thrown herself wantonly on the bed and indulged in what Ella used to call 'afternoon delight', the look on Leigh's face and her imagination being sufficient to satiate the burn.

'Ah, that's where you are. I've been looking for you all over.' Doris pushed her frame into the room and Isla blushed at being caught drifting off into a world she had revisited on more than one occasion since the date.

'Hey, Doris.' Isla coughed. Opened a window. 'What's up?'

'You're the talk of the home, you know. You and that Leigh.'

'Us? Really?' Isla pretended to find the scatter cushions particularly engaging as she rigorously plumped and tidied them.

'Yes, you two. Hang on a second, let me take the weight off me sling backs.' Doris dropped down into one of the wingback chairs and rearranged her cardigan.

Isla straightened up some books.

'The delivery lad had to leave extra copies of today's paper cos so many more of us are wanting to read the goings-on. It's not just you two, of course. There's that couple Diana and Andrew. Don't think that's going anywhere. He seems a bit too much like a grown-up and she is clearly wanting to reclaim her youth. You know they were supposed to go dancing in Leopold Square. Apparently there's often live music there?'

Was there an update about her date too? Isla had checked online this morning but hadn't seen anything. 'Oh, is it in today's paper? I forgot about that.'

Doris looked at her disbelievingly.

'Diana and Andrew got to Leopold Square and he'd put his back out or some such so Diana ended up having to dance on her own. She was furious and that was the end of that.'

'Right.' Isla could feel her phone in her pocket but didn't want to let on to Doris about how desperate she was to check the website again. 'I should probably get on—'

'Then there was those teenagers. Eighteen, the pair of them. Too young for this kind of a social experiment really.'

'Eighteen's not too young to date. I really do need to—'

'No good can come of mass media scrutiny at that age.'

'Mass media scrutiny? It's the *Sheffield Gazette*, not *Love Island*.'

'Well, thank goodness for that! I've heard awful things about that programme. I don't know why they don't just bring back *Blind Date*. Cilla could always spot a match from a mile away.'

Isla looked at the door, then wondered whether to just pull out her phone regardless of Doris being there. In fact, she was surprised Doris hadn't brought in a copy of the paper if she was so giddy to talk about it. 'So . . . what do you think about this social experiment then, Doris?'

Doris scoffed. 'Social experiment. It's a way for the paper to get new readers. And it's working, by all accounts. Rita's grandson works for them, did you know that?' Isla shook her head. 'Well, anyway, he said something about hits on the website going through the roof.'

'Nice.' Was the fact Doris wasn't telling Isla what Leigh had said in his interview a bad thing? She should probably just ask. She should probably have a full debrief about him with Doris to be fair, but first she wanted to keep the date to herself, and savour it just that little bit longer. She wasn't sure if she was ready for other people's opinions just yet.

Doris pulled out a pack of Polo mints, popping one in her mouth before offering one to Isla.

Actually, Isla *really* wanted to know what Leigh had said. 'Doris . . . '

'We all really like the sound of Leigh, and you two clearly get along.'

'Yeah?' It felt nice to think Doris approved. It reminded Isla how much she missed her own grandparents. How there was something reassuring about approval from someone who's seen the world from pretty much all angles.

'Yeah. And it must be going well if you had a bit of a snog. How was it? Did he knock your socks off?'

'Doris!' Isla could feel herself colour and wondered why Leigh had told them that. Did it matter that he had? They were grown-ups, after all, it was nothing to feel awkward about.

'Come on, spill it.'

'What do you want me to say?'

'Why are you being all coy?'

Isla's shoulders dropped. 'I'm not.' She rubbed at her neck, which was itching with the combination of embarrassment and nerves. 'I haven't read the interview yet. And I've been terrified in case my version of how it went was not the same as his.' She stuffed her tongue in the hole of the mint, then rolled it around in her mouth waiting to hear what Doris said.

'Oh, I see.'

'Like, I think it went well . . . ?'

Doris shook her head at Isla. 'Go on, get your phone out and read it. I'll keep a look out.' Doris huffed herself out the chair and took up position by the doorway. 'The suits are back, have you noticed?'

But Isla's head was in her phone. She scrolled through all the date roundups until she got to hers then looked up at Doris.

'Go on!'

And as she began to read, her heart leapt. And then she smiled to herself at his description of her. Lovely. That was their in-joke, right? Please let it be their in-joke. She finished reading, scanned back over it again, then looked up at Doris, glowing.

'See. He likes you. As well he should, you're quite the catch. Everyone's ever so chuffed for you, you know.'

'Are they?'

'Of course! People are invested. We all love a bit of love. And we all love you, so come on,' she glanced back out the door before judging the coast clear to head back to her chair. 'Tell me everything you know about him?'

Isla leaned against the wall by the window, indulging in a bit of storytelling. 'He's a designer. For an ad agency. He . . . erm . . . '

'Go on.'

'Well,' She stopped leaning. 'I suppose I don't know that much, really.' She wracked her brains. 'He lives on his own. He likes cheese and ham sandwiches. And digestive biscuits.'

'Is that it? Haven't you been on the internet and stalked him, isn't that a thing nowadays, googling potential suitors. Could've done with that in my day, I can tell you.'

Isla thought about the page on her phone for Leigh's company. The team he worked with. The women looked like the kind of women Isla always imagined she might be if she ever got a job that required suits. Before she realised she never wanted a job that required suits. 'I mean, I've had a *little* look, obvs.'

'Of course you did. No different to us asking around the village if there was someone we liked. Only these days, nobody needs to know about your secret crush.'

'Apart from everyone who reads the *Gazette*.'

'Well, yes.'

'I'd rather have you here with us.'

Isla caught Doris's eye. She smiled back, reminded that she didn't have to fake anything to impress her. 'Me too.'

'You need to make a list of things you want to know about Leigh. Make notes, there's no shame in that. What's he done in his life? What does he want to do? What are his goals?'

Isla wondered if she should mention to Doris about Leigh's marriage. Because really, that's all she wanted to know about. Who to, what happened, how did it end and how long had he been single? It's not that she thought Doris would judge him if she told her, it's just that she felt like it opened up too many questions. She had enough of her own without adding in any from somebody else. 'I feel like he's a bit of an enigma. He seems open and honest. Like, I can tell it's really him that I see on our dates, but there's this side to him. A part of him that's off limits.'

'Right.'

'I don't know, what if he's a tough nut to crack?'

'You'd like to crack him, then?' Doris asked this with every bit of lascivious intention she could muster. Isla grinned, wickedly. 'Well then, that's all there is to it. I wonder when you'll find out about date number three?'

'I'm not sure. I'm waiting on the email.'

'Well go on, check! Maybe they've messaged you now the story is live?'

Isla took out her phone again. She refreshed her email. It pinged. She shared a nervous look with Doris before realising it was a marketing email from HelloFresh – months ago, she and Sophie had taken advantage of a temporary discount on meal boxes. Disappointing.

'Well?'

'Nothing. Oh wait, hang on.' She opened the email that came in straight after. 'Oh, we're going to be dog walking.'

'Dog walking?'

'Yeah, a volunteering thing, apparently.'

'Well, there you go then. That'll show you if he's a tough nut or not.'

Isla's heart swelled, nerves tingled through her body.

Doris pulled herself up to standing with a groan. She paused to catch her breath. 'Slow and steady wins the race. Love is a marathon not a sprint. I'm sure there are more clichés I could share but I'll leave it at that for the time being.'

'Slow and steady. I'll remember that.'

'Yeah . . . at least until it gets fast and furious.' Doris winked and moved towards the door.

Isla laughed – Doris never ceased to surprise. 'Hey, speaking of fast and furious, how's Ged?'

Doris's face broke into a wide smile. 'Oh, you know, we seem to have found what works for us.'

'I'll bet you have.'

'Romance is not only for the young, you know.' She straightened up. 'Now if you'll excuse me, I've got to freshen up and polish off the Boggle set. He's popping round shortly. If I'm not back down for afternoon tea, well, don't you worry about me.' She got halfway through the door and turned to Isla. 'Maybe worry about Ged, though, eh.'

And with that Doris shuffled off as fast as her walking frame would let her. Isla buried her head in her hands, a complex mix of embarrassed, amused and scandalised.

'Yeah, OK, thanks.'

She hurried out the shop and up the hill towards home. Normally she'd have stopped and had a little rootle through the bag to see what she'd got first, but the young lad had followed her out and stood, one foot resting against the wall, vaping and texting as he watched her walk away.

By the time she made it home, she was engrossed in the knotty question of what to wear for dog walking. Something comfy and practical, but that would also somehow confirm in Leigh's mind that she was the same strong, sexy woman who'd kissed him at the end of their last date. She wondered if she'd dare do it again, like she had before, or if he'd take the lead, perhaps bolstered by her making it clear she was not messing about. She hadn't put him off, clearly, and date number three was going to be a real chance to see what kind of a human he was. She'd always thought you could tell a lot about a person by how they were with dogs, and perhaps more so, how dogs were with the person. She'd missed owning a dog, having grown up with a miniature poodle that didn't realise it was a miniature poodle. She'd once tried to persuade work that a dog would be an excellent addition to the home, giving residents something to fuss over if she took it in with her each day. They'd not been convinced, and she'd had to stop looking at the ads on Facebook for dogs that needed rehoming.

Maybe volunteer dog walking would be a good solution? Something she and Leigh could do together? She imagined them heading out in the car on a Sunday, both togged up for a romp through the woods, an elderly neighbour's dog in tow. They'd throw it a ball and laugh at it bounding after it into the streams or undergrowth. They'd take it home and as Isla made tea for the elderly neighbour, showing them photos of their beautiful walk in the woods, Leigh would be out in the yard, washing the dog off.

Then she called herself out for daydreaming with such stereotypical gender roles and switched it up, imagining him bringing her out a hot mug of tea as she finished drying off the dog. They'd lean against the wall of the house, feeling great about their good deed, then they'd go home and make a pie and drink wine and watch films, chatting about where they might take the dog next.

She knew she was going to have to stop getting carried away. They'd only had two dates. It's just that the whole 'cheap dates' set up seemed to be granting her a real insight into what he thought about her, or so it seemed. There was a confidence she could take from that. Plus, he'd said yes to a third date and experience told her this was a good sign. Could she really let herself believe that she'd met someone who liked her, that she liked in return, someone who didn't want to play games?

She unpacked her Too Good To Go, putting wonky carrots, on the edge of their 'use by' tomatoes, and a couple of boxes of pre-packed sandwiches (smiling at the ham and cheese), away in the fridge. That's when she noticed a piece of paper at the bottom of the bag. Scrawled in only just legible handwriting was a name, Dave, a mobile number, and the sentence, 'Let me show you how a cheap date could go'. He'd tastefully drawn a penis beside his number, presumably certain that this would be the deal clincher.

Tempting though it was, Isla shrugged, screwed the paper up and threw it in the bin. She had a third date with an actual grown-up man who she doubted would ever dream of writing a note like that. She headed into her room to get ready.

20

The Cheap Dates Club: Date Three, Isla and Leigh

It was out into the fresh air for our daters this week as they took to Graves Park in order to help out some local elderly owners of companion dogs. The Cinnamon Trust approached us, asking if any of our daters would enjoy a dog walk through the park, and we thought the idea was paw-fect (sorry!) for Isla and Leigh.

While neither Isla nor Leigh have their own dogs, both were excited to spend time with a furry friend, and each other. They told us they enjoyed getting to know even more about each other, learning new things about patience, compassion and kindness as they each cared for their dogs.

'She seems to have this incredibly empathetic side to her. It was beautiful to see,' said Leigh.

'All the dogs loved him,' said Isla before adding, 'They're clearly a great judge of character.' Though when asked about a moment that made her laugh, Isla also told us that the look on Leigh's face when it came to using the poop-a-scoop was priceless.

So, is this puppy love? Or is our couple barking up the wrong tree? Early days, but as our other daters fall by the wayside, Isla and Leigh are the only pairing to suggest they want to meet up for a fourth date. Are they proving that you don't need to spend money to find love? We're pretty paw-sitive about them. Check out next week's paper for your latest instalment.

And if you think you can help the elderly owner of a dog, the Cinnamon Trust are always on the lookout for volunteers and foster carers. Check out cinnamon.org.uk for more information.

Don't forget our socials, tag #TCDCIslaAndLeigh with your thoughts!

21

Leigh sat in his Rachel's kitchen as she and Jim pottered around him. They'd not be able to see what Leigh could: the way they dance around each other as if knowing the moves each one will make. She goes to the sink as he goes to the fridge, as she moves back to the hob, as he gets something out the oven, as the cat hops up onto the side, as Rachel swats it away, as Jim goes over to feed it. Life just seemed to move in harmony in their open-plan kitchen, its bi-fold doors flooding the space with light.

Leigh used to have bi-fold doors.

Though he wasn't sure he and Serena were ever as in sync as Rachel and Jim.

And it should probably be her that he missed, not south facing, eye-wateringly expensive joinery.

'So what did you say you did? Dog walking?' Rachel paused over her sautéed vegetables as she took a slug of Pinot. Leigh tried not to feel envious of the life his sister had built for herself. 'I always thought you were more of a cat person.'

'I've always liked dogs. It was Serena who didn't.'

'Go on then. When did you last walk a dog?'

What was it about siblings that could turn the most benign of questions into something so confrontational? 'I can't remember. Must have been Grandma's.' Leigh swallowed mild irritation. 'Do you remember that grumpy thing she had? What was it?'

Jim topped Rachel's glass up and she kissed him on the cheek. Leigh didn't begrudge her happiness, not at all, even when she was being obstinate. Jim was basically his best mate now, it's just . . . he'd hoped for the same when he got married; not rocking up to theirs, single, for a roasting over roast dinner . . .

'Sandy coloured. Coarse hair,' he said.

'Border Terrier.'

'That's it!'

'Magnus. Scruffy, but very cute.'

'Magnus. Yes. Cute – when he wasn't trying to steal toast from straight out of my hands. Or growling when he'd had enough fuss, despite being the one to come to us for that selfsame fuss in the first place. Funny bugger.'

Leigh had imagined getting a dog. He'd imagined a lot; Sundays where he, Serena, Rachel and Jim would all hang out together. He'd imagined persuading Serena that Soho was no place to bring up kids so they'd buy a nice place on the edge of Sheffield and all the cousins could play together, grow up near to each other. He never imagined a bedsit and a parrot.

'Do you remember how sad we were when they had to put him down?'

'You asked her if she'd buy a chocolate Labrador before Magnus was even cold!'

'Zoe Hubbard's parents were breeding them! I had to ask before they were all sold!'

Jim passed Leigh a can of Elvis Juice, swigging from his own. 'What dog did you have to walk on the date then?' he asked, adept at diffusing their sibling rivalry.

Rachel shot him a look, turning her attention back to the dinner.

'An Airedale Terrier called Derek, and Isla had an Italian Greyhound.'

'Called?'

'Monty.'

'Nice. And what did you talk about?'

'Oh, I don't know. All sorts. We didn't get so much one on one time, there was a group of us. Not daters from the paper, but other dog walkers. It's a charity thing, they meet up twice a week, apparently.'

'But you still like her?'

Just as he was about to answer, Leigh's phone rang and any warm feeling he might have had bubbling about Isla, the belly laughs they'd shared over the memories of kids' TV shows they'd both watched, and those first nights out drinking alcopops and sharing kebabs with strangers, were fast replaced with the thud of cold dread.

'Serena.'

Jim and Rachel glanced at each other then began acting disinterested, but Leigh was fully aware that their fussing over the dinner prep had suddenly got much quieter.

'I'm at Rachel and Jim's. It's Sunday. I just don't think I can . . . but I have plans . . . Serena, it's nothing I can't do tomorrow. So tell them they'll have to wait. That's not reasonable. Why should I? They're literally cooking it now—' He held the phone away from his ear, adjusted his composure and said, 'I might need to head off shortly. Something's come up.'

Rachel was about to say exactly what was in her head; Jim reached across and clasped his hand to her mouth.

' . . . Yes. I understand. Just email it through. I'll make a start as soon as I get back.' Leigh put his drink aside, knowing he was going to have to slow down if he was to keep a clear head and focus on work when he got home.

'I know they're important. And yes, I appreciate that. I suppose I think you could've—right. No. I hear you.' Leigh looked at his watch. 'You'll have it by nine.'

He threw his phone on the table and reluctantly took the glass of sparkling water that Jim had just poured him.

'I see she is still calling the shots,' hissed Rachel, stirring the gravy with some rigour.

'It's just work, Rach.' Leigh wasn't about to give Rachel any mileage by agreeing. As much as he'd imagined them all hanging out together, Rachel had never taken much to Serena. That their marriage ended had given Rachel an irritating sense of *I told you so.*

'It must be important,' said Jim, giving Rachel's hip a gentle pat to say he agreed, but wasn't going to make dinner awkward by joining in in quite the same way.

'So she says.'

'So she says!' Rachel scoffed.

'It's a huge client. I know that much. She says she needs her A Team on it. She can't lose them or it'll impact the whole business.' Leigh grabbed knives and forks to set the table.

'Nice. Just the kind of relaxed evening we were aiming for,' grumbled Rachel, taking the roast potatoes out of the oven and roughing them up, even though they were already golden. 'Go on then, when are you going to leave?'

'After dinner, it's fine.'

'I meant the job. When are you going to leave. Get a new job!'

Leigh prepared himself. 'I'm looking. Haven't found much of interest yet.'

She slammed the potatoes back in the oven. 'Honestly, Leigh. What is it going to take?'

'Shall I take the chicken out, love?' Jim positioned himself between Leigh, Rachel and the baster she was wielding.

'Look Rach,' Leigh sighed, 'I'm only just getting into a good place, where I feel better about things, about me, after the break-up. And the idea of disrupting all that with another big change – I don't know, it just feels like moving jobs would be massive.'

Rachel said nothing; Jim took the chicken out of the oven anyway.

'And believe it or not,' Leigh went on, determined to state his case before Rachel rallied again, 'there just aren't many well-paid, senior in-house designer roles out there. Especially ones that will let me work from Sheffield. People aren't recruiting like they were, not at the moment. Clients aren't spending as much as they used to on ads and design. I couldn't just jump ship even if I wanted to.'

'Look pal,' said Jim, 'I've got a mate with a taxi firm. He's always after drivers. I can get you some shifts if you want. It's not difficult, it's good money on a weekend. And it'd get you away from Serena. Just while you look for the job you really want.'

'It's easier to find a job when you're still in the industry, remember.'

'Yes, but . . . '

Jim went back to the hob and Rachel took over, her tone a fraction less abrasive now that she'd put down the baster. 'We just think you can't move forward while you're still connected to your old life. Of course it's going to be massive, this whole year has been huge for you and I get that you have needed some time, but . . . You're so close to getting your life back on track. This is one last hurdle.'

She was right, Leigh knew it. But that didn't make it any easier to do as she told him. Rachel took a deep breath and fixed him with a look.

'How does Isla feel about you working for your ex-wife?'

And this was why Leigh tended to avoid conversations about Serena with Rachel.

'She needs to feel safe, doesn't she?'

'Oooh, these parsnips look good,' tried Jim.

'What do you mean safe? We barely know each other. I'm not a threat!'

'No, but Serena is.'

Leigh reached for his beer. Sparkling water wasn't going to cut it. 'Serena's not remotely a threat. Of course she isn't! And besides, Isla doesn't know about her, does she?'

Jim winced and turned off the oven.

Leigh wished he'd quit while he was behind.

Rachel put her hands on her hips. 'How can you start a new relationship with someone without being honest?'

'I have been honest. She knows I'm divorced. I just haven't gone into detail about any of it. We're not in a relationship, we've just been on a few dates. I want to know if it's going anywhere before I start offloading all the baggage I come with. I don't want to scare her off.'

'How many?'

'What?'

'Dates. How many dates?'

'Three.'

'So?'

'So what? I'll tell her then,' Leigh slammed his can down. 'Yes, I was married but I was so shit at being a husband that my wife of five years went off with her personal trainer. So I must be a) rubbish in bed b) oblivious to anything and anyone around me, or c) all of the above. Excellent, what a catch. Isla will be bowled over.'

'Hey! If being rubbish in bed was the reason for the end of a marriage . . . well . . . ' she paused, Jim looked up from behind the oven door. 'I know a lot of women who'd now be single. Not me,' she added in Jim's direction.

'You don't get it, Rachel.'

'Leigh,' Rachel's tone had softened. She leaned across the worktop to squeeze his hand.

'Look,' said Leigh. 'I didn't tell her because I didn't know how I felt about her yet. Or about dating. Or getting into a relationship.'

'I can tell you how you feel because it's written all over your face.' She moved around the island to give him a hug. 'You like her.'

'Of course I do. So would you if you met her. But I don't know if I like her, or if I *like her*, like her.'

'There's a difference?'

'Of course there's a difference.'

'Then, I'd say you *like her*, like her.'

His sister had always been able to wind him up, and worse, always able to read him. As a kid, he'd hated it. As a grown up, he hated it. But supposed it had its uses. It was just a shame it often took them to fall out before they got to the root of the issue.

'You've liked her from the get-go. There's obviously something about her.'

'There is. I have! She's funny and smart and arresting. She has this way about her, like she has no idea how cool she is, or how beautiful. And she looks at me in this way that I know means she's going to be able to see me. Really see me. She feels stuff. Her dog, an Italian Greyhound. It got really bad cramp halfway around the walk and she didn't panic, even though it was howling like someone was murdering it. She just really calmly let it lean against her while she massaged its leg until eventually it stopped crying.'

'Sweet.'

'The gravy's ready,' said Jim, stirring it.

'Then she had tears in her eyes cos she felt so sad for it.'

'I'll pop it in the jug, shall I?'

Rachel gave him a thumbs up. 'Was the dog OK?' she asked

'Yeah. Fine. Totally fine.'

Leigh thought about how Isla kept checking in with it after. How they'd talked and she lit up when telling him about her mum and dad, how passionate she was about her job and the people she worked with. He smiled at the story she told him of the two residents at work that were sneaking about having an affair that apparently nobody else in the home knew about, and he could still feel her pressed against him when they found themselves alone in a wooded area, out of sight. She hadn't been so forthright as the first time they kissed, maybe because this time it had been more mutual. But it was like they were teenagers again, hiding, snogging in the park hoping that nobody would see, and he hadn't felt like that in so long. 'Honestly, I think she's pretty fucking magical.'

'But that's amazing, Leigh.'

'Is it?'

'What else would it be?'

'It's terrifying!'

'Why is it terrifying? I've read the interviews. She likes you too! What's to lose?'

'Me? My dignity! My ability to ever trust anyone has already gone, how do I open up to her? How do I believe that I can let go?'

Jim picked at the resting roast chicken. Leigh's belly rumbled.

'Trusting you can let go takes time. And for the record, you lost your dignity when you played Widow Twankey in Year Nine.' said Rachel, handing him a knife.

Leigh started carving the chicken. 'And I tried getting out of that part but Mr Whitfield said I had to do it because nobody else could sing.'

'You can't sing.'

'He hadn't realised that yet.'

The three of them giggled; the tension in Leigh's shoulders relaxed a little.

'Didn't take long 'til he did. What was it you had to start off with?'

'"Gimme! Gimme! Gimme!"'

'"A Man After Midnight", yes!' she finished with a guffaw, reaching for her phone.

'Don't play the video now. I'm not in the mood. I can't believe you've still got that.'

'Recorded it off the telly before you stole the video evidence.' She tapped her nose wisely.

Jim passed him a plate, taking Rachel's phone out of her hands. 'You shouldn't be afraid to fall in love, mate.'

'You've been watching too much Oprah,' said Leigh.

'I listen to her podcast when I'm working. But seriously pal, it's time to be vulnerable again. To be open.'

'And if you like Isla this much,' Rachel said, 'why don't you take a risk? What's the worst that can happen?'

22

Leigh jog-walked across the tram tracks in the direction of Park Hill flats. He didn't want to arrive all hot and sweaty, but he was determined to be at Cheap Date number four before Isla. There'd been something lovely – lovely! – about seeing her waiting for him in the Winter Garden, a glimpse of the version of her she was when she was alone. He had also taken a memory snapshot of the moment her face lifted with relief at his arrival. But he'd had the sense she was anxious while she waited, and he wanted to take that away.

Checking his watch, he waited for a tram to trundle by before running the last stretch up the wide driveway towards the developers' office. Park Hill, once revered as the new way to build communities 'in the sky', was a brutalist concrete icon that stood on the hill, overlooking the city centre. It had fallen into a complex state in the eighties and nineties. In disrepair, poverty-stricken and, at times, a dangerous and uninviting place to be, yet still, in certain quarters, lived in by people who'd raised families, built friendships and remained fiercely protective of their home. Leigh had read somewhere that a quarter of the flats had been promised to social housing, though couldn't help feeling it should have all stayed that way. He kind of loved it. He'd been once, as a kid with Jonny Hardwick from school whose grandma lived on the top floor. They'd sat eating fish and chips, drinking lukewarm sugary tea, both kind of mesmerised by the view: the hospital buildings, the university, and right across to Hillsborough on the other side of town. Looking up at it now, there was a whole new lease of life about it. And he was there first. Perfect.

He thought over their last date roundup in the paper, how his hands shook as he brought up the page on his phone. How his heart had swelled reading the part where they'd both said yes to another date.

He couldn't help but smile as he saw her walk up the road towards him, her smile matching his when she realised he was already there. 'Hi,' he said. She wore a pair of cut-off jeans and a baggy Pulp T-shirt, her hair scraped up onto the top of her head in an effortlessly stylish way, eyes peeking out from beneath the heavy fringe that he loved. He leaned towards her, kissing her on her cheek. Her smell was growing familiar – kind of vanilla and musk and something else that he couldn't put his finger on, but that basically drove him crazy.

'Now, I don't want you to think I've not made an effort,' she started.

'You look . . . ' he glanced her up and down again, any excuse. 'Amazing.'

She blushed and he wanted to pull her into him and take a long, deep breath, take in her smell, her vibe, feel her body next to his. She was dangerous. Not literally, of course – she clearly couldn't hurt a fly – but she was special. And no matter how scared he was by that fact, seeing her in front of him again today, there was no denying it.

'I just wasn't sure what they had planned and didn't want to wear anything that would get spoiled. They mentioned paint to me, did they say that to you?'

'No.'

'And full confession, I have been known to sleep in this T-shirt, which on reflection, may be more information than I should have given you.'

Leigh laughed. 'You've come to a date in your nighty? Is that what you're telling me?'

'No! It's just massive and comfy.' She looked down at her T-shirt. 'There are women on Pinterest who wear over-sized tees like this and somehow look like sex on legs.' She looked up, suddenly. 'I don't know why I just said "sex on legs". Who even says that anymore?'

'So you want me to think you look like "sex on legs"?' he teased.

'Oh my god. I wonder if I could walk away and turn around so that we could start over again. Or maybe go home and get changed?'

'Nope, afraid you're stuck here with me.' He was feeling pretty brave, she gave him a boldness he'd forgotten he ever had. He closed his eyes and nodded his head. 'Yeah. Yep. Pretty good actually.'

'What are you doing?'

'I was just taking a moment to imagine what you'd look like wearing just the T-shirt.' She giggled. 'And yeah, it's working. I can see it.'

'You can't see anything.'

'Well . . . ' He winked at her and she smacked him playfully across the arm.

'I think we're supposed to go in here, aren't we?'

'I think we are.' She shook her head at him, still smiling. He placed his hand on the small of her back, holding open the door to the development office.

'Ah, Isla and Leigh?'

'That's us,' she answered.

'Excellent. We are thrilled you're spending time with us today, have the paper told you what is happening?'

'No,' said Leigh. 'Just that we have to dress casually.' Leigh looked at Isla. 'Clearly some of us have taken that more literally than others.' She rolled her eyes, grinning. He loved her sense of humour. That he could tease her and she could take it. He wasn't a natural flirt – maybe once upon a time he had been, but Serena had pretty much eradicated any of that towards the end of their marriage. Maybe teasing was a playground version of flirting but while Isla still smiled, he was going to make the most of it.

'Perfect. Hang on, right, here you go.' The woman – Susie, according to the nametag pinned to her shirt – handed them an envelope.

> Dear Isla and Leigh,
>
> Welcome to date number four. Today you will become part of Park Hill team glow up. Armed with paints, brushes and overalls, you will be cleaning up graffiti to make way for street art especially commissioned for the area. Enjoy!

'Overalls?' said Isla.

Susie stepped out from behind her desk and passed over two plastic wrapped packages. 'Yes! Overalls. If you want to pop through there, one at a time, when you're both ready, I'll take you up to meet some of today's painting crew.

He watched Isla look down at the overalls. There was something in her eyes, the playfulness dissolved for a moment, replaced with a sudden nervousness.

'Shall I go first?' he asked. The relief across her face told him he'd made the right call.

A minute later, he came out from the back of the office, head to toe in white, paper-like overalls. An outfit that can only be described as ideal for cleaning up blood in a mass murder situation. He'd resisted putting the hood up as well. 'I think you'll find this is exactly how one should dress for a date and I can only apologise that I didn't make this kind of an effort before now.' He opened his arms to show Isla just how ill-fitting the overalls were. 'Now if you can hurry up and get into yours, so we can match, like all couples who barely know each other should, and we can really get this date started.'

The joke was lost on Susie, who threw him a baffled side-eye, but Isla nodded. Her shoulders relaxing again, a certain playfulness returned. 'OK,' she said, checking him out. 'But you may want to sit down before I come out.'

'Yeah?'

'Well, I was nervous when I first heard overalls because who really wants to look a tit on their fourth date, but if I look even half as fit as you do in that, you're not going to be able to keep your hands off me.'

Leigh belly laughed.

Susie went back to her laptop with just the flicker of disbelief in her eyes.

'Right, now, as I said, you may want to sit down for this,' came Isla's voice a few moments later.

'I can take it.'

'Well, I don't know if you can, actually.'

'Trust me. I've got this.'

'OK, if you insist.' And out she came. In a suit the same size as Leigh's, which worked fine (ish) on six-foot something, but less so on what he guessed must be five-foot five?

'They only come in one size,' explained Susie.

'No, no.' Isla held up her arms. 'This is how I wanted it anyway.' She presented herself to Leigh. 'As you can see, I've styled mine with a sleeve roll up. And here,' she bent down to straighten out her trouser legs, 'you'll notice a generous turn up, which is of course all the rage in Paris.'

She gave him a twirl. A lesser woman would have complained. Serena would have refused to even put it on.

'But I think we can all agree,' she said, now back to facing him. 'That *this* is the pièce de résistance.' And with that, she pulled up the hood, yanking on the strings so it tightened around her face. 'What do you think.'

'Definitely hotter than a Pulp T-shirt.'

'I knew it. Just go steady there, no funny business, right?'

'If you insist,' he laughed.

'Right, where do we go?'

Susie came out from behind her desk again. 'If you'd like to follow me.'

And the greatest sight Leigh had seen that day was Susie, in mad high heels and the tightest skirt, tottering up the driveway, with Isla, dressed like a giant flump, happily chatting away about how amazing the Park Hill development was, her eyes bright and her heart open. Like he'd said before to Rachel and Jim, she was pretty fucking magical.

Later that evening, high on the date and on a possible future he hadn't seen before, Leigh sat with multiple job sites open on his laptop. He had no idea if or how things were going to move forward with Isla, but he absolutely wanted them to. And one thing he knew for certain, as a direct result of that afternoon, was that he owed it to himself to make this move. To feel the fear and find a job anyway. Something in her made him see that for sure. Not that he dared look too far ahead, but he wasn't going to let fear get in the way of him at the very least trying to build a version of his life that might give Isla the best version of himself.

Tarquin was doing his best to distract him, however. 'Let's play!'

He glanced over at the bird, flapping his wings in the anticipation of whatever havoc he planned to wreak the moment he left his cage. He'd been in a particularly feisty mood for days now. 'Maybe later?'

'Sad face.'

Leigh also had a web page open for an animal rescue. A charity that found new homes for exotic pets. Leigh had typed out several messages to them and deleted them all, because no matter how much he wanted to get rid of Serena and all that represented her, he had surprised himself with some sadness about the idea of Tarquin's cage no longer taking up too much space in his flat. In his life.

'Look, you've turned me all sentimental,' he said, digging out some mashed banana from a bowl he kept in the fridge. 'Here, have this. Guilt banana.'

Tarquin hopped off his perch and shoved his beak into the tray that hung off the side of his cage. Leigh went back to his laptop and, clicking off the rescue page for now. The job pages weren't exactly brimming with opportunities, everyone seemingly preferring cheap labour to serious experience. Maybe he was going to have to set his net a bit wider? It didn't have to be forever . . . 'New starts all round, eh Tarquin.'

23

The Cheap Dates Club: Date Four, Isla and Leigh

I love you, will U marry me? No, don't get excited, this isn't a direct quote from Isla and Leigh's recent date, but a clue as to their date activity. Who remembers this iconic piece of graffiti on Park Hill flats, back in the day. Well, while that famous message of love now sings in neon, there are some other, slightly less romantic quotes that don't entirely fit in with the estate's new look.

Now, don't get us wrong, we don't want to get caught up in the argument about graffiti: is it art, or isn't it? What we want to do is give our daters an opportunity to get to know one another in unusual situations that might just bring out a version of themselves that they would otherwise keep hidden. We're pretty certain painting over graffiti is a unique dating event, but it sounds like it went pretty well.

Our sources say that Isla and Leigh enjoyed playful banter, were often found deep in discussion, and even disappeared for a questionable length of time, only to return looking – how do we put this? – a little hot under their overall collars. Both were tight-lipped about where they'd gone when pressed by our post-date analyst, so we'll leave it all up to your imagination. Perhaps the resident that sent us a snap of the couple could add more to the story but in the interests of privacy, (and because the lawyers said we weren't allowed!), we've resisted sharing it here.

Suffice to say, our last standing couple are on to their fifth and final date and, by way of thanks for showing up for each and every date, we might just have something special in store for them this time . . .

If you fancy checking out the Park Hill flats regeneration, take a wander, grab a coffee, splash the neon on your Insta! And for the chance to win a meal for two, tag us and a friend in your socials to share the #TCDCIslaAndLeigh love story! The more tags, the more chances to win!

24

Isla could never have imagined that painting over graffiti on a housing estate could have such aphrodisiac effects. The way Leigh had taken the lead with those god-awful overalls had completely dissolved her own panic about how terrible she'd look in them. From then on, they'd been so relaxed in each other's company, covering all kinds of topics in their chat, from family and the time he visited the flats as a kid, to politics to music to their favourite TV shows. He had a smile and an 'eh up' for anyone who passed them. He'd downed tools at one point so he could help a young woman with a pram and too much shopping, rebalancing it all for her, offering to carry it if she preferred. The point at which he crouched down to hand the toddler in the pram his teddy back, making the teddy talk and the toddler laugh, may have been a move too far for Isla's ovaries, which had for so long lain dormant. She'd asked him after the interaction if he'd thought about having kids, worried it was a bit of a gamble question, not everybody wanted to talk about that stuff, but he'd been so direct: yes, he liked them, he'd love to be a dad one day, if he was lucky enough to be so. How he talked just lit a fire in her belly again. How he looked at her and waited until she'd finished speaking before he said what he had to say. She loved how he teased her, too. He'd initiated a paint fight by dashing her overalls with council beige, and she'd finished it by drawing her brush down his cheek as he held her tightly in his arms, before they sneaked off to a quiet corner and snogged like teenagers again. God, she hadn't been kissed like that in so long. His body pressed up against hers, his hands holding her face while she traced the line of his shoulders and back. She remembered how, when they came up for air, her head was spinning and they agreed they should probably get back to what they were actually supposed to be doing. He'd kissed her gently, one last time, then taken her hand, fingers clasped through fingers, back to the paint pots and the spot of graffiti they'd basically just been adding to. Tags and swears replaced with blocks of beige and cream in varying sizes.

After all that, getting ready for her fifth cheap date had reduced her to a jumbled mixture of giddy and nervous and shaky and determined. Butterflies thrashed in her stomach and when Sophie popped over to offer her free access to her Spotify sexy-time playlist, the butterflies turned into a herd of elephants stampeding in her chest. Because for all the dates she'd been on in recent months, it had been a while since she'd actually got intimate with anyone. Apparently sex dreams about Harry Styles didn't count.

And it wasn't that she and Leigh were definitely going to have sex today. Though she was enjoying bringing out the soft, white, flirty summer dress that Sophie said made her boobs look banging, (take that, Date Number Five), she had purposefully not put on her good underwear in order to dissuade her from the possibility. When she told Doris of this plan, she'd been outraged. *You're young. You're single. You should definitely make the most of it*, Doris had said. But actually, Isla wanted to take her time. Leigh wasn't like anyone else she'd dated. He wasn't pushy. Despite all their flirting on their last date, there wasn't a moment where she felt like he was going to try and edge things on to the next level, even when she had him up against that concrete wall, and she couldn't remember the last time a boy, a man, had ever respected her boundaries.

Had anyone?

And she loved getting him talking about his job. He'd been so reluctant before, but she'd broken through a barrier and he'd given her an insight into how much he loved the creative process of design work. It was all about getting to know a company, getting under the skin of the people who worked there, where they'd come from, what their ambitions might be. He wanted any design work he created to embody more than just the product, it was about the people and the spirit and energy behind a team's journey. People mattered to him. Only then could he deliver a full campaign that would have the impact and legacy people were paying him for. It was this kind of commitment that meant he was often working late, or travelling for meetings. Like a project on his desk at the moment. He was loving it but he didn't want to bore off about it. Most of the men she'd dated either slagged off co-workers and their job or built up what they did as if their entire being was created through their career. The times she'd sat and listened to men showing off about all the things they'd achieved, all the places they'd been. And of course, in some cases there was probably some merit to the celebration, maybe some of them had done incredible things, but as someone whose work was one small part of who she was, Isla respected how little time Leigh dedicated to talking about his.

Devonshire Green was packed. Tramlines Festival always flooded the city centre with activity, although the main event took place in the suburb of Hillsborough. She'd always preferred it back when it was a small platform for local talent, but she could see what it did for the city year on year. The footfall, the excitement, the big names playing the main stage. Since the cutlery and steel industry's glory days were long gone (and Henderson's Relish remained relatively on the down low), Tramlines put Sheffield on the map. And thankfully, the old traditions still lived on in pubs across town, where free live music by local bands could be enjoyed by all throughout the weekend.

She looked around, searching out Leigh from the crowd. It didn't take long before she saw him coming towards her, mindful always of those around him. He walked with an assuredness that seemed to have grown with each date they went on, arriving before her, the sun casting a glow around him as he leaned in for a kiss.

'That's a shame,' he said.

Her stomach flipped. 'What's a shame?' she asked, squinting through her knock-off Ray-Bans.

'I was rather hoping for another outing of the overalls.'

'Were you now?'

He pulled her into him and her whole body tingled. Despite the fact they'd only just arrived and were stood in the middle of a bustling green, Isla absolutely leaned into the moment, enjoying the reminder of how intoxicating their last tryst was . . . and the one before that . . . and the one before the one before that.

'I've still got mine,' she said, eventually.

'Yeah?' His eyes were closed. Did he feel that kiss fizz in his head too?

'Mhm.'

'I'll bear that in mind.'

At that, Isla feared she may spontaneously combust, but then a tipsy woman, wobbly on wedged espadrilles, toppled into them and they were forced apart. The interruption brought them both handily back to reality. Devonshire Green. Hot July day. Tramlines Festival. Their fifth and final Cheap Date.

Leigh ruffled the back of his hair and Isla fanned herself with a flyer for the Frog & Parrot pub that she'd been handed on her way there. 'Look, the Everly Pregnant Brothers are playing.'

'Incredible. I love their song "Oyl Int Road". It's such a nostalgia trip. Shall we head that way?'

'Definitely.'

'Isla and Leigh?' Isla turned around to see that a young lad, late teens maybe, was jogging their way.

'That's us!' Leigh put his hand in hers. They'd had a few people come up to them since the married woman in the gallery. Sometimes when they were together, but more often when they were apart.

'Nearly missed you. Here, it's from the *Gazette*.' He handed over an envelope then sloped off.

'Still weird!' said Isla.

'Getting recognised?'

'Yup.'

'I was in Aldi the other day, and a woman asked me for a selfie in the middle aisle.'

'No!'

'It was so awkward!'

'Any good deals?'

'If you like hedge trimmers.'

'I haven't got a hedge.'

'No, then.'

Leigh ripped open the envelope. There was no quiver to his hand this time. He pulled out a card. Opening it up, there were two crisp twenty-pound notes. 'Bloody hell!'

'I haven't seen a purple one for yonks,' said Isla, eyes wide.

Leigh looked at her, deadpan, for just long enough for her to realise what she'd said. Then blinked away his amusement and read:

Dear Isla and Leigh,

It's Tramlines! Your home city is buzzing with free live music. And as the only couple to make it through to the fifth and final date, we would like to reward you with actual cash you can spend on your date. Enjoy some delicious food and a few drinks, celebrate your time together, whatever you fancy - and budget allows. Please take this as a token of appreciation for taking part.

Isla nestled closer into Leigh so she could read too:

All you have to do today is decide if you will continue to see each other, now the experiment is over.

'Experiment,' said Leigh, sarcastically.

Isla took the letter from him, not quite able to look at him. She thought she knew enough about him to assume they'd see each other again, but this was final. It made it real. At this point, they could actually go their separate ways. Surely they wouldn't? Surely this was the start of something?

'Can I keep this?' she asked, avoiding his gaze but holding up the letter.

'Course,' he said, smiling.

She folded it up, tucked it into her back pocket and reminded herself that her life wasn't over if, for some unexpected reason, things didn't go any further. As Doris said, she had enjoyed these dates. She was going to enjoy this one. She was going to live in the moment and enjoy the ride.

25

An hour later, Isla and Leigh tumbled out of the Frog & Parrot. 'God, I bloody love them. They're so funny,' she said. 'I reckon "Personal Cheeses" is my new favourite.'

'Yeah, or "No Oven, No Pie". Do you like pie?'

'Big fan.'

'You ever had one from the Broadfield?'

'Nether Edge? Have I! Bloody lush!'

'Maybe we should go some time . . . '

Isla flushed. It could have been the suggestion of another date beyond this, their final Cheap Date. Or it could have been the second pint of Guinness she'd had because although she loved a Guinness and could generally manage two or three at a steady pace, the sun was so hot today and she was fairly sure it had gone to her head. 'I think maybe we should get food now?'

'Yeah? What do you fancy? Might be a smidge warm for pie?'

'Probably. Oh, wait! Pizza at the Forum, just up here!'

'Good shout.'

They grabbed for each other's hands and, navigating the crowds, they dashed over the road to bag a table.

They were in luck. Minutes later they were ensconced in a blue leather booth, knees touching under the table as they scanned the menu. Isla was finding it really hard to concentrate and wondered if he was too. Just the touch of his leg, the closeness. There was this energy between them, a definite spark. He had to feel it too, surely.

Or was it the Guinness?

Or the heat?

It was really, really hot.

She fanned herself again with the cocktail menu.

'You want to sit outside?' he asked.

'Probably hotter there, to be fair.'

'True. And the music out there sounds great but . . . I'd kind of like to chat.'

'Yeah. Me too.'

'OK, we'll stay here then. What you having? Let me go order.'

She watched him at the bar. He let a young woman go before him, but unlike some men she'd dated in the past, he didn't stand there taking a side glance at her. And Isla couldn't have blamed him if he had. She was gorgeous. Long blonde hair and effortless, casual style. When she left the bar to move back to her table, Leigh paid no attention. Just gave his order to the barman, paid, waited for their drinks, then made his way back to Isla with a smile on his face and a gentle pink hue to his cheeks. The heat, or maybe he'd caught the sun earlier.

'A pint of lime and soda.' He passed her the drink and she didn't come up for air until she'd nailed a good half of it. 'Thirsty?'

'Just a bit!'

She played with the straw and her ice. The bottom of her drink was much stronger than the top, the lime having gone in first. She stirred it, aware he was watching her. And there it was again: coyness.

'So, it's our last date,' he said.

'It is.'

He nodded. She nodded.

He paused.

'How do you feel it went? This "social experiment"?'

'It's been interesting. Very . . . scientific.'

'Do you think we've given the Cheap Dates Club a good return on their investment?'

'I think we've given them a few new readers. Albeit, most of them are the octogenarian residents of the care home. Doris says hi, by the way.'

'I'd like to meet her sometime,' he ventured.

'You would?' Isla's hands shook a little.

'Isla,' he reached for them.

'Sorry, they're a bit damp. From the condensation on the glass.'

'Oh, erm. Nice.' She wiped her hands then placed them back down in his. 'I'm not very good at this,' he began.

'At what?'

'At telling people how I feel, or what I'm thinking.'

Isla wanted to tell him she felt like that sometimes. Especially if telling people how she felt was going to leave her vulnerable. But even more, she wanted to ask him why he felt like that here, now? Because she wanted to know every last detail of what he thought and how he ticked; what made him not good at telling people how he felt. She bit down on her bottom lip, sensing he wasn't done.

'I'd really like to see you again. Outside of the Cheap Dates Club. We can still do cheap dates. It doesn't have to be anything flash. I just . . . I'd like to get to know you even more. If you want to. And it's totally fine if you don't want to it's just . . . I think that maybe you do?'

'I do. Want to do. I do.'

He laughed at her clumsiness which meant she could too. Then he let out a sigh of relief just as their food arrived. 'Oh, that was quick. Thanks.'

Perhaps relieved for a moment to divert from the heavy lifting of the conversation, they turned to their food, each one making all the appreciative sounds good pizza invites.

'Oh my god!' Isla pushed her plate towards Leigh. 'This is to die for. Do you want a slice?'

'I'll swap you for a slice of this one.'

'Amazing.'

They dipped into each other's plates, stringy cheese colliding and twisting as they picked out their slices.

'Everything all right with your food?'

They both nodded and gave a thumbs up to the waitress who had followed universal law of 'wait until punters have their mouth full of food before asking if they're enjoying said mouthful of food'.

Four slices in, Isla was beginning to slow down. But also, while eating, she'd realised that she wanted to be brave. She wanted to be honest about how she felt . . . if she could find the right words.

'There's something I need to tell you,' started Leigh.

Leigh's face was serious. Not a look she recognised on him. Her heart dropped a little.

'It's not a big deal, not really, I just . . . I don't even know why I've not said anything before now except, I think I didn't know if there was any point and then when I realised I liked you I was worried that it would cause an issue and then it felt like I'd left it too long and—'

Isla wiped her mouth, pushing her plate away. 'It's only been a few dates. We don't have to know everything about each other. That's part of the fun, finding out. On more dates . . . '

'I know, but . . . so, I told you I'd been married.'

She nodded.

'And that we're divorced.'

She nodded again. Then she crossed her fingers that he wasn't going to tell her he was in fact still married, or that they were going to try again, or worse, this whole experiment was in fact a ruse in order for them to find a third person to join their relationship and she'd inadvertently fallen for someone looking for a sister wife.

Was she falling for him?

'My ex. Serena.'

Serena? Serena. She knew the name.

'She's also my boss.'

'Oh. Oh! Serena! The immaculate one from your company website who looks like she could break balls with one look . . . ' Isla trailed off, aware how she just sounded. Leigh stared. 'I just wanted to find out a bit more about you.'

'Right.'

'I wasn't stalking.' She wiped her hands with a serviette.

'It's OK.'

'Sorry.'

'It's fine. But, yes, that's Serena.'

Isla sat back. 'Wow, she looks . . . I mean, she's . . . ' she thought for a moment. 'She's literally everything that I'm not!'

'Mhm.'

She tried not to read too much into how quickly he agreed. 'Why would you be remotely interested in me, if that's the kind of woman you were married to?'

He smiled at her, taking a moment to flash his eyes over her face. 'Exactly because you're everything she's not.'

Isla fiddled with the serviette.

He took a deep breath, stretched his arms out, and laid them on the table forcing his back into the chair. 'She left me. For her personal trainer.' As soon as he'd said it, his whole body seemed to relax somehow. 'I mean, things weren't great between us before that, hadn't been for a long time but . . . could there be any lamer an end to a relationship? So clichéd. Such a—'

'Bitch!' As soon as it came out did Isla's hands fly up to her mouth and she pinched her lips shut.

Leigh looked up. Stunned.

'Oh my god,' she said, wide-eyed. 'I am so sorry. I didn't mean to . . . it's just, how could she do that? That's awful. Her PT! What a . . . sorry. I mean . . . '

Leigh looked at her. He started to giggle, then laugh. Then couldn't stop himself and that made Isla laugh too and soon enough the pair of them were sat, tears rolling down their cheeks, unable to breathe or get a word in. A table of women beside them stared over and still, they couldn't catch hold. Maybe it was the relief on Leigh's part, or on hers.

'Is he fit?' Isla squeaked, in between snorts.

'He's massive. Like a brick outhouse. Huge. He's like The Rock,' said Leigh, howling.

'Does he drink Huel and eat raw protein at midnight.'

'Undoubtedly. With baked beans on the side for extra . . . '

' . . . Oh god, I can't.'

'Like, he'd not touch a pizza,' said Leigh, lifting up a slice. 'Pizza?' He offered.

Isla leaned forward and took a massive bite, cheese dripping down her chin. Tomato catching in the corner of her mouth. Leigh reached forward to wipe it clean then held his hand on her face, the laughter beginning to subside. 'Even with cheese down your face and tomato on your cheek, you are so much more my type!'

She wiped her chin clear.

'Not that I'm comparing.'

'No. They say it's the thief of joy.'

'They do. But . . . you are better. For me. I think. So far.'

He let go of her face, brushing crumbs off the table onto the floor, clearing his throat and shifting in his seat.

Isla laid her hand on his arm. 'You don't have to be embarrassed.' He turned back to her. 'About any of it, you know. And, for the avoidance of doubt, you know with you working together, I think it's worth saying that I'm really not the jealous type.'

'You're not?'

She thought about Brian the Monster. 'Well . . . I mean, maybe I have been in the past. A bit green-eyed monstery, but I called him Brian so he'd stop causing problems.'

'You called your green-eyed monster Brian.'

'I mean, now I say it out loud, it sounds ridiculous. I've basically never told anybody that before.' She looked down at their hands, clasped tightly together. 'I suppose I've had my fair share of "bitches" – no personal trainers, but plenty of blokes who put it about far too much.'

'Plenty?' He flashed.

'Well, you know. My fair share.' She grinned. 'But you're different, somehow. And I'm different with you. I feel like I can trust you.

She took a moment, safe in the knowledge she didn't have to rush to fill the gaps in their conversation, even now, talking about something like this. Could she really could ignore Brian when he inevitably began his diatribe of viciousness? It was so hard to say for certain but she really did believe that Leigh brought out a different version of her. A version she really liked. One that could see how she might actually feel secure in a relationship, maybe for the first time ever.

He squeezed her hand. 'I'm going to leave. Get a new job.'

'And you'll find one. When the time is right. And it can't have been easy trying to find a way to cut her out of your life if she's still the person giving you your annual review.'

'She said that sometimes I stare out the window too long during Zoom meetings, and that I should filter what I say more when talking to clients. Be "*a bit less Yorkshire*" was an actual sentence she once used.'

'What's wrong with being Yorkshire!?'

'Right!'

'And I love it when people say what they're thinking.'

'Me too.'

They stared at one another; a cool breeze came out of nowhere.

'Say what you're thinking now.'

He swallowed and looked down at her hand in his. 'I'm thinking we should . . . '

'Yes?' She bit her lip.

'. . . go for a walk?'

It wasn't exactly what she hoped he was thinking in that moment, but she would rather be with him, now, together, going for a walk, than anywhere else in the world.

They stood outside the Winter Garden and watched the fountains for a moment. Young teens played and flirted between the spouts of water. Toddlers tried dragging parents perilously close. Couples lounged on the grass and a group of older teens sat cross-legged, cradling food from McDonalds that they practically inhaled.

Leigh put his arm around her. 'Our second date. I was really nervous. I thought you'd stood me up when I didn't see you outside the door and then I got closer and there you were, watching that newly married couple. I wondered what you were thinking.'

'I was worried you'd not find me. And worried I'd make a fool of myself again.'

'You didn't make a fool of yourself on the first date!'

'May I remind you of my face.'

'There was nothing wrong with your face.'

'That is not my memory of it.'

'I was nervous today, too,' he said.

'Yeah?'

'I don't know why, you kind of make me feel like that. And not in a bad way, I don't know, maybe it's not nerves, but it's something, definitely something.' She looked up at him. 'I kind of feel caught off guard around you.'

'Yeah?'

'Yeah.'

'Leigh.'

'Isla?'

'Walk me home?'

By the time they made it back, they'd barely spoken. Hands clasped together, walking in unison, comfortable in silence; but also knowing.

She opened the front door, hoping the coast was clear, then led him into her bedsit, not caring that she hadn't scooped up the clothes from her sofa, or made her bed before she came out.

'Can I get you anything? Coffee?' she asked, locking the door behind him.

'No.'

He stepped towards her. Her heart raced. Her whole body longed for him to touch her yet neither one of them was in a hurry. Both wanted to savour every moment of the intensity, the burn. He moved closer, his breath against her neck, the touch of his hand as he ran it down her spine. Connected at the hips, mouths barely touching; his breathing heavy, hers almost caught in her throat. As she took her fingers through his hair, he walked her backwards towards her bed, lifting her gently, as she wrapped her legs around him.

And they were lost, to each other, the only place either wanted to be.

26

Isla didn't want to open her eyes. She knew that as soon as she did, she would have to acknowledge that it was the next morning, and the day would have to start and Leigh would probably have to leave and she would have to go to work and Doris would want to know all the details that she didn't want to tell. She wanted to stay in this bubble of loveliness reliving last night over and over again.

Leigh stirred beside her, so she propped herself up on his chest. 'Now do you want coffee?'

Eyes still closed, he scooped her up, pulling her onto him. 'I mean, I suppose so.'

Her hair fell across his face, creating a momentary hideaway for them both. 'How are you this beautiful, even first thing in the morning?' he asked, finally blinking at her.

'Because I got up at four and put a full face of makeup on.'

'If that's true, you may need to reevaluate your technique because that definitely looks like day-old mascara to me.'

Isla sat up, Leigh between her thighs, as she wiped around and beneath her eyes, ruffling her fringe back into life. 'How do you take it?'

Leigh's eyebrows raised, his hands firmly on her hips.

'Your coffee.'

'Oh. Disappointing.' She leaned down to kiss him, knowing she was going to have to drag herself away. He let her go, their fingers the last to break apart as she threw on a T-shirt and some shorts. 'White. One sugar. I usually follow it with incredible sex, so I don't know if that's your thing, I mean . . . I know that's definitely your thing but . . . '

She grinned at him. 'I'll make you coffee then I'll be getting in the shower.'

'The shower is good. I mean, call me vanilla but it's not my go-to, it's awkward and obviously there's an element of danger – slipping hazards and so on. But you know, I'm willing if you are. Do you have a grab rail?'

She laughed. 'I'll be having a shower because I have to get to work, as I believe do you. I'll make you your coffee first, though.'

Leigh sighed good naturedly. 'It's probably for the best. The last time I had sex in a shower, I put my back out for two weeks.'

When Isla got back to her room after her shower, the bed had been made and Leigh was gone. She searched for a note, checked her phone for a message but nothing. Her shoulders dropped. She tried not to feel sad, or panicked. It was fine, it was fine. She'd told him she was going to work; he knew he couldn't stay . . . though she'd sort of thought he might say goodbye.

She shook off the noise in her brain (Brian!) telling her that that would be the last she would see of him, threw on some clothes, tried to shake herself clear of doubt and headed back to the kitchen to satisfy her grumbling tummy instead. 'Morning,' she said, rubbing her eyes, aware that Sophie would be sat at the table; she usually zoned out over a bowl of Crunchy Nut around this time.

'Morning,' said Sophie. 'We were just getting acquainted.'

Isla spun around from the sink to see Leigh sitting beside Sophie; Jay stood by the toaster.

'I was searching for bread so I could make you something to eat,' said Leigh. 'And also because I was starving and needed something to eat. Then I was just loitering in the kitchen like a spare part when they came in – sorry about that.'

'No, no. Not a problem. Was it, Jay?' said Sophie.

'Not at all.'

Though thrilled to see Leigh had not absconded – Isla: one; Brian: nil. She was a little less thrilled to see Sophie and Jay there too. Not because she was embarrassed. She'd found Sophie in the kitchen with random strange men many times before, and vice versa as it went – but this was different. There was something about Leigh that she wanted to keep all to herself for as long as possible.

He stretched, then stood up. 'I should probably go, to be fair.'

'But you've not eaten anything yet.' Isla looked in her cupboards for anything remotely like breakfast. 'BelVita biscuit?' she offered.

Leigh grinned at her. 'While it's hard to say no to such culinary delights, and you know I love a biscuit, I think I'll get something on my way back, thanks. Nice coffee though.

I mean, I might need to give you a few lessons on exactly how I like it, but it was a start.'

There was a flirtatious glint in his eye and Isla had to turn away, rinsing out her mug suddenly felt like a very important task. Regaining her composure, she turned back to him. 'Come on then.' She ushered him out of the kitchen. 'If you've got to go, you've got to go. And you know, me too, so . . . '

'Bye Sophie, Jay,' he said over his shoulder.

'Bye, Leigh,' they answered in unison.

Isla put herself between Leigh and the front door. 'So, I had a great time.'

'Me too. It was . . . lovely.'

'Lovely?' She pulled back, narrowing her eyes at him.

'Well, you know. I don't want to give away exactly how I feel about the last', he checked his watch, 'sixteen hours.'

'Right.'

'Your honour.'

He pressed her up against the door as they kissed.

'I really should go,' he said with a groan.

'You should.'

'When can I see you again?'

'When do you want to see me again?'

'Let's call in sick to work.'

'I can't. We've got a man coming in to give a talk about Sheffield history through the ages. It's my job to set up the projector for his PowerPoint.'

'Oh. Fascinating.'

'Could have been worse, last month's talk was about St Pancras.'

'The station?'

'The fourteen-year-old boy martyred in Rome in AD304.'

'Wow. Way to get a station named after you.'

'Bit desperate if you ask me.'

'And I suppose I do have to pretend I'm working while I send my CV off to every design agency in Yorkshire, so I guess we've both got responsibilities. Tonight, then? My place. I'll cook for you.'

'You cook!?'

'I'm basically Nigella Lawson!'

'I've always fancied Nigella Lawson,' she said, laughing.

'Basic, but same.'

'OK. Yeah. Tonight.'

He reached for the latch behind her as he gave her another kiss. 'I'll text you my address.'

'Can I bring anything?'

'Nope. Just you.' He jogged down the steps. 'And maybe that Pulp T-shirt?' he added before disappearing down the street.

Isla closed her eyes and held onto how full her heart was for as long as possible. This was going to be different. He was going to be different.

Please let him be different.

'Isla! Get in here now!' was the sound that interrupted her thoughts.

Sophie and Jay sat side by side at the table, she with her Crunchy Nut, him with his toast. A newly brewed cafetière sat between them and they looked at her expectantly as she walked in.

'What?' She feigned innocence.

Sophie crossed her arms. 'All. The. Details.'

'No.' Isla gave a look to Sophie that said, not this time.

'I mean, we don't need *all* of them,' suggested Jay.

'Oh, we do,' corrected Sophie. 'And if it's too much for you, you can leave me and Isla to it!'

Isla shook her head. 'I'm not giving you any detail so you can stay where you are, Jay.'

Sophie pulled her not fair face. 'But we tell each other everything!'

'Do you?' Jay gave them both a panicked look.

'No, not "everything".' Sophie patted his leg which did little to reassure him.

'Just most things, Jay.' Isla looked at him just long enough to make him wonder. She knew it was a low blow, but she was feeling mischievous. 'This time, I'm saying nothing. Other than we had a lovely time, and it looks like I'll be out this evening.' She poured herself a fresh cup from their cafetière, winked and flounced out of the kitchen.

'We like him!' came Sophie's voice before Isla had shut the door to her room.

'Yeah! He's cool,' added Jay.

But Isla didn't need their approval. She was falling hook, line and sinker. And couldn't wait to see him again. She picked up her phone, pressed and held Tinder, removing it from her home screen. With the possible exception of those few messages with Rupert before he deleted it, it hadn't even been fun while it lasted.

27

Leigh stood back to check out Tarquin's cage. 'There. Clean, tidy, perfect to meet the new woman in my life.'

'New woman! New woman!' Tarquin hopped about his cage. He'd been pretty extra all day. 'See her again!'

Rolling his eyes, Leigh nipped over to the hob to give the pan a stir. He hoped Isla wasn't going to be put off by the fact that in the end, all he'd decided to cook was a spaghetti bolognese. It's not that spag bol was all he was capable of, more that he knew his take on it was good. And he wanted something he could rely on while tidying the flat, making Tarquin presentable and checking in on his emails. He'd also been looking out for some volunteer work, wondering if it was something he and Isla could continue to do together. There was a soup kitchen nearby that often needed people on a weekend, and he was up for it if she was.

Last night with Isla had given him the final push he needed to turn leaving Serena's company into a reality.

He splashed the bolognese with a bit of red wine, the all-important Hendo's, and his secret ingredient: a dusting of seventy per cent cocoa to bring out some depth of flavour. He was going to plate it up paired with a nicer bottle of red he'd been saving for a rainy day and then tell her all about the conversations he'd had. The meetings he'd got booked in. He was most excited about a chat he'd had with an old colleague who now owned his own design studio. Dave, brilliant designer, a skater back in the day. Loved whiskey and playing guitar and led a team of young, brilliant things doing edgy, irreverent artwork and graphics. Leigh wasn't sure if he would be up to the mark, but he'd give it his best shot if Dave was prepared to take him on. And if not Dave, there were others. There was a new agency based near the train station. And an advert he found on LinkedIn for a company he'd not come across before down in Chesterfield. It was a bit further away, but he'd go if they could offer him the salary. It would be worth it. He'd ask Isla what she reckoned. He wondered what kind of advice she'd give. They'd not had to ask for each other's opinions on life choices before – would she tell him what she thought or what she thought he wanted to hear? She didn't strike him as being the kind who'd pay lip service, she was smart, she knew her mind . . . God, he'd missed her. He couldn't wait for her to come round. He wanted to see her in his place. He wanted to sit next to her. Feed her, pour her wine, play her music, kiss her. He really wanted to kiss her and—

The doorbell went. He checked his watch, then his face in the mirror before straightening out his T-shirt and giving his room a final once over to make sure it was tidy as he went to open the door. He thought he'd said seven but didn't care that she was so early. The earlier the better, they'd have more time together. Maybe she'd stay over? Could they ring in sick tomorrow?

'Serena!' Leigh stared, holding the door open, as his ex-wife pushed past him into the flat and stood tall in the centre of the room. 'What the hell are you doing here?'

28

Sophie was tucked up on Isla's sofa, giving her feedback on each outfit. 'I think the catsuit is a bit much, but you do look fit in it.'

'It's a pain in the arse if I need a wee.'

'And not particularly quick to get in to . . . or out of, I shouldn't wonder.' She raised an eyebrow and Isla threw it back on the bed.

'Just go for that dress. The linen one.'

'They get so creased though.'

'He won't care. I mean, he literally won't notice. He is obsessed with you; you do know that?'

Isla beamed, dropping onto the sofa beside Sophie. 'How do you know?' she asked, well aware she was fishing.

'It's not so much what he said, as how he said it. It was like you were an angel sent from above or something. A magical fucking unicorn. And not in a creepy, put-you-on-a-pedestal kind of a way, more in a, this-is-a-woman-I-want-to-fall-in-love-with kind of a way.'

'Fall in love with?' Isla swelled. 'It's only been five dates; I think it's all a bit too early for that.'

'Well, of course it is, I suppose I just think that he's hoping to stick around. It's always hard to know for certain but he looked pretty smitten to me. When we found him in the kitchen, he was just staring out the window at nothing. Think we took about ten years off his life expectancy making him jump.'

'Ahhh.' Isla jumped off the sofa and went to plug in her straighteners. She'd seen Dawn O'Porter give fringe styling tuition and wanted to try it out. 'So, while I've got you alone, tell me how things are going with Jay.'

She'd been so reluctant to ask before now, since jealousy monster Brian had firmly taken up residency in her soul when she'd first learned Sophie and Jay were an item. It had felt so much in recent months like everyone except her was finding a man and, aside from that, Brian also liked to remind her how much she missed having mates that she just call up and go out with. Maybe if she had someone too, there'd be chances for double dates. She could get all the Christmas Girls and their partners together without having to wait for their annual get together.

The look on Sophie's face told Isla pretty much everything she needed to know. 'He's great. I mean, I really like him. He's thoughtful, bought me a notepad the other day because he knew that I'd finished one and saw it and thought of me.'

'Ahh, nice.'

'I mean, it had an alpaca on it and said: "An adventure? Alpaca my bags".'

'Oh god.'

'But the thought was there.'

'I guess.'

'We've talked about going away for the weekend. To the Lakes. I love it there and he's never been. I was thinking that maybe I'd swing by Mum and Dad's on the way back so that they could meet him.'

Isla paused, mid straighten. 'Introducing him to your mum and dad? Woah!'

'Don't burn your fringe.'

Isla set the straighteners aside and played around with pinning her hair up, then leaving it down. Either way it didn't matter, her fringe looked so much better now.

'Do you think they'll like him? Your mum and dad?'

'Who knows. They've always been a bit guarded with their opinion, but I'd like to know this time. This time feels . . . different.'

'Yeah?'

Sophie nodded. Then went a bit giddy.

'Well, I'm happy for you. Brian would have been raging by now were it not for Leigh.'

'Brian?'

'Never mind. And I know it's early days, I mean, it really *is* early days, but I think I might feel the same about Leigh.' She checked her watch. 'Oh God, I'd better get a shift on. I don't want to be late for him. OK, so I'm going with the jeans and Rebellious Hope T-shirt. But with heels for a bit of added sex appeal.'

'Strong choice.'

Isla poked around in her makeup bag. 'Dark red lip?' she said, reaching for her phone as it dinged.

'No. Course not. It'll be smooshed around your face and you'll be stuck with it for days.'

'Oh yeah. Cos for once in my life, I'm pretty sure I am going to have se—Oh.' Isla read her message. And read it again. She deflated instantly.

'What's up?'

She bit down on her lip, disappointment wrapping its hooded cloak around her. 'It's from Leigh.' She held the phone out for Sophie.

'"So sorry for the short notice, but can we take a raincheck? I'll call you."' Sophie read it twice too, frowning. 'Is that it? I'll call you. Not even a kiss at the end of it? Or an emoji? I mean, I know emojis are old school now but he's what, mid-thirties?'

'Thirty-two.'

'So he's probably still using emojis.' Sophie passed the phone back to her. 'What are you going to say?'

'What can I say?' She went over to her bed, picked up her pyjamas then dropped them down again. 'It's no problem. He's rainchecked, so, that means some other time. Doesn't it?'

'Well . . . yeah . . . '

'And I can hardly get arsy with him, can I? We barely know each other.'

'But it doesn't make any sense?'

'Doesn't it?' Isla pulled up sharp, folded her arms and bit down hard on her cheek.

'He likes you. I'm sure he does.'

'Soph,' Isla laughed to herself, knowingly. 'Don't be so naive.' She turned away pretending to sort out her clothes, clumsily hanging stuff up as her heart raced and frustrated, disappointed tears threatened. The Pulp T-shirt fell off the side of the bed and she grabbed for it, frustratedly throwing it at her cupboard. 'I had sex with him. The chase is done.

He's got no need to pursue any further. I should have held out, though I suppose it wouldn't have changed the outcome. He's like all the rest of them.'

'What?'

'Men!' Isla caught Sophie screw her nose up. 'OK, like most men. Some men. He's been . . . ' She tapped out her reply, clicked send and threw her phone on the bed. The same bed that last night she'd had the most amazing sex of her life on. The same bedsheets she hadn't yet changed. The same bed she'd got home from work and lay upon, then within, just to take her back to the moment he—

'What did you say?'

'What?'

'To the text, how did you respond?'

'I said, "No worries. Another time." No kiss. No stress. Honestly, Sophie, I'm a fool.' Her heart was racing. 'I do this every time. You should have reminded me I do this every time and next time, it's your job to remind me of how I get and how men can be. Yes, I know! Not all men.'

'I wasn't going to say that.' Sophie's voice was quiet.

Isla spun around. 'What you doing tonight? You want to get takeout? I can ransack my books and see if I hid any more cash between the pages of the ones I only buy to make myself look smarter.'

Sophie looked down at her fingers.

Isla laughed to herself. 'Of course you don't. You'll have plans with Jay. Don't worry about it. Go on, get yourself ready. I'm going to change my sheets and order food.'

'I'm really sorry, Isla. I'm sure there's a perfectly good explanation for it.'

'Of course there is. What is it they say? He's just not that into me. It's fine. I got great sex, some food, and a chance to see the Everly Pregnant Brothers, who, I might add, were excellent. So there we go. Like that Kris Hallenga woman says on her podcast, I've found the glitter.'

'You don't always have to find the glitter, Isla. Sometimes you're allowed to think a situation is a bit shit.'

Isla opened the door, standing by it for Sophie to leave. 'Go. Have a good evening. we'll catch up properly about it in the week. I'm fine.'

Sophie got up, reluctantly. 'Isla.'

'Go on! I'm a big girl. I've been here before. I survived then. I'll survive now!'

Knowing there was nothing she could say, but still not happy about leaving, Sophie went to give Isla a hug. 'Bye then.'

Isla went through the motions. And as the door shut, she clamped a hand over her mouth to muffle the sound of a dramatic sob. She must be hormonal, or overtired.

He wasn't different after all.

29

'Leigh, I still love you. I've always loved you. I don't know what I was thinking, I got caught up in . . . I don't know what. Marriage is hard. Being with that same person, day in day out. We'd been together for so long.'

'We'd been together for five years.'

'It was the longest relationship either of us had ever had.'

'You went off with your personal trainer!'

'I know. I know. And I've regretted it every day since.'

Leigh watched on as Serena performed her one-woman show, with occasional input from her audience of one (two if you counted Tarquin, who was uncharacteristically quiet.) She'd step towards him, cradle his face in her immaculate manicured hands. She'd step towards the window, gazing out of it forlornly. She was one soft-rock ballad away from a cheap film that would have gone straight to DVD in the days DVDs existed. She bit her lip, she dabbed at her eye, she paused for effect, somehow resisting taking a glimpse out of the corner of her eye to see how the performance was being received. If she had, she'd have seen Leigh's review: two stars.

'You will never know how sorry I am for what I've put you through. I would do anything to make it up to you. Simon's nothing like you—'

'I know this.'

'I lost sight of what was important.'

'When you gained sight of his six pack.'

'That's unfair, Leigh.'

'Is it? Because from where I'm standing, that's exactly what happened. Things weren't great between us, I know that, but I wasn't about to give up.'

'I know.' She stepped towards him; he folded his arms. 'And that's what I love about you, what I miss about you. You're so . . . ' She paused. He waited. 'Reliable.'

Almost as sexy as lovely.

'Whenever I needed you, you were there. If I was having a bad day, you'd cook, you'd run me a bath. You'd put on the music I liked even though you hated it.'

She was right. He did hate Backstreet Boys.

'When all that stuff was going down with Mum, Dad and Lexi—' (when Serena was trying to sneak inheritance that should have been split with her sister) 'you helped me to see how I could fix things.'

'You couldn't see that on your own? That you needed to be upfront and explain why you needed the money?'

'I didn't want to admit that the business they'd helped me to set up was failing. That I was failing. But look, look at me now. Look at us, what we've achieved.'

'I've done nothing but show up every day and do my job.'

'Exactly! Which was what the business needed. It was what I needed. You're all I've ever needed, showing up, doing your job.'

'I wasn't your employee, Serena. I was your husband.'

'I know that, Leigh. But you are more than that, you're also my best friend.'

Leigh looked at her, puzzled. They'd barely shared two civil words that weren't about work since she left. He certainly wasn't the person she shared her innermost secrets with. 'Serena, you know as well as I do, there is nothing between us.'

She sighed, dramatically flopping onto the sofa that he'd procured from eBay when he first moved in. Took him an hour to get it up the stairs and he, Jim and Rachel cried laughing with the reenactment of the 'pivot' bit from *Friends.* Yes, it had seen better days. No, it was not from Ponsford, or whatever equivalent independent furniture shop she preferred down in London, but it was his. And it was really comfy. And it should be Isla sat there right now, not her. Serena needed to go. Then he could message Isla again and explain. He'd fired off the first text too quickly, flustered at the thought of her arriving on the doorstep and bumping into Serena. He hadn't wanted to ruin the mood between them, the rhythm they'd found. Maybe if he explained they could have dinner as planned and—oh! Dinner. He dashed over to the bolognese which had been simmering so long, half of it had welded to the pan. 'Oh, Serena!'

'What?'

He looked at her, then his pan of concrete ragu. 'Nothing.' He threw his wooden spoon into the pan then dropped the pan into the sink a bit more forcefully than he intended.

'I can see that you're angry.'

Leigh felt his jaw flex.

'And I get it. Maybe it's time we started again. Moved you back away from here.'

'I like it here.' His voice was flat, he was clinging on to his temper. She would not ruin his mood; not any more than she already had.

'We could start again. I'll buy us a new place, somewhere nice in London.'

'Because Sheffield isn't nice?'

'Well, it's . . . ' she didn't complete the sentence, presumably because on this occasion she knew better than to lay into his home city. 'Stay up here? I might start sounding like you!'

She offered up a smile as if she was joking, but Leigh had endured far too much of her ignorant northern-bashing, including alleged jokes about his pronunciations of words like mug, cup and bath. He wasn't taking it anymore. 'Look, Serena, Sheffield is real. It's honest. I'm connected to it. There's nothing flashy about it – with the possible exception of Whirlow. Some of the houses up Whirlow are pretty flashy. And you know, Dore and Totley have some nice places too. But you never gave it a chance, you never saw it for what it is. An amazing place to live, green, rich in a culture of its own. Characterful. Soulful. You've always acted like it's a surprise we can get decent coffee and good food up here. Like the only place with anything to offer is London.'

'Well, you have to admit when we first opened the office up here, nobody had oat milk.'

Leigh looked to the ceiling.

'I feel about London like you do about Sheffield, Leigh. It's my home city.'

'You're from Norwich!'

Serena stood up defiantly. 'You know full well I've lived in London since I was fourteen. It's my home.'

'And Sheffield is mine. It's in my blood.'

They stood face to face, a stand-off. In the old days, a row like this would have ended in sex wherever they happened to be. Fiery, angry, burying their feelings until the next time.

She took a step towards him; he took three steps back.

'OK. OK. I hear you. I do,' she tried. 'If you don't like London, fine. Whatever. We could meet in the middle and live somewhere in zone five? In the countryside, even. We could buy a big house with loads of land and start a farm.'

'Why would I want to start a farm, Serena? And more to the point, why would I want to with you!? Have you looked in a mirror? What about you, your fake tan and lashes and nails, says "farm"? I mean, I know, you like to take care of yourself.'

'There's no shame in that.'

'Of course there's not, but also, have you seen me, recently? Like, have you really seen me?'

He turned to face the mirror. 'Look.' Serena looked away. 'Look at us,' he repeated, more forcibly. 'We don't fit. We're not a match. You're . . . you. And I'm . . . '

She turned to face him. 'I love you, just the way you are, Leigh.'

'You hide my clothes and buy me designer ones. I'm one dropped *t* away from being sent for elocution lessons.'

She studied him. Her eyes glazed slightly, glassy, emotional, a technique he knew she was capable of drawing on to order. He'd seen her do it with her dad many times over the years. She bit her lip, which he knew she was doing because once, when they were first together, he'd told her it was hot. But that was before he realised she already knew it was something some men liked and she'd trot it out anytime she wanted something from him. It stopped being hot when he realised it was an affectation. (And he'd never really worked out why he'd ever thought it was in the first place.) She closed her eyes and she moved towards him, parting her mouth gently going in for the kiss.

'Absolutely not!' Leigh ducked out of her direction of travel and she pulled up short. 'I think you should leave, Serena.'

'But—'

'What we had,' he sighed, exhausted. 'It didn't work for either of us. We weren't good for each other. We weren't happy.'

'I was happy, Leigh.'

'You were the one that left!'

She went to bite her lip then thought better of it.

'It's over. It was over before you left. Let's be kind to each other and let go. Move on. Find someone you can be truly happy with. And . . . ' He cleared his throat and braced himself. 'You need to know that I'm looking for another job.'

'You're doing what?'

'I'm looking for something else. I think it'd be better for the both of us.'

'Is this *her* idea?' Serena folded her arms. Her face changed. Everything pinched.

'Whose?'

'That girl you've been seeing. I read all about it online. What was she called? Isla!' Serena sneered. 'Your "cheap date". I mean *really*, I don't know what possessed you. Was it a dare? Did Jim put you up to it?'

'Nobody put me up to it! And how did you even hear about it?'

'I was chatting to the head of sales at the paper, they're trying to get me to take out some ad space now that they've got all these new readers. I asked how, he showed me. And there you were.' Leigh clamped his jaw tight. 'And I've got to tell you, Leigh, I wouldn't trust her as far as I could throw her.'

'You know nothing about her.'

'I'm a woman. I can see what she's doing.'

Leigh stuffed his hands in his jeans pockets because he absolutely was not going to give Serena the satisfaction of him asking her what she meant.

'And you can look for another job, but remember, it'll be me giving you a reference. And you have to, at the very least, give notice first, which, if I remember rightly, is three months? Yeah, I'm pretty sure that's what you signed, which is great, actually, because I have some work for you to do before you go, if you even get yourself another job. You're not known for being proactive, are you?'

Leigh moved away, anger and frustration boiling in his blood.

'We've a potential new account. Up in the Shetland Islands. It's for their tourism board. It's a critical opportunity which would open up a whole new sector for us. They've seen some of your work and we think you'd be perfect for a project launch they've got on. I said we'd go out there tomorrow, for the rest of the week at least. If we get the job, you'll need to stay out there for a good few weeks, maybe even the full length of your notice period, to make sure we really get our claws into them.'

'You'd let me spend time with a new client when I'm leaving? Why not just put me on gardening leave?'

'Oh, you'd like that wouldn't you? So you can lay around watching films, playing computer games and not having to answer to anyone. You seem to forget that I picked you up from the gutter, Leigh. You forget that it was me who gave you an opportunity and I've been propping you up ever since. Even after I left. Well, you owe me.'

'I what?!'

'And you can repay me by finding out every last detail about this new client and coming up with a report that details how we can manage them moving forwards.'

'You have account managers for that.'

'They're busy. You're more than capable.'

'I think it's time you left.'

'I was going. I've got to pack anyway. As, I'd suggest, have you.'

'What do you mean?'

'I'll have the car pick you up at six.'

'Serena, I can't just go.'

'Of course you can. That's what I pay you for. I presume you still want to get paid, don't you? Maybe one day, if you decide to keep seeing that woman, you'll be able to afford to take her on something more than a cheap date.'

'She doesn't care what kind of date we go on.'

'She would if you were totally broke, trust me. We women don't like a man who can't pay their bills. And that's where you'll be if you don't come on this trip tomorrow. Because I'll withhold your salary.'

'You can't do that.'

'I can if you're in breach of contract.'

Serena headed for the door.

'In that case,' Leigh wrestled with Tarquin's cage, wishing it didn't look as comedic as he knew it undoubtedly would. 'Take him. Your prized parrot. I won't be able to care for him if I've got to drop everything and fly out for work. Your pet, you sort out who looks after him.'

Serena looked at Leigh, then Tarquin, disgust writ large across her face. 'As if I'm taking that flea-infested thing.' And with that, she flounced out of the door and off into her car, leaving Leigh standing there alone with Tarquin.

'Breach of contract. Breach of contract,' Tarquin squawked.

30

The Cheap Dates Club Roundup – Isla and Leigh

When we set out on this journey with eight hopefuls looking for love, we could not have foreseen how it would pan out. It's fair to say that our love matches were not entirely successful across the board, some feeling that cheap dates didn't exactly spark romance; and we very much hope that both Andrew and his lower back make a speedy recovery from his disappointing date. But we had high hopes for our Cheap Dates Club stalwarts, Isla and Leigh.
As did so many of you.

Our social media accounts blew up each time we updated their story. At one point, after date number four, #TCDCIslaAndLeigh was trending, it looked like the matchmakers had hit a home run. And despite some reluctance to commit to how they felt early doors – something we attributed, perhaps naively, to nerves – both Leigh and Isla talked so positively about each other after the last couple of dates. So much so, Jenny in accounts was about to buy a hat.

But we have bad news for you.

Despite a last date in which they enjoyed live music, great food and each other's company – one reader spotted them walking hand in hand, away from town at the end of the afternoon, and told us 'they only had eyes for each other' – it looks like they've tripped at the final hurdle. We asked them if they wanted to continue seeing each other outside of the experiment and according to Isla, they had agreed to a date the following day but at the eleventh hour, Leigh cancelled with barely an apology and besides a couple of feeble attempts to contact her, she's heard nothing from him since.

Even our own post-date questionnaire has been ignored. Leigh had been quick to respond in our earlier correspondence with him, but now? Radio silence. Is he ghosting us too? One of our team heard from an anonymous source that Leigh's past is not quite as tidy as he had us believe. Rumour has it, there might be the rekindling of an old flame going on here . . .

Whatever his reasons, we think it's a pretty poor show. We were swept up in their romance, all as eager as you to get the updates each week. And now, we're left with that hollow feeling you get when drinking substandard decaf coffee. The buzz has gone.

Well, we're gutted for you, Isla. We hope that you find your perfect match soon. We're only sorry it didn't happen on our watch, on a budget.

#TCDCTeamIsla

31

Isla padded through to the kitchen, rubbing her eyes and trying to force some energy into her body. She'd taken a couple of days off as sick leave because when she'd tried to get up to work the morning after the night Leigh sent that message, she'd not been able to stop crying, which she was furious about, because how ridiculous to cry over a man. He'd tried calling a couple of times while she had her phone off, left her a voicemail saying he had to go away with work. That he was really sorry, it came out of the blue, blah, blah, blah. After many hours spent watching old films she'd not seen in years, which included realising that *Weird Science* hadn't aged particularly well, she'd begun to wonder if she was being rash, overdramatic, too quick to judge. Then she saw the write up from the *Gazette*. To not even bother talking to them? Rekindling of an old flame? So what had she been? A chance to see if he could slum it? After all he'd said about his ex and how different she was to Isla. Or was it a chance to show his ex that he could move on, in the hopes it made her jealous and she came running back to him? Had he really gone away with work, or was he hedging his bets? Keeping Isla hanging on, without committing, on the off chance a reunion didn't work. The idea made her feel sick, but it just wouldn't go away.

As she filled up the kettle, there was a rustle of paper and whispering – Jay and Sophie arriving, trying to act casual. 'Morning,' Sophie chirruped. 'Nice to see you up and about. You look great, actually. You off to work today?'

'Yes. Thought I should get my act together and stop moping. And you don't have to hide it.'

'Hide what?' Jay said, carefully folding something beneath the table.

'The *Gazette*. The one I left on the doormat that you're now hiding under the table.' She poured coffee and dropped a slice of bread into the toaster.

'Oh, I was just . . . '

'Looking for jobs. He was looking for jobs. Weren't you?'

'Yeah.'

'In the *Gazette*?' said Isla.

'You're right,' agreed Jay, quickly. 'Silly really. Probably find better options online. One of them job websites. Or . . . '

'LinkedIn?' offered Sophie earnestly.

'The pair of you are rubbish liars. You got it to have a read of the Cheap Dates roundup. I've already seen it online, so go ahead.' Isla bit down on her toast, sitting in the chair beside them. When Jay guiltily put the paper on the table, open at the Cheap Dates Club roundup page, Leigh's photo stared back at her and her heart flipped. Then sank.

'I'm not reading it.' Sophie reached for Isla's hand in solidarity. 'I don't care for what he's got to say.'

'There's nothing to read; he never got back to them,' Isla said.

'He what?' Sophie, changing her mind, flipped through the paper to read for herself. 'That's just rude.' She read on. 'Team Isla,' she added, her voice cracking with sympathy.

'I don't need anyone taking sides, Soph. It is what it is. I just wish someone would have talked me out of it before I got all wrapped up in it. Then unceremoniously dumped after someone has managed to unlock level sex.'

'Isla.'

'That's what it feels like! He played a game and kerching! He hit the jackpot, collected his winnings, moved on. The only casualty here is my dignity, which I could cope with if it weren't for the fact that everybody's bloody well read about it.' Isla screwed up the paper and threw it in the bin.

Her back turned away from Sophie and Jay, she made a packed lunch with the leftovers of cheese that had started to go hard at the corners, and bread that she first had to pick the mouldy bits off. Roll on pay day. Again.

'Just remember, today's news is tomorrow's chip paper,' offered Sophie.

'They don't wrap chips in newspaper anymore, Soph. And the internet lasts forever.' Isla appreciated her support but she wasn't in the mood for the platitudes.

'You had fun,' Sophie tried, again.

'While it lasted,' agreed Jay.

Sophie nodded. 'Exactly. And just because he was only in it for the cheap dates, doesn't mean you have to give up on love.'

Isla turned, knife in hand like a pointer. 'Cheap dates *and* a one-night stand. Let's get it right.'

'Well . . . the next date you go on might be different.'

'Oh, I'm done.' She wrapped her sandwich up in a reusable beeswax wrapper that her mum had sent her, months ago.

'There's someone for everyone, Isla.'

'Soph, I'm done. Honestly. Totally done. I'm fine on my own. I've *always* been fine on my own. I don't know why I've been so obsessed with *not* being on my own. It's been embarrassing, really. What kind of feminist am I if I can't envisage a future *on my own*? Well, I can. And I do. And I'm fine with it.'

Then Jay got up and moved towards her. He looked like he was coming in for a hug. Isla's heart stopped. She did not want consoling by anybody right now and especially not by him. However well-meaning he thought he was being. She picked through the fruit bowl for an apple that hadn't gone wrinkly, leaving Jay to stand awkwardly by the fridge.

'Right, I'd better go. Got to pick up a load of jigsaws that some woman in Totley is donating to the home. They were her late mother's, and she wants them to still be enjoyed. Lovely idea, isn't it.'

'Isla.'

'Sophie. Don't. I'm fine. I just got carried away. It was silly and I've learned my lesson.' She didn't bother painting on a smile but did at least give them both eye contact so they could see she was serious; and fine, totally fine. 'I'll see you both later.'

Her phone pinged with a message. The Christmas Girls.

```
Ella: Just seen the paper, Isla, are
you OK? Do you need anything? We
could set up a Zoom?'
```

A Zoom. Because that's as much time as they can muster for her.

Isla grabbed her pack up, shoved it in her bag in her room then legged it out the front door before Sophie, Jay, or any of the Christmas Girls for that matter, could catch up with her.

32

Pushing through the double doors to work, Isla was immediately hit by the slightly fusty smell of her 'home' from home. She opened some windows, drew back some curtains that had been left closed. Dust particles lingered in the shafts of light, disturbed by the slow and steady arrival of Doris who stood between Isla and her office (cupboard) door.

'Well, thank goodness you're back in today.'

'Hi Doris. Nice to see you too.' Isla checked the rota to see who else was in. 'You been bored without me? I've got two bin bags full of jigsaws, bloody murder carrying them up from the bus stop but that'll keep you all quiet for a bit, eh.'

'You feeling better then, love?' asked Doris, pointedly. 'What was it?'

'A cold. Just a cold. And yes. Loads better, thanks.'

'Lucky it's passed so quickly.'

'I suppose so.'

'Now you'll be able to smell those.'

'What?' She could feel Doris watching her as she pushed open the door. 'Oh!'

On top of her desk, swamping it entirely, was an enormous bouquet of flowers. Roses, greenery and some pretty things she didn't know the name of but that smelled divine. In fact, her entire cupboard smelled divine. She'd once fancied working as a florist because of this smell, until she'd realised how early you have to get up and how cold you have to store flowers to keep them fresh – she hadn't fancied a lifetime in fingerless gloves.

'I wondered who they were from,' mused Doris.

Isla stared at the flowers.

'But I figured it wasn't my business to know.'

Isla peered beneath them to see if her desk was actually still there. Of course it was, but the volume of these flowers was ridiculous.

'I could guess, I suppose.'

They were without doubt, the biggest bunch of flowers she'd ever received.

'I'd hazard that someone's feeling guilty.' Doris folded her arms, pursing her lips, tightly. 'As well he should, treating you like that.'

Isla bit into her cheeks. Part of her didn't want to believe they might be from Leigh because then she'd have to decide if she could believe he really meant it. Did she dare be drawn in again?

'It's typical. They always think they can just send a few flowers and it'll all be OK again.'

'Doris.' Part of her also wanted to believe that the past few days had all been some awful mix up and he'd blown an entire month's salary on an unnecessary, but – if she was being truthful with herself – desperately welcome apology.

'Though I can't fathom how someone entertaining cheap dates can afford to send a bouquet this size. Seems a bit deceitful if you ask me. Like he was hiding something to see if you really liked him for him. Do you think he's a millionaire?'

How would Isla feel if he was? Was that why they went to her place not his? Was that why he'd disappeared suddenly, to organise a grand reveal? Would she be relieved, or feel like she'd been manipulated? She'd kind of enjoyed the sense that they were both in pretty much the same situation, the same boat, financially. Like it could have made them a team . . .

'One of those secret ones off that TV show that pretend to be a regular worker then surprise someone who doesn't have very much with a car and a cheque and enough opportunities to change their lives. Well,' Doris crossed her arms and utched her chest up disapprovingly, 'I don't think he's going to be changing your life anytime soon, I wouldn't trust him as far as I could—'

'Doris!'

'Yes, love?'

'They're from Rupert!' She held the card out for Doris to see, her heart sinking back down to her battered Converse.

'Rupert?'

'Prudence's nephew.'

'Oh! Rupert!' Her eyes glittered. 'Well, how very generous of him.' She paused, thinking. 'Though I'd say it'd be even more generous if he'd sent them to Prudence too. You know she had a funny turn while you've been off. It's that room. It's cursed!'

'Is she OK?'

'She's fine. We read some *Lady Chatterley's Lover* out loud together, that soon perked her up.'

'Oh. OK. I don't remember that section on my first-aid training . . . '

'I'd still be moving rooms if I was her, mind. So come on, what does the card say?'

Isla studied it. 'He still wants to take me for dinner.' There was boredom in her tone. A weariness. If love was as hard, and as continually disappointing as it had been so far, maybe she shouldn't bother.

Doris snatched the card from Isla. 'An "expensive" date is what he's actually put. "The antithesis to your recent experience."' Her tone was gleeful. 'Blimey. I wonder where?

'I wonder why!'

'Well, he's said why, hasn't he.'

Isla looked at Doris pointedly.

Doris handed her the card back. 'He's been keeping an eye on your cheap dates and wants to cheer you up. I think it's very lovely.'

Lovely. Isla's heart tripped at the word.

'Did you ever call him?'

Isla shook her head. Aware his business card was still in her drawer at home. She'd been going to throw it out after her night with Leigh but got distracted with work and it remained tucked beneath last year's diary and a half-eaten packet of Starburst.

She tried to move the flowers to one side, searching out her laptop. 'All very sweet but—'

'Don't you dare.'

Isla looked up sharply. Doris had never used that tone with her and there was a look in her eye that said she was not to be messed with.

'I've seen that look on your face. And you have not had a cold. You've been off with a broken heart. Or if not broken,' she said, holding a hand up to Isla's protest, 'bruised. A bruised heart. And we get it, we really do. We've all been there.'

'We?'

'Us lot, here. In the home. We were so sad to read how things had turned out with that other fella.' Isla groaned again at the reminder that *everyone* at work would know all about what happened with Leigh. Why, oh why, had she signed up for such a public opportunity to shame and embarrass herself? 'We know you thought you'd met someone special.'

Isla screwed her eyes shut.

'But if he's gone silent on you, and the paper, maybe he's just not the one. It happens. The *Gazette* certainly seemed to think there was something fishy going on and if that's the case, you just don't need it, or him.'

She took a deep breath, picking the flowers up and looking for somewhere to put them. 'It's fine, Doris.' There was a coffee table in the entrance, they'd look nice there. 'In fact, I'm fine. Totally fine. I just want to get on with my job.'

'I know it is. And I know you will be. You're made of strong Sheffield stuff, you are. You'll not go down without a fight, but maybe, sometimes, you can stop fighting. Maybe, sometimes, you can accept the offer of a slap-up meal with a handsome suitor who sends obscenely expensive flowers and therefore can clearly afford to pay. Look, he's said it himself, you won't owe him a thing.'

'Doris . . . ' Isla was tired. 'You don't get owt for nowt.'

'He's not taking no for an answer.'

'Bit predatory.'

'Or romantic.' Doris moved to reposition the flowers, irritated. 'You young uns. It's not all bad men being bad men.'

'I know that, Doris.' Isla strained to shift a load of old copies of the *Gazette* that hadn't been picked up. Her face was on the front page, top right beside a side headline. She couldn't bear to look at it.

'There are still some good ones left.'

'Hard to really believe that what with recent evidence, though, eh.'

Doris steadied herself against the reception desk. 'A little bit of embarrassment killed nobody. Yes, you've had a bad experience.'

'Many of them.'

'A few bad experiences, but why let that put you off some nice food with a nice-looking man. That's all it needs to be. No high hopes, no expectation. Sometimes we need a little palate cleanser between meals. If you get my drift.'

'Are you saying Rupert is a palate cleanser.'

Doris winked.

'You're basically calling him a sorbet.'

'Pretty fruity one, if you ask me.'

Isla shook her head. Ged shuffled down the hallway towards them.

'At least think about it, Isla. You look like you could do with a bit of fun. And if he's offering it, take it up, on your own terms. Make your own rules. Don't let this business with Leigh—' Isla prickled at the sound of his name. 'Don't let this business with him colour how you move about your world. Rupert may not be the love of your life, but he might just be the boost you need.'

Ged arrived beside Doris, patting the hand that grasped onto her walking frame.

'Still playing Boggle?' Isla asked wryly.

'It's good fun, isn't it, Doris,' said Ged, oblivious.

Doris adjusted her composure, and her walking frame, before saying, 'Don't knock it 'til you've tried it.' She offered Ged a cheek to kiss, before the pair pottered back up the hallway, nattering to each other.

Isla kicked herself for feeling a wisp of jealousy about octogenarian 'Boggle' and tried to busy herself tidying the reception area instead. Thoughts of Leigh pushed their way into her mind again, the same questions she'd been battling with for the last few days: where was he, what was he doing? Had seeing their Cheap Dates in the paper made his ex realise what she was missing out on? Isla tried to think back to the dates they went on, desperately searching for red flags. His reluctance to open up should have been one, the fact that he hadn't just left his job when they split up, another. Who really wanted to stay working alongside an ex? Unless there was some hope that things might rekindle?

The phone ringing interrupted her thoughts, she jogged over to answer. 'Hello, Nether Edge Residential Care Home. This is Isla.'

'Isla, do you have a few minutes?' Isla's boss, Bill. They didn't tend to have that much to do with each other, him usually stopping at one of the other homes in the group until he'd joined the suits for some meeting or other. 'I'm in the back office, I could do with a chat.'

Had he seen the newspaper too? Was he going to call her out for taking time off sick when clearly nobody believed it? Isla checked her face in the mirror, to be fair, she was looking rough. Tired eyes, her face still a bit puffy from crying. She hadn't bothered with much in the way of makeup that morning, and certainly didn't look her usual self. She straightened out her blouse, wishing she'd at least ironed it that morning.

33

Isla stared at Leigh's number in her phone. She'd heard nothing from him since the voicemail on Monday night. She'd deleted it in anger, then couldn't work out how to get it back from her deleted folder and ended up deleting all messages, forever, from everyone. Then she'd had another cry, because maybe if she listened to it again, she'd hear something different in what he said or the way he said it. She'd sent him a text on the Tuesday, a moment of weakness where she wondered if she'd just read it all wrong. But it didn't look like he'd even read her message and he'd certainly not bothered calling again. Surely if he'd cared, he'd have tried harder?

He hadn't.

Hands shaking, quickly, so she couldn't think about it too much, she blocked him. It wasn't fair to Rupert. She'd accepted a date with him, she shouldn't be hanging on to some fantasy version of Leigh that she'd created. He didn't deserve any more of her energy.

She threw her phone down again and turned to face the full-length mirror. Her reflection did not please. She'd eventually agreed to the date with Rupert and Sophie had convinced her to put on the catsuit as some kind of 'stub you' to Leigh, but it just made her look a bit desperate. She took it off in favour of her jeans, tired, and not really up for going out. In fact, she wasn't up for anything much. Bill had wanted to let her know that as a direct result of the increase in costs of running not only the home she worked at but also all homes across the organisation, they were having to begin some pretty tricky conversations about where they might need to cut corners. Since telling him she understood and leaving the office nodding, smiling and generally being very amenable to whatever decision the senior management team needed to make, she'd gone back to her office, panicked, set the residents up with some marathon jigsaw puzzling and hidden herself away to type up a whole list of reasons why she should be allowed to stay in her role, and what she brought to the organisation.

Now was not the time to lose her job.

She'd put it all in an email, being clear about all the areas of her work that were vital to the residents' mental and physical wellbeing. Healthy, happy residents were surely cheaper to look after and support. She'd let it sit in her inbox because she was too scared to click send until she did it in a brief flash of courage, just before she went out the door.

For now, there was nothing more she could do.

She tried to shake off the niggle of fear that sat in the pit of her stomach since she'd had that chat with Bill, staring at herself in the mirror. The jeans weren't cutting it. She should probably make more of an effort if she was going to get the most out of this 'palate cleansing' date.

Back in the catsuit, she stared at herself from all angles. She fluffed up her hair, pouted, then shook her head at herself and flung open her wardrobe doors. However hot Sophie claimed Isla looked in it, and however much Doris thought she should go for it, no holds barred, it was not a first date outfit. Even just speaking practically; they were going for food, and she planned on eating as much as she possibly could. The skin-tight catsuit did not, therefore, a first-date-slash-stuffing-her-face-session outfit make.

In fact, thinking about it, why had she even bought it? On a whim in the New Year sales when she still had some Christmas money left. It was unlikely she would ever wear it for anything other than fancy dress, topped off with cat ears and kitten heels. In the cold light of day – or the average warmth of late afternoon – she'd be putting it up on Vinted.

After rejecting a number of alternative outfits, she finally settled on a pair of linen trousers she'd got at a clothes swap, paired with a high-necked vest top. Chunky, strappy sandals, some layered necklaces and a jacket she borrowed from Sophie finished the look and actually, when all dressed up, she looked good. She felt good. She was going to go and enjoy this date without any expectation.

Her phone pinged. She jumped on it then remembered she'd blocked Leigh. Now it would never be him calling or messaging, which was absolutely fine. Totally, totally fine. In fact, she thought, Leigh who?

> Call me if you need me, I'll definitely be available. Promise. xxx

In fairness to them, all the Christmas Girls had been messaging her since the newspaper printed her update. Ella was furious with Leigh and wanted to hunt him down. Poppy was being reasonable and supportive: *just let him go. You're worth so much more.* And although things were going well for Molly with Intercity Matt, she'd been checking up on Isla the most. Offering to cook her food. Suggesting they went on a spa day, apparently oblivious to both Isla's financial situation and the fact that nobody had died. Isla had pointed out that she didn't want any fuss, though she did briefly imagine what a post break-up spa day might look like: champagne breakfasts and healing saunas. Some other time. Maybe.

One of the roses from the flowers Rupert had sent sat in a tall shot glass on her bedside table. It was a kind of dusty peach, not traditional red or ostentatious white. Just peachy, with a soft, floaty scent to it. It had put a smile back on her face, even if she did think it was all a bit over the top. But maybe she deserved that kind of treatment, every now and then. And if the Cheap Dates Club was anything to go by, she wasn't going to be getting bouquets as big as her desk sent from Leigh.

Not that he'd have needed to.

She'd never wanted flashy from him. She'd kind of liked that all that side of things had been taken away with the Cheap Dates.

And yet, it hadn't changed the outcome.

Maybe Doris was right. Maybe she'd been too quick to dismiss Rupert.

When Leigh had arrived in her world, she had immediately veered towards him because he seemed safe. He seemed straightforward and the kind of person that had the same goals as her in life. She'd read into them both subscribing to the Cheap Dates idea and, it seemed to her now, made assumptions about what that meant. She'd seen serendipity. He'd seen a challenge – or a chance to make Serena jealous.

Rupert on the other hand, he'd backed off as soon as she made it clear she wasn't interested. He didn't try and pursue her or change her mind. He respected her boundaries even though she'd not really given him a chance. And he'd always been sincere. He'd always just made it clear that he liked her. And he knew about Leigh but hadn't got arsey or jealous over him. Not that he'd have had any right to, she knew that, but some people would have. And yes, the flowers were showy. But maybe she shouldn't assume that just because someone can afford to do something so excessive in a cost-of-living crisis, that they can't offer her what she really needs, too.

She tried to ignore the part of her that also kept thinking how nice it might be to date someone who didn't have to worry about money. Not that she wanted any of it – she was a fierce, independent woman who could absolutely cut her cloth to live to her means.

She looked around her flat. A spent plate with stale toast crumbs and cheap baked bean juice sat on her bedside table. No matter what anybody said, Heinz made the best beans and having to buy budget was really getting on her nerves.

She shoved her phone in her bag. Sprayed a cloud of perfume to walk into. Took a deep breath and headed out the door. She wasn't sure if love had any more chances with her, but she certainly wasn't going to let Leigh dictate her 'happily never after'.

34

Rafters Restaurant was pretty well known in Sheffield. Michelin stars, AA Rosettes. If you were a foodie, you'd most likely have been. If you were a foodie and rich, it might be a regular haunt. Isla once googled the menu to see taster plates of dishes she couldn't pronounce or even picture. It wasn't really a world she'd ever imagined inhabiting.

Rupert had invited her to go in first, then not batted an eyelid when she suggested he go before her. She'd always hated walking into a room before whoever she was with, and hated it even more when, in acts of outdated chivalry, men insisted. *No, please. Ladies first.*

Lady? She'd never been a lady. She never would be a lady. (Though agreed with Lisa Stansfield, she was very much all woman.)

'Can I take your jacket?' asked the waitress, smiling at Isla as if she came here often.

Rupert helped remove her (Sophie's) jacket in an entirely gentlemanly fashion. A mode he'd been in since they met outside the care home earlier that evening. They'd agreed to meet there, as he'd been to see Prudence beforehand, but she'd immediately regretted it. Upon arriving to wait by the entrance, she realised that Doris could, if visiting Ged, position herself in his wingback chair perfectly to watch the scene play out.

Isla had tried miming actions to 'go away', 'close the curtains' and less successfully, 'go off and play Boggle'. This being the action she was taking when Rupert appeared in the doorway.

'If you'd like to follow me?' The waitress led them past a handful of tables, some occupied, many awaiting their evening's guests.

Rupert pulled out Isla's chair, perfectly timing the moment where he pushed it in for her to sit. The waitress went to the bar and collected a tray with two flutes.

'This is a champagne made up of a blend of Pinot Noir, Chardonnay and Meunier from the Champagne region.'

The drink, a kind of straw yellow with slowly rising bubbles, had a gentle floral smell to it, Isla thought. Then she laughed at herself because she had no idea what she was talking about and instead wondered if it would be considered crass to clink glasses. Rupert clinked them anyway.

'Thank you for agreeing to come out with me.'

'Oh, you know. I had nothing better to do.' She gave him a raised eyebrow and a smile that she hoped was borderline seductive. She had no intention of actually seducing him – no matter how well he filled his sharply tailored suit, and how temptingly touchable his hair looked as he ran a hand through it – but if she was doing this, she was doing it on her terms.

He leaned in, seemingly enjoying her flirtation. 'You know, I don't think I've ever been made to wait for so long for anyone to agree to go on a date with me.'

She leaned in too. 'Yeah, well, I'm not just anyone.'

'That's why I waited.'

He held her gaze for a moment. She sat back, faux confidence fizzling a bit.

'I got the impression from your last few dates that a bit of extravagance wouldn't go amiss.'

That suggestion irked her, as if it was a veiled dig at Leigh. She might have blocked him but she wasn't quite ready to pick him apart. She blinked and wrinkled her nose, aware that she couldn't really argue with it, though. There'd been nothing wrong with the Cheap Dates Club formula. She'd seen a side to Leigh that she might not have seen were they dancing around each other in bars and restaurants. But she *had* liked that Rupert was inviting her somewhere nice for a change. What was the harm in that?

'Sorry,' he said hastily, sensing his faux pas. 'I didn't mean to make you feel uncomfortable.'

'It's fine.' She took another sip of wine and glanced out the window, reminding herself she was here to have a nice time. 'Honestly. I'm not uncomfortable at all.'

He smiled at her. Isla wasn't quite sure how he made her feel. Excited? Nervous? Both?

She broke the look, taking in the room. The red-brick walls bounced a kind of golden glow around them. There were a few more tables than she'd at first realised, but not many. It was a small restaurant with discretely busy staff who flitted about caring for customers and each other with effortless efficiency. There was the smell of rich food which intensified as a waiter passed by with two plates for a couple at the table opposite Isla.

Rupert reached for Isla's hand briefly, bringing her back to him.

'Dating's weird, right?'

'So weird.' She let him thread his fingers through hers. He had one of those small, gold signet rings on his little finger that all the blokes on *Made in Chelsea* wore.

'Like, we both know we must like each other because otherwise why would we be here, but we've made those decisions on arbitrary details like a photo and a dating app bio that only ever says the things you want people to know like "I enjoy travel. I like brunch".'

'I do like both of those things. Should have added them to my bio.'

'Go on then, why did you want to come on a date with me?'

'It was the lavish displays of flowers because I am woefully shallow like that. Oh, and your business card.'

He cringed, not unattractively. 'Yeah . . . regretted that as soon as I walked out.'

'The flowers were lovely though. Thank you.'

'Good. I'm glad you liked them. And I suppose I had an advantage with Aunt Prudence. I got to ask her all about you.'

Isla wasn't sure she liked the fact he'd spoken about her to a resident, even if it was his relative. There'd been enough chat about Isla's love life in that place already.

'She thinks you're pretty great. Exactly what I suspected.'

She sipped at her champagne, which was delicious. A waitress brought them bread with a Henderson's butter; also delicious.

'So what is it you're looking for in a man then? And how can I make sure that's me?'

Isla took another bite of the bread and butter, enjoying his attentiveness. And how comfortable she felt to make him wait. She made a show of thinking about her answer.

'Take your time,' he grinned.

She grinned back, in spite of herself. 'Just . . . don't be a dick?' Her voice was a little louder than the guests at another table would have liked.

'Don't be a dick,' he said, pointedly for all to hear. 'Noted.'

She liked that he had her back. 'I mean, honestly, it's pretty simple. I don't think we're asking for much.'

'We?'

'Women.'

'And yet so many people get it wrong?'

'So. Many. People.' She loaded her bread up with more Henderson's butter. 'Also, we need to work out the recipe for this, because oh my god, it might be the best butter I've ever tasted in my entire life.'

Rupert loaded more butter on his bread before finishing his slice. 'Yeah, that's . . . wow. I am definitely recreating this at home!'

They both took a moment to enjoy the bread. Isla was suddenly very aware of how hungry she was. And how thirsty. She drained her champagne.

Before she'd put her glass down, Rupert picked up the wine menu. 'What do you like? Wine? Red or White?'

'Aren't we supposed to drink whatever matches the food in a place like this?' She looked around at the other diners, who looked utterly bewitched as the waiters delivered them dish after beautiful, carefully crafted dish.

'We can drink whatever we like. I'm sure they won't mind. And if they did, the customer's always right, so . . . Do you have a preference? More champagne?' he asked, motioning to her empty glass.

'Oh no! No. I'll drink whatever. I drink most things, to be honest. Apart from whisky. Though I'd love it if I could enjoy a nice malt.'

'Beside a roaring fire in the Scottish Highlands?'

'Exactly that. I mean, that would be . . . yes!'

'I'd love to take you. You don't have to drink whisky, though.'

'We should probably see how tonight goes first, eh?'

'Of course. Though, I already think tonight's going great.'

Isla swallowed then scanned a wine menu. She tried not to feel a rise in panic. It was good that he said what he thought, how he felt. Things went wrong when people didn't. When they kept secrets.

'I like white. Or red,' she said. 'Or rosé to be honest, so . . . '

'Me too. Let's go white to begin with. If we go by the glass, we can try a few different types, if you like?'

'Wouldn't a bottle be cheaper?'

'Who's paying?'

'Well . . . '

'So don't worry about it.'

After two hours of the most incredible food Isla had ever tasted, and four glasses of the most incredible wine she'd ever drunk; plus, the champagne starter and a light yet sweetly moreish dessert wine, Isla was that perfect level of full. Not so full she could barely move or needed to undo a button but leaving no room for a slice of toast when she got back which was good because she knew that after that menu, even something as basic as bread and butter was now ruined for life. 'Literally every bite was, just . . . I mean . . . thank you!'

'Wasn't it? It's been so nice to do this with you. We should come again sometime, if you'd like?'

Isla was going to have to admit it to herself: Rupert had been a surprise. He'd listened to everything she said and proved it by remembering tiny details about her uni years and that she always told people her favourite film was *Withnail and I* because it felt a little more highbrow than *Legally Blonde*. And she did like *Withnail and I* but was charmed when Rupert said he too preferred *Legally Blonde*, and that it was one of the earliest feminist movies of its time. Some men would say this to try and get in her pants, but with Rupert . . . He'd flirted, oh, he'd definitely flirted, and he was good at the flirting. And the making her laugh. And the giving of compliments that felt truthful, not loaded. But it felt like these were all a part of a journey, not boxes ticked in the hopes of a sexy destination.

And the more he talked, the more handsome he became, which wasn't bad going, considering that his starting bar was so high. Definitely out of her league, but unlike most men out of her league from a visual standpoint, he didn't appear to know it. She wondered how hard he had to work to maintain the beautiful shape of his arms, just visible through his sweater. Was it cashmere? It looked expensive. How did he wash it without shrinking it? Maybe he had staff. Money didn't seem to be an object to him, but he also didn't seem like the kind of man who'd want people to wait on him hand and foot.

'What's your favourite thing about living in Sheffield, then?' he asked, after motioning to the waitress for their bill.

'The Peak District. Right on our doorstep.'

'You like the outdoors?'

'I like pubs within easy walking distance of the outdoors.'

'Right. So a casual Sunday walk through a dale, followed by lunch—'

'As opposed to a hike up Kinder, exactly. What about you? What do you like about living in Sheffield'

'I love all the old houses that are nearby – Haddon, Chatsworth. And the little villages with a real sense of community. I'd love to live out there one day.'

'Yeah? Me too.'

Rupert had a very specific smile that he deployed whenever she said something he particularly liked. It was small, a kind of hint of one. Like he wasn't afraid to show her he liked her, but he didn't want to make her feel uncomfortable by going all in, too soon. He wasn't all show and fluff and bluster. She didn't feel like he was a game player.

And the more he gave her those smiles. The more he laughed at her jokes, and really laughed, no performance. The more he reached across to give her hand the occasional touch while making direct eye contact. The more Isla fancied him. He had deep brown eyes, the kind of eyes you could get entirely lost in.

Maybe it was the wine.

They had had a lot of wine.

But as he offered her a hand to steady her down the steps. And checked his phone for the Uber he'd ordered for her. And asked if it was OK to hold her when she shivered. Isla couldn't stop wishing he'd lean down and kiss her.

Was this a palate cleanser?

A car drove by, lighting up his face. They caught sight of each other in the moment and he moved his face towards hers, and she made it clear she would reciprocate, and as their lips met, he wrapped his arms around her, pulling her into him. And she couldn't help but press her body into his, and he couldn't help but let out the smallest sound of appreciation. And neither of them noticed at first when the taxi, finally, arrived.

'Erm, well, you are . . . ' he took her by the hand, leading her towards the car. 'I think you're incredible. And I am so grateful you agreed to meet with me. And . . . ' a flirtatious look spread across his face. ' . . . for that. Yeah, I'm pretty grateful you kissed me too.'

'I think you'll find that *you* kissed *me*,' teased Isla, relieved that very soon she could sit down in the taxi and rest her legs, which had now turned entirely to jelly.

'Don't tell Aunt Prudence,' he said, with a wicked grin. 'She'd be scandalised at such displays. And out in public too!'

He opened the door for her, leaned in for another kiss that she thought was going to be on the cheek but was in fact just on the top of her neck and dear god, she was not prepared.

'When can I see you again?' he said, his voice part muffled by her hair. And by the pulse racing through her entire being.

'Oh . . . I don't know.' She got in the car and tried to buckle up, nervous hands failing her resulting in Rupert leaning across her. There was something obscene about the way he put the buckle into the holder, slowly, firmly, his eyes on hers the whole time. It shouldn't have been at all perverse and yet she very much needed a lie down.

'I'll message you. Like, I don't want to overwhelm you, but . . . I'd really like it to be soon.'

'OK. Sure. Yeah. Message me.'

As the car pulled away, Isla pressed the back of her head into the headrest and tried to recapture her breathing.

'Good night?' asked the taxi driver, casually.

'Oh, you know,' she shrugged, as nonchalantly as she could muster. 'It was all right.'

35

'You're all I've ever needed,' squawked Tarquin from the corner of the hotel room as Leigh held his phone up in the air, trying to find a decent signal. 'I still love you.'

'Yes, all right. I love you too, Tarquin. I must do, or why the hell would you be here? Oh my god! How can there still be no signal *or* Wi-Fi? They said it was getting fixed!'

Tarquin hopped off his perch and started pecking at some leftover broccoli the kitchen had given him until the boat came in with bird food. In the rush to get packed, and the distraction with trying to get Serena off his back and Isla to pick up her phone, Leigh had forgotten to pack any. He was still annoyed with Rachel and Jim for saying they wouldn't look after him. 'As if we're going to make it easier for her to drag you away. Just tell her you can't go,' Rachel had said. Had she *met* his ex-wife?

And that's how Leigh ended up sharing his room with Tarquin. Special dispensation from the hotel who had not taken kindly to the bird's arrival, but Serena had insisted that Tarquin was not going to be left to starve to death, just because Rachel and Jim couldn't put an animal's welfare before their own selfish selves.

Leigh had been too tired to argue, too tired to appreciate the beauty that was the Shetland Islands. They'd arrived on the plane from Aberdeen then took a thirty-minute drive, along the coast, up to Lerwick to make a final crossing on the boat over to Bressay where the tourist agency had a base. He'd noticed the sea, the moorlands, the clusters of houses and expanse of land, the soft peaks of hills in the distance, but he'd been more interested in keeping focus on his phone, desperate for a signal that meant he could check if Isla had responded to the voicemail he'd left her before being entirely removed from civilisation. Should he have been clearer? Or told her again how much he liked her and couldn't wait to see her when he got back? Should he have explained he was there with Serena in case she somehow heard or found out and read the wrong thing into it? The longer he was out of contact with her, the more chance there was that she'd think he wasn't interested, or that she'd lose interest in him, she'd said how shit it was when blokes just stopped calling or messaging, how worthless it made her feel. That was the last impression he wanted to give.

The was a sharp knock at the door.

Leigh's heart sank; it was Serena.

'I just want to brief you before we go to meet the team.'

'Hang on.' Leigh tried clicking send on yet another message to Isla. The send bar crawled along his screen before eventually throwing up an exclamation mark again, adding to all the others that hadn't gone. 'For god's sake!'

'Leigh, I don't have time for this.'

'I still love you.'

She scowled at Tarquin. 'Can you just put his cloth over him? I don't want him interrupting my flow today. Honestly, you do realise that I've had to pay extra to the hotel for you to bring him, in case of damage to the room.'

'He's your pet, Serena! And now that you're not with Simon and his pigeon fancying lungs anymore, you could take him back!'

'Pigeon fancying what?'

'Never mind.'

'He was Mother's bird, Leigh, as you well know. And Simon still has things at the house.'

He tried the message again. Leigh held his hand in the air by the window, desperately hoping for a tick that said 'delivered'. 'He still has things there? You didn't mention that when you were trying to get me to move back in with you. And for that matter, you didn't mention Tarquin. Was the invite extended to him or were you imagining I'd get a permanent carer in to cater to all his needs?' The message threw up another exclamation mark. He threw his phone on the bed.

'I don't appreciate your tone. I don't appreciate you throwing company property around, and I don't appreciate your attitude in general since we got here. This is an important meeting. A vital new client. And now that we can't even email them to confirm we've arrived, the least we can do is remain professional.'

'We're in the arse end of the Shetland Islands. It's taken us more than a day and a half to get here and the only tower serving this part of the island with any kind of contact with the outside world is down. How on earth do you expect me to be excited? Or for that matter, do my job properly? I need the internet for research, Serena!'

'I don't expect or even need you to be excited. But I do need you to be focussed. When we finally meet with them tomorrow, I want you to get fully under the skin of what they are wanting to achieve with this new brand identity. We need to understand their aims and objectives. We need to know the personality, *you* need to understand how to create a full campaign that is ambitious and gives them a return on their investment.'

'I know how to do my job, Serena.'

She stepped towards him, her voice softening. 'Come on, Leigh. I don't want us to be against each other. Look, we're here. It's just me and you. Maybe this is the time we need to reconnect, to learn how to communicate again.' She reached out to him. He didn't move. 'I know you're mad at me. I know you think that I've blown it for you with Ira.'

'Isla.'

'That's what I meant. But if it's really meant to be, like you say it's meant to be, then she'll wait for you. Send her some flowers or something.'

'Flowers? All right, the 1990s called, it wants its tired old dating cliché back.'

'Women like flowers, Leigh.'

'I suspect she'd rather I was there.'

'Honestly, Leigh. I just think that sometimes life throws little signs, little opportunities in your direction and maybe this is our opportunity.'

'I've handed my notice in. Is that not a big enough sign for you?'

'You were angry.'

'I haven't changed my mind.'

Serena moved over to where Leigh's clothes hung in the wardrobe. She ran a finger across the T-shirts that hung next to a pair of chinos and his best trainers. Leigh clamped his teeth together. 'I know. You've made your decision. I believe you.' She turned back to face him, dabbing the corner of her eye in such a way that her (invisible) tear wouldn't smudge her makeup. 'You can't blame me for feeling hurt.'

Tarquin did a little cough, then said. 'I still love you.'

Leigh scratched at the back of his head, despairing. 'I'm taking a shower and getting ready for this meeting. In the meantime, if you could find out when we might have some internet or maybe even a dash of wobbly 3G, that would be something.'

He sidled past her, irritated when their bodies brushed, opened the door and waited for her to leave.

The sooner he got this job done, the sooner he could get back to see Isla.

He just had to hope she was interested enough in him to wait that long.

36

Isla's heart felt like it might explode. 'Really? Oh, Mum. That would be lovely.' Her parents were coming home after ten months of touring the Mediterranean.

'Well, your father really missed a good northern winter last year and of course, we both miss you like mad! We put some feelers out,' her mum said, her face comically close to the camera in her phone. 'And there's a little house on the other side of Bakewell that we could rent.'

'Just for six months or so,' said her dad, popping up behind her mum. 'We'll be off again after that. We're fancying a full tour of Germany next year. But there's a spare room in the rental, so you could come stay whenever you want.'

'We could spend Christmas together. Your dad could prep dinner for us while we drink Bucks Fizz and watch all the National Lampoon films. Plus, there's a log burner, isn't there Peter?'

'There is, Marion.' He tried adjusting the phone so Isla could see them both but it dropped on the floor instead.

As they wrestled with it, a close up of her dad's nostrils, her mum's hand as she tried to take back control and wedge it properly, Isla pictured herself waking up on Christmas morning, padding downstairs in her pyjamas, and finding her mum and dad downstairs with bacon sandwiches and their first drink of the day waiting. The log fire would burn majestically. Her dad would be making crosses in the bottom of sprouts and her mum would pretend she wasn't checking he'd properly parboiled the potatoes. Maybe it would snow. They could walk to a pub for Christmas drinks then home to enjoy a feast, together.

Would Rupert join them?

What would he look like in Christmas pyjamas?

What did he look like, out of them?

'Isla?'

'Sorry. Sorry, yes, that's lovely. Amazing. Oh, Mum, Dad, I'd love it. I'd really love it. To see you at Christmas, and actually, just to see you, to give you a hug. We could spend so much quality time together, yay!'

'You seem very chipper today, love,' said her mum, narrowing her eyes. She studied Isla across the screen. Isla tried to act casual. 'Who is he, what's his name, will we meet him, and how do you know he's any good?'

'Mum!'

Isla's dad nudged her mum's arm off the cabin table in their camper van. 'You can't go off like that, maybe she's just in a good mood. Not all good moods have to be connected to a new man, Marion! This is the twenty-first century.'

'I know that but look at her. She's been like this for weeks now.'

Isla shifted in her chair. She had avoided FaceTiming them when she was moping about Leigh, despite the fact that she craved their love and wisdom. So all they had seen was her good mood during the Cheap Dates, and her good mood now. Which also meant that her dad was, on this occasion, wrong. Seemingly her good moods had been connected to a new man. Men. Eurgh.

'Tell us everything. Is it that Cheap Dates thing you told us about?'

'Mum, it's early days.' She wasn't about to tell them everything. She didn't feel quite ready.

'There is someone new! I could tell!'

'It might come to nothing.'

She was trying really hard not to get ahead of herself this time. When she'd got back from her date with Rupert she couldn't help but wonder if she'd just got caught up in a moment with him: a moment of relief that someone was distracting her from Leigh and how sad she felt about him. A moment of gratitude for being made to feel worthy of nice things. But unlike Leigh, Rupert was there. And Rupert clearly liked her. And he did funny things to her lady bits so she was going to ignore the voice in her head that questioned if he was maybe just a 'palate cleanser', as Doris had put it, and embrace the bit that had rather enjoyed his adulation. He'd clearly told Prudence he liked her too and had suggested he was going to take her somewhere she'd love for a second date, if she agreed to one.

Which of course she would.

'You don't have to tell us anything,' said Isla's dad.

'No. No. Course not. You don't have to tell us a thing,' agreed her mum.

Then they both went silent.

'You two!' Her parents gave her their faces of innocence, which she knew were not remotely innocent. 'He's called

Rupert. He's thirty-three. He does something in acquisitions.

'Oh, how fascinating.'

'He has an aunt here, actually, in the home, so, I've seen him a couple of times at work, too.'

'So long as you're happy. That's really all me and your dad care about. Someone who treats you well and maybe who'll enjoy spending a bit of time with us.'

'Oh, it's very early days yet, Mum.'

'I know, but . . . you've got a sparkle back. A mother can see these things.'

Later, Isla was setting up the day room: pulling curtains closed, moving chairs and tables about for the afternoon film. She felt all warm and fuzzy inside after chatting with her mum and dad, and Rupert had sent another text, just to say hi. Nothing specific, just letting her know that he was thinking of her, which she loved. It was so nice to get messages like that and to not feel like she had to respond, even though she did. With a 'hi' back. Followed by an 'x'.

Ged arrived first, taking up a chair with a table and pouring a bag of ready-made popcorn into a bowl. He offered some up to Isla who popped a few pieces in her mouth before bringing another chair over ready for when Doris arrived.

Prudence ambled in, smiling and waving at Isla. Isla had felt a bit uncertain about seeing Prudence after her first date with Rupert, but Prudence had really put her at ease. She told her that Rupert was a lovely nephew and a really nice young man and if she were fifty years younger (and, presumably, not his aunty) he'd be just the kind of man she'd have gone for.

A few more residents arrived. Isla passed the time of day with them. Sat them down. Doris was the last to take up her seat next to Ged, patting his leg and stealing a bit of popcorn.

'All right everyone, so this week's film is one I think you're all going to love. No singing this week, so you can just relax, sit back and enjoy.' She picked up the remote ready to press play on *Cocoon*, a film about a load of old age pensioners who'd found the elixir of life in a hotel swimming pool.

'Aren't you missing something?' said Doris wryly.

Isla pressed play, then looked at the blank wall where the TV should have been.

'Somebody's been daydreaming again,' said Doris, nudging Ged.

'Oh! Ha! What a silly thing to do. Just a second, I'll just . . . ' Isla felt her cheeks burn. She fumbled with the door to the TV cupboard, then around in her pockets for the keys. 'Honestly, what am I like?' she said, her palms getting sweaty.

'Away with the fairies, I'd say, or with a romantic suitor.'

'Doris!' gasped Isla, glancing over at Prudence who simply raised her eyebrows. 'I just . . . forgot.'

As she left the day room to find the key to the TV cupboard, Isla could hear the hubbub of gossiping, before Doris's voice, above everyone else's said, 'I think your Rupert's putting a bit of a spring in our Isla's step, if you know what I mean!'

37

Isla stared at her inbox, a sick feeling creeping inside her. She read the email again, her eyes glazing over. Bill, her boss. He'd thanked her for the *information* she'd sent over, saying *it would be useful for the senior execs to have in mind while planning the future of the organisation in the current climate.* And then the worst bit: *there will be some difficult decisions to make in the coming months.*

Difficult decisions?

She shut her laptop screen. What did that mean? Difficult decisions. She tried to think about it from a positive angle, but a difficult decision always ends badly for some people, and if it was going to end badly for some people, there's no reason some people weren't her. Who were they most likely to keep: the fully trained carers, or the girl who set up the Guess Who? tournaments and tidied away jigsaws? She worked hard and loved her job but staff are disposable. She was disposable.

Which was really what it all boiled down to.

She opened her laptop back up and resumed reading some guidance about a small grant she wanted to apply for. A pot of money that might help the home invest in some new exercise equipment designed for older people. But she could hear the little voice in the back of her head, reminding her how pointless it was, how surplus to requirements she was. She shook her head and adjusted her position, sitting up straight, shoulders back, shaking her head a little to try and regain focus. She read the words on the grant guide over and over without taking them in.

Leigh thought she was disposable, too.

She stood up so she could close her door, reaching for a bit of blue roll at the same time, then buried her face in the paper as she let out a muffled sob that seemed to come from nowhere.

She rubbed at her eyes, scolding herself for the dramatics.

He'd not even tried to call or message her for what, ten days? That's how disposable she was despite what she thought was a real connection. How could she have been so drawn in by him?

Not that she was going to waste a single bit more of her energy thinking about him. If her bosses had difficult decisions to make, maybe she did too. Maybe she should start looking for another job. Maybe she should pull herself together and update her CV. Check out the job pages. She could do that now, it would be a good use of her time; just get a feel for what was out there, what she might be able to do, what the salaries might be like. Hey, maybe she could even earn more money. Maybe she had been holding herself back by staying at the home, maybe this was exactly the push she needed . . .

She scrolled one job page. Then another. And another.

She didn't want to leave.

She really didn't want to leave. She loved it there. She really loved it.

How the hell was she going to pay her bills? Make her rent? Would they give her any kind of payout, or even a good reference? They'd have to, wouldn't they?

She was going to be fine. This was ridiculous.

But did senior management really understand? How could she make them? Why was she crying?

Gah! *Why* was she crying!?

It was her mum's birthday soon too – if she lost her job, that would be another year where she'd have to apologise for not buying her anything. Last year it was because her car broke down and she had to pay to fix it, only for it to completely give up the ghost two months later. She still hadn't found the means to replace it. And of course her mum didn't mind, but just once, she wanted to show them that she was an actual grown-up, capable of supporting herself and doing nice things for others. Moving forwards in her life, forging her way. How long would they have to wait to see her succeed in life? They'd given her so much. They deserved to see their energies pay off.

A knock on the door made her jump. She panicked, wiping her face with more blue roll, hoping that it had not done that red blotchy thing it normally did whenever she had a cry. She shuffled over to open the door.

'I was just passing and—Oh! Are you OK?'

Rupert. Standing at her office door. With a look on his face that said that yes, her face *had* done that red blotchy thing.

'What is it? Is everything OK? I mean, clearly it's not but . . . '

'No, no, it's OK. I'm fine. Everything's . . . really it's fine.'

Rupert looked at her with kind eyes and that made it all a thousand times worse.

'No, really. Please don't. I'm fine, I just, I'm quite busy actually, I have a million things to—'

'Isla.' He reached for her hand. An act that completely undid her. 'What's happened?'

She turned back for more blue roll, hoping he hadn't noticed her nose was running, or felt how clammy her hands were.

'Can I give you a hug?'

Isla wiped her face again and looked at him. To be fair, it could have been anyone stood there in that moment, offering to give her a hug, and she wouldn't have been able to help it. The part of her that felt like this was a total overreaction to the email was drowned out by the part of her that was tired and worried. She gave a shallow nod.

She stepped towards him, he wrapped his arms around her, she hid her face in his chest and wished she'd got round to actually buying waterproof mascara because if there was any left on her eyes, it would definitely now be crushing itself into Rupert's very lovely shirt, which smelled very nice. He held her tightly, resting his chin on her head, just gently. He said nothing. When her breathing had begun to stabilise, she relaxed her grip on him, moving him to do the same.

'What time do you have lunch?'

'I don't really. I tend to take a quick break whenever there's a gap, or when there's leftover food from the residents.' She fiddled around with some papers on her desk, now embarrassed at the state she'd got herself into.

'What they eating today?'

'Smells like fish pie.'

'You want fish pie?'

'Not really.'

Rupert looked at his watch. 'Well, it's almost twelve now. Let me take you for a sandwich.'

'No, no, I can't. I shouldn't,' she sniffed with a little hiccup.

'You're no use to anyone here in this state. Look at you! You don't have to tell me anything about it if you don't want to. I just want to get some food down you and a bit of fresh air to brighten up your face.'

Oh god, her face. The state of her face. She was the world's least attractive crier. 'I should probably just give my face a wash and push on. I've got stuff to do . . . ' She wanted to respond to the email from Bill. Acknowledge the situation then maybe go chat to a few people, ask them if they'd heard anything about what was going on.

'I'll have you back within the hour. Everyone is entitled to a lunch break.'

Isla looked at her desk. Her watch. Her laptop with the email that implied there was every chance she'd be out of a job soon. 'I don't know.'

'Come on. There's that deli round the corner. It's nothing fancy, but they do an incredible hot pork roll.' He raised his eyebrows. 'If you're lucky, there'll be crackling too.'

'OK, OK. I'll come. Give me two secs.'

'I'll wait outside.'

She nodded and watched him go. He was the kind of person whose energy just felt reassuring. Like a proper grown-up who could fix a problem if required to. She darted down the hall and told a couple of people where she was going, promising to be back within the hour, then met up with Rupert out front.

'Come on,' he said, offering her an arm.

She took it and they walked. A breeze dashed across her face and she let her eyes close for a moment, safe in the knowledge that he had her. They walked to the deli in silence and though they barely knew each other, it wasn't at all uncomfortable. They passed a group of students leaving the shop with white paper bags stuffed with toasties, rolls and baguettes. The smell of hot roast pork lifted Isla's mood. They had dandelion and burdock in the fridge and despite the fact she was not thirteen anymore, she reached for one, placing both hands around the cold can as she gazed up at the menu.

'Hot roast pork for me please,' ordered Rupert. 'Isla?'

'Yeah, same, please.'

'Owt else, love?' said the woman behind the counter.

Isla watched as Rupert amiably chatted to the woman, reaching for his own drink, making her laugh as he paid. She was loving his attention, flirting and giggling as she made up their sandwiches. Isla looked down at her feet, wishing she'd carried on saving up for a new pair of shoes because the battered converse were looking even more battered than she'd realised now she stood beside him with his posh suit and shiny boots.

If she lost her job, she'd need new clothes for interviews.

Back out in the sunshine, they found a bench to sit on, part sun, part shade. 'Which side?' he asked.

'I don't mind.'

'Go on, you choose.'

Isla sat in the shaded side, grateful for a bit of respite from the heat. They each ate their sandwich and drink, quietly. Eventually, when she'd finished, she said, 'It looks like they may be making some redundancies at work.'

'Oh no, Isla. I'm sorry. What does that mean for you?'

She held her breath for a second. 'I don't know yet. I mean, I get it. It must be hard running a business at the moment, what with everything how it is, and I don't want to be naive about it, sometimes redundancies are inevitable in difficult times. So maybe I'll just start looking for something else anyway.' As soon as she said that out loud her bottom lip quivered. 'I just, I really like it there. I really love my job.'

'I can see that.' He paused, thinking. 'What ambitions do you have in life?' he said eventually.

'Oh, I don't know. I guess I've never really been that ambitious. I just want to be happy.'

'Yeah, but we're all allowed dreams. Sometimes it's fear that stops us from having them. You do know that you're great, don't you?'

She took a sip of drink.

'And that you could do anything you wanted to.'

She laughed, cynically. 'I think my days of really believing I could take on the world are behind me. That sort of thinking is reserved for teenagers, isn't it? You get older and realise maybe it's not that easy.'

Rupert shifted position to look her dead in the eye. 'Maybe this is a chance to do something different?'

'I don't know that I want to do anything different.'

'Maybe you could marry someone super rich and then you wouldn't have to worry about all this? You could dedicate your time to a charity of your choice, maybe have some children too?'

'Super rich?' she said, looking at him.

He shrugged, playfully.

'I'm not a Real Housewife.'

'You could be.'

'Not really my thing. I might not be ambitious, but I don't want to be beholden to anyone, you know?'

Rupert studied her, then smiled to himself in a way she couldn't quite put her finger on.

She nudged him, gently. 'Thank you for this. It was just what I needed.'

'You're welcome. I'm sorry we didn't go somewhere nicer.'

'No, not at all. A good sandwich and some fresh air, and this,' she held up the dandelion and burdock, hoping he didn't notice the small burp she swallowed down. 'It's the taste of my youth. A bit of nostalgia when you're feeling overwhelmed. It's good. Thank you.'

'Anytime.' They fell silent again, before Rupert said, 'This isn't exactly what I'd have planned for our second date, is all.'

'Second date?'

'Yeah, I mean I had hoped to take you on one of those casual walks followed by delicious lunches you were talking about, and I guess in a way that's what we've done. I just didn't think it would be a five-minute trip up the hill for a pork roll.'

'It was a very good pork roll. I'm a simple girl with simple needs.'

Rupert raised his eyebrows, looking away.

'Anyway, is it even a date if you don't kiss me?' She surprised herself by being so bold but in that moment, she didn't care that they were sat in the middle of the street, on a bench that people walked by. She didn't care that she was in her work gear with scuffed Converse and a face recovering from the cry blotch. If Rupert liked her, he wouldn't care either. And she really could do with feeling wanted right now.

'Is that how you define a date? Kissing?'

'Yes. I've just decided.'

He nodded. Folded up his sandwich bag and dropped it in the bin beside them. Then moved closer to her, lifted her face to his, and slowly, gently, kissed her.

When they moved apart, he smiled at her. 'What are you doing Sunday?'

'No plans.'

'Can I take you out again? Let me cheer you up.'

'OK,' she said, a rush of warmth settling in her stomach. 'That would be really lovely, thank you.'

38

Garlic and onion sizzling in a splash of olive oil filled the kitchen with all the smells and sounds as Isla chopped up leftovers of veg from her drawer in the fridge. There was always something so satisfying about creating something from nothing, a trick she'd learned from her mum back in the day. She'd definitely share a photo on the family WhatsApp when it was done. Take that tinned chilli con carne and beans on toast. Plus, focussing on chopping and stirring, lining up songs she could sing along to on her phone was exactly the kind of distraction she needed. She had to stop obsessing over whatever was going on at work, stop thinking about Leigh, and stop wondering about Rupert – slowly, slowly.

The front door slammed so she called out, 'Hey! Want a brew?'

'Hey,' came Sophie's voice. She edged into the kitchen, loitering by the door. 'Go on then, I'm gasping. So. . . how was your day?'

Isla groaned, flicking the kettle on then throwing a load of peppers and courgettes into the pan.

'That good?' Sophie sidled beside her, pulling out a mug and teabag.

'Oh, I dunno. There's stuff going off at work that's a bit of a worry. Lots of hushed meetings and then I got an email this morning saying that they were going to be making some "tough decisions". You got any passata?'

'Oh.' Sophie's tone vindicated Isla's panic as she handed over a carton of Tesco's own-brand chopped tomatoes. 'Only these, any good?'

'Aye. Cheers. I'll replace 'em.' Isla wondered how easy it would be to replace stuff like a tin of chopped tomatoes, if she lost her job. Or how pleasurable fridge surprise tea was really going to be if the surprise became less about using up the contents of her fridge and more about scrabbling about in the bottom of it for anything that didn't contain E. coli.

'"Tough decisions" sounds ominous.'

'Right?' Isla turned to face Sophie, spatula in hand. 'And it could all be totally fine, but you just worry, don't you.'

'Of course. And you love that job.'

'That's what I said to Rupert!'

'Oh yeah?' Normally the mention of a conversation with a man Isla had dated would have seen Sophie pull up a chair but instead, she leaned against the wall by the door.

'Sorry, do you need to get on?'

'No, no,' Sophie replied in singsong, checking her watch. 'I've got a few minutes.'

'He came over to surprise me today, found me crying in me cupboard.'

'Oh, mate.'

'I know, I'm being ridiculous really, there's no guarantee I'll lose my job, that's not what they've said at all, I'm just feeling a bit touchy.'

Isla went back to her pan, throwing in a bit of damp salt from the windowsill.

'You've not heard owt from Leigh then?' said Sophie, after a moment.

'Nothing.' Isla wasn't keen on how much her heart twisted at the question. She just needed to move on.

'I just don't get it.' Sophie shook her head. 'It makes no sense to me. I can normally tell if someone's a dick and I just didn't see it with him.'

'And yet, here we are.'

'I know, right. So bloody disappointing. Jay can't believe it, but like I said to him, this is the shit we deal with all the time. He's one of the good ones . . . ' Sophie's voice trailed off as if she realised that sounded a bit clumsy. 'Sorry.'

'You're allowed to be happy, Soph. It's good to have a bit of love around the house. When I'm not feeling insanely jealous it actually gives me a bit of hope, seeing you two love birds together like you are.' Isla wasn't sure she totally believed that, but she kind of really wanted to.

'So what about Rupert then?'

'You don't have to change the subject, either.'

'I'm not!' Sophie coughed and smiled. 'So are you rebounding, or do you actually like him?'

Isla tasted some of the concoction in the pan. 'Well, that's average.' She added pepper then tried getting some juice out of a definitely past it lemon she found in the back of the fridge because she'd once heard a TV chef talk about how it can lift a dish. 'Honestly? I'm not thinking about it. I'm going with the flow. And if all it ends up being is a nice distraction from Leigh, then whatever. But he is making an effort, like he really wants to do nice things for me.'

'*To* you, you mean!'

Isla spun around to see Sophie, phone in hand, thrusting like a sex pest while giving Isla a look. 'Absolutely not. I am not making that mistake again. Not unless I genuinely can't resist it . . . Actually, he's so hot, I'd better not. I'd only disappoint him, after all the fit women he's guaranteed to have been with.'

'Shut up!' Sophie scoffed, tapping out a message as she talked. 'He should be so lucky. When you seeing him again?'

'Sunday.'

'Oh right.' She inched towards the door, still messaging. 'What time?'

'I think he's picking me up at elevenish and has planned a walk and then a pub lunch somewhere.'

'Nice. Lovely.' Sophie looked at her phone, then back up at Isla. 'You gonna be out all day then?'

'I guess. You can have the place to yourself, make as much noise as you like.'

Sophie laughed. 'Well, I'd better get on. You need the bathroom?'

'Nope.'

'Cool, I'm going in the shower then heading out to meet Jay. Enjoy your fridge surprise.'

'Anywhere nice?'

'Oh, no, no, not particularly. Just . . . just out. Right, I'd better get . . . off. Ready. I'll see you later, then, bye.' She hurried out, her bedroom door slamming shut quickly afterwards.

Isla tasted dinner again. The salt, pepper and lemon juice hadn't miraculously turned it into a gastronomic success but in the absence of anything else in the cupboard, it was going to have to do. One of the residents had been telling her how their teacher grandson had been referred to the foodbanks to feed his family. She was under no illusion as to how much worse it could be for her.

39

'I can't believe we saw that many,' said Isla, still breathless from the magic of a herd of deer galloping across the road in front of them as they'd driven away from their walk round Chatsworth Park. 'I had honestly forgotten how beautiful the house is too. We're so lucky living close to it.'

'Aren't we?' grinned Rupert, holding open the door to the Rutland Arms, an imposing hotel and restaurant on the main roundabout in the Peak District town of Bakewell. They'd parked up, and meandered through the streets and shops before he'd guided her to lunch.

'We have a booking for 3 o'clock, under Parker?' He said to the maitre d'.

'Ah yes, I see your reservation. Right this way, Mr and Mrs Parker.'

'Oh, we're not—' Isla said, quickly.

Rupert winked at her, hooking her arm through his. She supposed it didn't matter if people thought they were married.

Then she wondered what kind of wedding they'd have.

Then she stopped herself because she was a strong, independent woman, and not a total loon. 'Have you seen the size of those Yorkshires!' she stage-whispered and tilted her head towards the magnificent roast dinners being enjoyed by the next table. Her mouth watered. With all the fresh air and talking and laughter, she had definitely worked up an appetite.

'My mother was terrible at Yorkshire puddings,' said Rupert. 'She used to get the au pair to make them up in batches and freeze them. If we ever had guests round for Sunday lunch she'd present them with pride, telling everyone they were hers.'

Isla sat back. 'You had an au pair!?'

'Oh. God, yeah . . .' Rupert looked suddenly bashful. 'Well, Mum and Dad both worked so much.'

Bashful was an endearing look on Rupert. Isla smiled. 'What did they do?'

'Dad had his own business. Hospitality.'

'So, hotels?'

'A few.'

'Right.' There'd been a few things he'd said in their conversation today that made her wonder if she'd entirely underestimated Rupert's wealth. He'd picked her up in a Maserati and she was fairly sure his walking boots were designer. 'You never went into the family business then?'

'I did. Kind of. It's all very boring.'

'OK then. What about your mum?'

'Lawyer. Litigation. Was a partner in her firm. Really showed me and my sisters what it was like to be a working mother. I could see how necessary it was to graft and that there was more to life for her than just being our mother.'

Isla leaned in.

'What?'

'It's good. Nice to get to find out more about you. Because so far, you've only seemed interested in me and my life. I was beginning to wonder what you were hiding!'

Rupert gave her a winning smile. 'You're just far more interesting than me!'

'So, you had an au pair. Was she like a teacher too? I have this image of you in a classroom in your home with a large blackboard and an abacus.'

'I'm thirty-four!'

'I know, but I feel like large blackboards and an abacus are synonymous with home schooling and privilege. Maybe I saw it on TV once.'

'I went to school. Just like anybody else.'

'Which one?'

'Birkdale.'

'Ah.' Isla nodded her head. She'd had friends of friends who'd been to one of the two private schools in Sheffield. Birkdale for the boys, Sheffield Girls High for the girls. 'So, I'm guessing you went skiing for school trips and all learned Mandarin.'

'Hey, no mickey taking. Skiing is an absolute scream. And Mandarin is a language spoken by over a billion people around the globe. Only just fewer than those who speak English. Now, what are you having to drink? I fancy a bit of fizz with lunch.'

'I could be persuaded.'

'I'll bet you could.'

He held her gaze a little too long, interrupted by the arrival of a waitress. He ordered a bottle of the prosecco and both their roast dinners, almost forgetting Isla's Yorkshire. She wondered if she'd have taken Mandarin at school if it had been an option alongside French and German. 'Latin?' she asked, after the waiter had gone.

'*Modicum*.'

'Pardon?'

'A little bit. Of Latin. In Latin.'

'Oh. Right. Of course. *Ich bin zwölf*.'

Rupert laughed, shaking his head. 'I don't think you are.'

'No. It's all I remember from German. And I'm not sure "I am twelve" would get me very far if I went to visit.'

'We have a place out there that we could go and stay at, up in the hills. You can try out what you remember.'

'Oh, really. You have "a place",' she teased.

Rupert screwed his nose up good naturedly. 'Does that come across as obnoxious as I think it might have?'

'Are you embarrassed?'

'Would it make it better if I was?' His hand dropped to hers.

'A little bit,' she grinned.

'Then yes, I'm mortified. But look, I can't help the family I was born into any more than you can.' A waiter arrived, separating the pair with two generous plates of roast dinner, placing them down on the table.

'Crikey, it's even bigger up close!'

'Well, you don't have to eat it all,' said Rupert. 'You might want to save yourself for dessert . . . '

She playfully ignored his suggestion. 'I'll manage.'

'Good appetite then?' he asked, eyes glinting.

'Good enough,' she said, shutting him down. She was going to have to be really careful, now. She could feel Rupert piecing her back together again after Leigh. Or maybe he'd got in there before she'd had time to fully break, which couldn't be a bad thing, could it? But she was not going to let herself get carried away this time, which had been hard to remember this morning as they lay on the picnic blanket he'd produced, with a flask of coffee and some shortbread, setting it down by a tree overlooking Chatsworth House. Shortbread wasn't really her favourite and kissing after coffee always made her feel a bit self-conscious but it hadn't taken long before she found herself on her back, Rupert nuzzling her neck in such a way that she had pretty much melted into him. A couple of dog walkers mooched past them, trying not to look and she'd had to put some distance between them, bringing Rupert back into the real world. He'd apologised, and she couldn't be cross about it, she'd lost herself too, just for a moment. All that fresh air, it had gone straight to her head but if this thing, whatever it was, with Rupert, was worth pursuing, she was going to do things differently.

Lunch had been gorgeous. They'd fallen onto a sofa by the fire afterwards, Rupert deciding he'd leave the car and pay for a taxi back so they could have a few more drinks. The prosecco flowed, as did the flirting. Their bodies connected, sometimes thigh to thigh, occasionally hand holding. At one point he'd reached across and moved her hair away from her face so he could see her better as they shared stories from their childhood. The year Isla found out Father Christmas didn't exist because she stumbled across the wrapping paper 'he'd' used for her Heelys. It was hidden in the understairs cupboard and her mum had been put on the spot, immediately crumbling with a confession when Isla had asked what it was doing there. And the year Rupert got a beach buggy from Santa even though he didn't live anywhere near the beach. 'How did you use it!?'

'We shipped it out to a villa we were renting in Cyprus.'

'Of course you did,' she'd laughed and he'd tickled her playfully. 'Hey, you!'

Their play turned to a kiss turned to her knowing without a shadow of a doubt that he fancied her as much as she fancied him, and she was determined not to overthink what someone like him saw in someone like her. 'God, you are . . . ' he shook his head at her. 'You make me feel all kinds of things I probably shouldn't be feeling in public.'

'Yeah?' She glinted at him, then rearranged her hair, grateful for a blast of cold air from the door as somebody left the hotel. 'We should probably go,' she said, thrilled with the idea of leaving him wanting more.

'Or . . . maybe . . . '

'What?' she folded her arms, good naturedly.

'Well . . . ' He paused. Then shook his head. 'No. Never mind.'

'Go on?' She was fairly sure she knew what he was thinking and while part of her, the part mostly fuelled by prosecco and lust, could thoroughly enjoy whatever it was he had in mind, the other part of her, the part fuelled by a newfound commitment for self-care, was not going to be swayed. And it felt good to know she was in the driving seat.

He edged closer to her, lowering his voice, taking hold of her hand, somehow suggestively. 'How about I show you a bit more of the high life. See if I can pull some strings and get us a room. The best room.'

'Show me the high life . . . ' She pulled back. How much prosecco had he had?

'I just mean, there's no point denying that money can get you things, you know? Pretty much anything, and I don't want to brag but . . . '

'What?'

'Well, I have money.'

She frowned at him. He'd definitely had too much prosecco. 'All right Daddy Warbucks.'

'Pardon?'

'*Annie*! Come on, tell me you've seen *Annie*. The orphan that gets swept up in a life of riches and high society.' He shook his head, so she began to sing, '*Tomorrow, tomorrow, I love ya, tomorrow . . .*'

Rupert half laughed, looking over his shoulder. Was he checking if anyone had noticed her singing? She felt suddenly self-conscious. And it was a different kind of self-conscious to the kind she'd felt when the dog walkers went past them . . .

Perhaps satisfied nobody had seen, he turned back to her. 'Well, I know you're not an orphan, but yeah, I don't mind the idea of showing a working-class lass how the other half live.' He winked at her, taking her hand and placing it on his thigh.

She stared.

'Now, be a good little Annie and wait here. Let me see what Daddy Warbucks can hustle.'

She took her hand back, a discomfort picking at her as Rupert winked, then swaggered off down the hallway. Showing a working-class lass how the other half lived? It surprised Isla how quickly the prosecco drained out of her veins and a moment of clarity could creep in. He actually just referred to himself as Daddy Warbucks . . . something wasn't right. And it was more than just the ick she'd developed.

She grabbed her handbag and jumped up.

Then sat back down again. She must have read it wrong. She'd misunderstood. But how could she have?

Before she could invent a satisfying answer to that question, a young woman tottered over from reception. 'Isla? Your husband asked for this.' She handed Isla a key.

Isla looked at it in the palm of her hand. It was brass. Heavy. And had the word 'Suite' on the keyring. She looked up at the young woman. Then back at the key.

'Wow. Impressive.'

'What is?' smiled the girl.

'How the other half live.'

The girl smiled but looked a bit confused. Then Isla remembered something: 'your reservation', the words the maitre d' had said to welcome them on their arrival. The penny dropped. 'Come on then, when did he book this?' she asked, smiling broadly despite how fast her heart raced.

'Well, I probably shouldn't say, but it was the day before yesterday.' The girl seemed thrilled with it all. 'He said that money was no object and that he only wanted the best for you. I don't want to give the game away but there's a nice surprise in the room, too. You're a lucky woman. Important to keep the romance alive, it's inspiring to be honest.'

Isla did not want to be inspiring.

'Happy anniversary. We hope that you both enjoy your evening.'

All her blood followed the prosecco, draining out of her face, leaving her sitting there, sober. Cold. With a deep sense of self-loathing. He could book as many fancy hotel suites as he liked, but he was not about to initiate her into the 'high life'. However much she had fancied him . . . before he'd done this.

'Please, pass this on to Rupert and say that I'll meet him up there. Just as soon as I've . . . ' She paused, trying to decide what to say to buy herself enough time to get out of there and away from Bakewell before he tried to track her down. 'Tell him I've gone to powder my nose.'

The young woman smiled, nodded and walked smartly away to find Rupert. Isla stood and caught her reflection in the mirror, curling her lip in disgust. How could she have been so stupid? Well, not this time.

She ran out the door, down the hotel steps, over the road, and on to the first bus that arrived at the bus stop. Turning her phone fully off and staring out the window, Isla left. Destination unknown.

40

By the time Isla made it home, she had been all around the houses, both literally and figuratively. It turned out that buses back from Bakewell took a lifetime, which was just long enough for her to have torn herself to shreds over getting drawn in by Rupert's flashy veneer. It's not like she'd never seen that kind of behaviour before. She'd actively pursued a bloke with a Porsche when she was eighteen and he'd reciprocated with a weekend in the Cotswolds and a pair of Manolo Blahniks. Shoes she'd never been able to walk in because a) they were obscenely high, and b) she'd accepted them the morning after their first night together and it all ended up feeling a bit *Pretty Woman*. She'd sworn then that she wouldn't get suckered in again by anyone with all the show and none of the charm.

But that's where Rupert had been different. He had all the cash, and he had charm. Like, he really did have charm. And after everything with Leigh, she'd enjoyed someone who seemed to be so certain about who and what they wanted. Until they showed her exactly who and what they wanted.

She'd arrived back home to some random stranger in the hallway with Sophie and Jay, relieved they seemed as keen to avoid her as she did them. When she tentatively put her phone back on there'd been a handful of phone calls from him since she left. Followed by a text that said

`I really like you, please come back.`

She'd stared at it for about ten minutes, trying to decide how to respond, when her mum FaceTimed.

'Hey love. You are not going to believe who we bumped into this morning. Oh, what's the matter?'

Isla screwed her face up and fought back the tears.

'Oh, love. What is it? Are you OK? Has anybody hurt you?'

Isla shook her head, sniffed up hard and tried to rub away the feeling of shame and ridiculousness.

'Oh, Mum!'

'What is it? Oh, Isla. Tell me what's going on.'

And just like that, Isla opened up properly for the first time since her parents had left home. She told her mum all about the months of dating, the lack of money, and the feelings of frustration that had been building up on both those fronts; and about how terrified she was that she'd be out of a job come winter and having to choose between eating or heating.

'Oh love, I'm so sorry you've been dealing with all of this on your own. You know you don't have to hide anything from us. And I know you want to stand on your own two feet, fight your own fires and all that, but you have to remember that you're one of the lucky ones. You're not going to find yourself on the street, or going hungry. Me and your dad are here to help.'

'I shouldn't need help. I'm a grown woman.'

'You must never feel ashamed for needing help. Or the fact that it's available to you. You're living in a different world to the one me and your dad grew up in.'

Isla sighed, heavily. 'All I've ever wanted was a steady job I enjoyed and to find someone that I can fall in love with and live happily ever after. Like you and dad.'

'You do know that there are some days that I could wilfully bury him under the patio, don't you, darling.'

Isla let out an unexpected laugh. 'Mum! That's a bit dark!'

'I'm just saying, happily ever after doesn't really exist. Not in the way people would have us all believe. Yes, we have been together a very long time. And yes, I still love him. But do you know where he is now?'

Isla shook her head.

'Cookery class. And do you know why he's there on his own?'

Isla shook her head again.

'Because if I have to hear him mansplain to the incredible Portuguese cook how to cook authentic Portuguese *bacalhau*, I might shove the *bacalhau* where the sun don't shine.'

'What's *bacalhau*?'

'Cod!'

Isla started giggling.

'Honestly. This is the man who wouldn't touch fish until he was fifty-four because he'd once had a bad experience with some Captain Birdseye. And I've tried to explain to him what mansplaining is, but do you know what he does?'

'Mansplains mansplaining?'

'Exactly! You see, you know him too well. No relationship is perfect. No man is perfect. Crikey, I'll even let you into a secret.' She looked over her shoulder. 'I am not perfect, either.'

'I don't believe it.'

'Well look, we can keep that between the two of us then, can't we? The thing is, Isla, you don't need a man.'

'I do know that.'

'So maybe it's time to just let it all go. Enjoy your life. Build your world. Be young and single and free of anyone who tells you how to load a dishwasher because I am telling you now, it is *not* essential to rinse all the plates first and dried on lasagne *will* come off if you put it on an intense cycle.'

'Mum.'

'Sorry.'

Isla carried her phone to the kitchen to make herself a drink.

'There's something else, isn't there? Come on, talk it out, before your dad gets back and tells me all about today's lesson. What else?'

Isla crossed her arms.

'Isla!'

Isla uncrossed her arms. 'I did meet someone.'

'The same chap you met through work? He had an aunt there or something?'

'No, through the cheap dates thing, remember?'

'Oh, yes!'

'Before the chap through work, I'd been on those cheap dates and I didn't say anything about them because I wanted to keep it to myself until I knew what was happening. I almost couldn't believe how well it was going. He was someone I thought might be really special. Well, anyway, it came to this horrible, abrupt halt. And then these last few dates with this other guy, well, they were lovely because he was handsome and funny and charming and I thought he was really interested in learning who I am, it kind of made the cheap dates stuff feel not quite so heartbreaking.'

'And?'

'Let's just say he turned out like all the rest.'

'But what about this "special" guy, then? What was the problem there?'

Isla let out a long groan, one she hadn't realised she needed. 'I really thought that we were on the same page. I really believed he liked me. I don't think I've ever felt so relaxed with someone. I don't think I've ever felt quite like I could be myself with someone as much as I could with him. Like, I know I said all this nice stuff about Rupert, but I think . . . '

'Go on.'

'I think I was just deflecting. I think . . . I think I really like Leigh. And I think I felt let down by him, which maybe was a bit unfair, he didn't owe me anything, but he just cancelled a date. Last minute. And it was so out of character, or so I thought. Then I felt so humiliated because . . . '

'You don't have to give me all the details.'

'I know. I know. I really liked him, Mum.'

'What was his excuse for cancelling?'

'Work.'

'Right?'

'He works for his ex-wife.'

'Oh.'

'And I've heard nothing from him since. He's just totally ghosted me.'

'Maybe he's just busy, love? Maybe it was an emergency.'

'He's a graphic designer. What kind of emergency could that be?'

'Well, I don't know, but . . . ' Isla's mum cocked her head to one side. 'Maybe you're right, maybe he has just disappeared and isn't interested but if your gut told you differently, maybe you need to give him a bit of time.'

'To do what?'

'Find a new job away from his wife, probably.'

'I wasn't bothered by that.'

'No? But as soon as something changed in him, you panicked.'

'Well . . . '

'Because you really liked him and then you worried you were going to get hurt. You pushed him away?'

'I don't think it was like that. I don't . . . '

Her mum gave her the look only mums can give when they're waiting for their child to catch up.

Had she been too quick to block him?

Isla groaned again.

'For every time I could have buried your father beneath the patio, there's been the time I could not have been vulnerable with anybody else. For every bit of mansplaining, there's been the days where I've needed him beside me, not saying or doing anything other than holding my hand. For every time he's cooked sub-par Portuguese cod, despite his claims to the contrary, I have reminded myself that I choose to be with him because he makes eighty per cent of my life better. That, to me at least, is true love. I can be vulnerable. I can be me. And I can forgive him for not being all of the things, all of the time. Maybe it is work that's stopping Leigh from calling, maybe it's something else.' Isla thought about the fact that she'd blocked his number. 'Maybe you need to take a moment, breathe, and listen to what your gut tells you.'

'Do you think?' sniffed Isla, wishing more than ever that she could get one of her mum's massive, tight and slightly too long cuddles.

'I really do.'

Isla nodded.

'Now look, your dad's back. I'll spare you his questions because he'll see you're not right as quickly as I did. Go on, have that cuppa and give yourself a break. To err is human, right?'

'Right.'

41

It had taken four hours, three more missed calls from Rupert and two comfort episodes of *Downton Abbey* before Isla decided what she was going to do. She'd replayed the conversation with her mum, over and over. She'd thought about the Cheap Dates Club and wondered if she'd been too hasty to just assume that Leigh was the kind of man who would sleep with her one night, then bin her off the next. And she knew why she'd done it; she'd just not wanted to admit it.

She really liked him.

And not in the same way she'd liked Rupert. With him, she'd been taken in by good looks and big gestures. When he'd finally realised she wasn't going to about-turn and fall into his lap, Rupert had sent her a string of angry texts asking her if she normally let a bloke buy her flowers and food and lavish her with attention then not return the favour. Apparently his mum had warned him about girls like her but he'd thought Isla was different.

She wondered if Great Aunt Prudence had any idea what kind of a nephew he really was.

But Leigh? They'd had that ridiculous first date where she'd sat, innocently talking and drinking tea in Sheffield Botanical Gardens, unaware that her makeup was sliding down her face. And each date after that felt . . . important. Like they were both really getting to understand new things about this new person in their life, and even though they knew they'd have to tell the newspaper all about it afterwards, and that more and more people were reading all about their dates, it hadn't stopped them being vulnerable with each other.

Maybe she needed to do that again. Be vulnerable. Maybe she just needed to outright ask him what was going on and give him a chance to just explain.

Oh God. What if he'd seen a side to her that he didn't like? A high maintenance side that he didn't have the time for. He said that was one of the problems with Serena, that she was too much. Was Isla too much? She didn't want to be too much!

She paused. Took a breath. If that was the case, if she was too much for Leigh, or anyone for that matter, they weren't meant to be. Simple as that. What was it her mum had said? To err is human.

She googled it, just to make sure she understood what it actually meant and yes, she did. To err. To make a mistake. She'd made a mistake. And to forgive was divine, or so Google said.

Hands shaking again, she reached for her phone.

She unblocked Leigh's number, embarrassed she'd blocked it at all. Like a teenager trying to prove a point that more than likely, hadn't even been noticed.

She dialled.

It rang once, then twice, then a third time and oh god, was it going to go to voicemail? Should she leave him a message? Would he listen to the message? What should she do!?

'Isla!'

'Leigh.'

Just the sound of his voice. She closed her eyes and took a breath.

'Isla, I can't believe you got through! The signal here, it's terrible. I'm not going to move, I'm literally standing with my ear pressed up against the window. I'm so happy that you've called.'

The relief in his voice gave her heart a squeeze. What had she been thinking? She'd acted like an idiot. 'I'm sorry. About . . . '

'No, no,' he cut her off. 'I'm sorry. I should have explained. It was all a bit sudden, and then it got . . . complicated. I mean—'

'You don't have to explain yourself to me. We barely know each other.'

'I know, but I wanted to, I just needed a bit of time to—'

'Leigh, honestly. I was too rash. I think I got frightened.' She paused. She could hear the sound of him breathing. Was she making him nervous?

'I'm away with work. The internet was down and until this morning, we had no signal either. It's still patchy, which is why I've got my face glued to the double glazing right now.'

'Where are you?'

'The Shetland Islands. It's beautiful. You'd love it. Well, you'd love it when freak storms haven't taken out loads of phone lines. Wait, can you still hear me?'

'I can hear you.' She closed her eyes and lay back on her bed.

'OK. We're just waiting for some satellite coverage to get organised so that I can complete this one project. As soon as it's done, I'll be home.'

'It's fine. Just, whenever.' Her eyes stung with tired, relief tears. She could trust him. She could surely trust him! 'I guess you're mad busy then?'

'Yeah, it has been pretty full on. A new client. I'm working in my hotel room at the moment, just trying to pull a pitch together.'

'Oh, I should leave you. I didn't mean to interrupt, I just . . . I just wanted to hear your voice.'

'No, no, you haven't interrupted. I'm just. It's just me, my laptop and . . . now you. I've really missed you.'

'I've missed you too. And I owe you an apology.'

'You don't. You really don't.'

'Just let me explain.'

The signal started breaking and she could hear Leigh move around his room. 'Wait, don't go. I'm going to try over here, hang on.'

She imagined him checking his phone, looking out for possible signal hotspots. She closed her eyes again and pictured him. His eyes, his hands holding hers. How it felt when he held her.

'You still there?'

'I'm still here.' She felt a lump in the back of her throat, and a longing to see him. 'I get frightened, really easily. Especially when . . . especially when I think something's at stake.'

'I get it,' he said, the line crackling.

'And after all those cheap dates, and all the conversations we'd had, and then that night at mine. I couldn't believe I'd found you; I couldn't believe that somebody like you might like somebody like me.'

'You're amazing. How could I not! Wait, oh god, this signal is going to be the end of me.'

'I still love you.'

Isla's heart stopped. Someone's voice had crackled on the line. And it definitely wasn't Leigh's.

'Who's that?' she said, sitting up, slowly. A coldness edged over her.

Leigh's voice again. Was he talking to somebody? 'Oh god, it's . . . ' crackle. Break up. Crackle. 'shut *up*! . . . you think.'

'Leigh?' She stood up.

'Isla, it's—' The line broke yet again.

'Who?'

Crackle. 'Serena's . . . ' Crackle.

She wasn't just naïve. She was stupid. 'Look, I'm sorry, I . . . I don't want to interrupt you. And I certainly don't want to come between you.' The line went silent a second then came back. Isla knew what she had to do. 'Look, I'm sorry I bothered you. I hope work goes well. And thanks . . . for . . . ' Isla ran out of words. 'Bye, Leigh.'

'Isla—'

She hung up.

She dropped down into her chair. She rubbed at her eyes, desperately trying to force useless tears back into her stupid face because what sort of man could lie so blatantly. It's obvious somebody was there. She'd heard her with her own ears. Leigh was not alone, and he did not deserve her tears, Isla knew it. She totally knew it.

She was not going to cry.

She was not going to cry.

She was not going to . . . She was crying.

42

Leigh dialled Isla's number. 'Pick up, pick up. Pick up!' She red buttoned him. He dialled again. 'Please, Isla. Pick up. And you, you flea-infested feathered shit bag. Zip it. I don't want to . . . '

'Hi, this is Isla. Please leave a message after the tone.'

'Isla, Isla, please. Let me explain.' He held the phone out to check the signal. It had gone. And nowhere in the hotel room gave him anything. Not even back at the window, phone to his ear, head pressed against cold glass.

'Sad face.' Tarquin hopped about his cage.

'Right. Come on then. You owe me,' Leigh opened the camera on his phone, flicking it on to video. 'Say it again.'

Tarquin looked at him.

'Speak!'

Tarquin hopped off his perch and fussed around with some bread at the bottom of his cage.

Leigh tapped on the cage to get his attention. 'Speak!'

Tarquin pecked at his finger.

'You little—' He stuck his finger in his mouth and instead took a photo. Tapping out a message.

> Meet Tarquin. A talking African Grey parrot that I have looked after since the divorce because Serena wouldn't take him and I felt bad about getting rid of him. He's a nightmare. He's with me here because it was such short notice, I couldn't get anyone to feed him and now I'm stuck up here, at the tip of the middle of nowhere and I can't do anything other than plead with you.

Leigh looked at the message he'd tapped out. A desperate attempt to justify his position. If he ever got a text like that, he'd have laughed. What a pathetic excuse it would sound like. A load of rubbish. She'd never believe him and why should she? Five cheap dates and a night of incredible sex did not a love match make.

Yet, Leigh knew that his connection with Isla had been different.

And once again, however tenuous it appeared to be, Serena had ruined it for him, or maybe he'd ruined it for himself. A bit more backbone and he'd never have taken Tarquin in. Even more, and he'd have left his job months ago.

Basically, this was nothing less than he deserved.

43

Isla left work bang on five. She was exhausted after spending the whole day pretending to Doris that she was totally fine, had had a lovely weekend and no, she did not want to talk about it, while avoiding Prudence, who didn't appear to know anything of her disastrous date with Rupert . . . yet. Surely it was only a matter of time?

Sophie was cooking when she got back. 'Pay day, I'm making a pie. Chicken, bacon and leek. You want some?'

'How uncharacteristically homely of you. Yes, absolutely. I think I have some slightly sad-looking cabbage I could attempt to revive with garlic, if you'd like?'

'Oh, OK. Sure. That'd be nice. Jay bought wine, too. Help yourself.'

'Wine as well. It's almost like you saw into my weekend, understood it for the pain and torture it was, and morphed yourselves into the best housemates ever. Honestly, this is so needed.'

Sophie nodded towards the wine. 'You want to tell me about it?'

Isla opened it and poured three glasses, making a mental note to return the favour when she'd been paid. 'Not really. I want to eat pie and drink wine and smash out a few more episodes of *Downton Abbey*.'

'Fair enough.'

They busied about the kitchen, relaxed in familiarity. 'This is good wine,' Isla said later, appreciatively, as she stirred up the shredded cabbage with bits of white onion she'd found at the back of the fridge. If she doused it all in garlic granules too, it would be perfectly acceptable. 'I feel bad, drinking it all.'

'No, no. Don't feel bad. Enjoy it. We have more.'

'Wow, you two won the lottery?'

'No, no, we just fancied . . . more?'

'You sure?'

'Of course!'

Jay arrived. He kissed Sophie on the cheek and squeezed Isla's shoulder in the kind of friendly way that she had grown to like.

'Oh, by the way, Mum and Dad are coming back for a bit.'

'Where've they been?' asked Jay, pouring himself the last of the wine before placing a new bottle of red on the table.

'Portugal. Well, they've been all over. Travelling Europe in a van. I can't wait to have them here.'

'That's going to be so nice,' said Sophie. 'I'm chuffed for you!'

'Yeah. Maybe we could have them over, cook them a roast here. I'd love them to meet you Jay. They adore Sophie so would really like to see her, well you both, happy.'

Jay sipped his wine. 'Oh . . . yeah, that sounds . . . '

'Can you get the plates?' instructed Sophie, and he obeyed.

'How hungry are you?' she asked Isla.

Isla thought about it for a moment. 'Starving.' She'd never been the kind of woman who lost her appetite. Happy = hungry. Sad = hungry. Hormonal = hungry with added wine, Cadbury Twirl and Cool Original Doritos.

'There you go.' Sophie passed her a plate with a giant slab of steaming pie on it. The cabbage had come up all right too and Jay had whipped up some gravy, and even though it was only Bisto, it smelled and tasted wonderful. There was a time and a place for gravy granules and that time and place was now. And there.

'Oh, Soph,' said Isla, shoving another mouthful in. 'This is . . . ' she 'chef's kissed' then coupled up more pie with cabbage and yeah, she'd revived it. She'd revived it good. And sometimes this was all you needed in life: good food and delicious wine and beautiful friends who'd found something lovely together. It was moments like this that reminded Isla she just needed to look at the positives and be grateful for all she did have, not sad for all she didn't.

'So, Isla.' Sophie pushed her plate away and cradled her wine. 'Jay and I need to talk to you.'

'Go on,' Isla said, passing Jay her glass because he'd offered her another one and as if she was going to say no.

'Jay and I are moving in together.'

'What? Your room's not big enough for the two of you! You'd never get all your clothes in, for starters. I suppose you could use his room as a wardrobe though, eh? Or better still, we can get another housemate in and drop the bills even more? Maybe I could move into one of your rooms and you could have mine? It's a bit bigger, I think?'

Sophie looked at Jay who looked at Sophie before they both looked back to Isla and Isla knew she'd got it wrong.

'Oh. I see.' She put her glass down, their generosity with the wine suddenly feeling a bit suspect.

'We didn't know how to tell you,' said Jay.

'Because we love you and we don't want to lie to you and I know this is shit timing for you, what with the last month or so.'

'It's fine,' said Isla, quietly.

'It just all happened so quickly because this place came up to rent through Jay's work and it was too good an offer to turn down.'

'It's fine,' said Isla again.

'And you'll be welcome to come over any time you like. We really want you to come see us.'

Sophie nodded enthusiastically. 'And maybe even stay. On a weekend. When we've all cooked and eaten and had wine and it's too late for you to walk home. There's a lovely little box room and I'll make sure the bed is super comfy for you and even though it's only a single bed, it's yours. Whenever you want it.'

Jay looked at Sophie and if Isla was going to guess what he was silently saying to her, it would be something along the lines of: not *whenever* she wants it!

Isla dug deep. 'This is brilliant, you two. Honestly, I'm thrilled for you, I really am.' Isla drained her suspicious wine on the basis that after that conversation, it was better than no wine at all. 'You two are perfect together.'

'And we don't want to leave you stranded. So we asked around at my place and at Jay's. There's a few people who might be interested to rent a room. And Mark is on the case. He says he's got a few people lined up to look. Someone came round the other day, I think she really liked it.'

Isla remembered the stranger with them both and could have kicked herself for not being more inquisitive of who she had been. Not that it would have changed anything. Not that the outcome would be any different. She was about to be left behind. Left to pay the bills on her own until their landlord found someone else and then who would that be, and how could they be as lovely as Sophie? And Jay, for that matter. Would they consider how long they were in the shower for, or how high they turned the thermostat? Would they be careful of switching lights off and would they ever want to share their delicious pie and tasty wine in exchange for on-the-edge cabbage?

'We're really sorry, Isla.'

Isla dug her nails into the palm of her hand. 'Hey. It's fine. You two deserve happiness and I just know that this is going to be great for you. You've definitely brought out the best in her, Jay. And I can't speak to what she's brought out in you because up until a few months ago, I didn't even know you.'

'We know it's all been a bit quick.'

'No, no. I didn't mean it like that,' Isla squirmed and bit the inside of her mouth. 'I'm happy for you. Honestly. I really am. Oh, did you hear that?'

'What?' Sophie and Jay listened.

'I think that was my phone. Mum said she'd get Dad to ring me tonight. I need to catch up with him about their plans, see if they need any help. Look, this was delicious. Thank you so much for sharing your wine. I feel a bit bad—'

'No. Please don't. It was for us all to share. A celebration,' said Jay, then seemed to immediately regret it.

44

Leigh stood on his bed, leaning against the wall, head as high as it would reach where the signal seemed to be most stable. 'That sounds amazing, no, I'm really chuffed. Thanks, Dave. Yes. I'll sort that out and let you know. I can't wait. I'm really going to enjoy the challenge. Thank you.'

Serena let herself into Leigh's room as he hung up his phone call and jumped down on to the floor.

'You could at least knock,' he said, turning the radio back on.

'It's the middle of the afternoon and I'm paying you to work, so forgive me if I don't feel like I need your permission to check up on you. And that didn't look like a work call.'

'It wasn't.'

'On your work phone.'

'They called me.'

Leigh sat back at his laptop and began resizing a logo he hadn't quite got the dimensions right on. Serena picked through some designs he had asked reception to print off for him earlier. 'They're only black and white, there's no colour printer. But I figured that, alongside my laptop, the client could see what it might look like in various formats. They may just have to use their imagination.'

'Because clients are notoriously good at that.'

'What else do you want me to do? Hand draw and paint every single one of them? Because that kind of design stopped years ago and I'm not much of a painter.' He stared at her for just a second too long. Serena thinned her lips as best as her filler would allow.

'I think we should keep it down to three options, tops,' he said. 'Too many and we'll confuse them. We need to be confident about what we're offering. *I* am confident about what we're offering.'

'We need them to be happy,' she said, tersely.

'They will be. Because I'm good at what I do. Look, this is the one they should go for.' He picked out one of the logos and passed it to her for inspection.

'I don't like it.'

'Serena.'

She looked at him. 'What? I don't. I think it's weak. I think that's not what they asked for and I think you're not focussing properly.'

'I'm in a hotel room with zero internet, a parrot that pipes up every two minutes, and the continual threat of you walking in whenever you want.'

'Let's play!'

'See.'

'You don't get to hand your notice in, then coast the time out, Leigh. I'm paying you fairly. You're a good designer, you're certainly better than this.' She cast the artwork aside.

'This is not me coasting. This is some of my best work and you know it as well as I do.' He paused, considered whether to add anything and decided, what the heck. 'You're just feeling sour.'

She spun around. 'What do you expect? I laid down my feelings to you, Leigh. I showed you my vulnerable side and you kicked me in the teeth.'

Leigh looked at her veneers.

'I'm going to have to cancel your flight out. This isn't good enough.'

'I can do this from anywhere, Serena. I don't have to be tied to this place, just to deliver you logos.'

'And that's where your problem is. This isn't about logos, Leigh. This is an entire brand identity. That's why I need you here, to keep you focussed.'

Tarquin squawked, 'Feeling sour!'

'For goodness sake, will you shut that bird up!'

'I could stuff him?'

'Don't be obscene.'

'Sorry, Tarquin.' Leigh went to move his sheet over the cage. 'I didn't mean it. Some of us give a shit about you. Despite . . . everything.'

Leigh filled his kettle up in the hotel bathroom. 'I am not stopping. I'm aware this is a full rebrand, not "just a logo", and also that you wanted a report. I'll do it all. From home. Even if I have to pay for my own flight.'

Serena gave him the kind of look that said yeah, sure, of course you have the spare money to do that.

'I've got a new job.'

'You've what!'

'I've just accepted it. For a pretty cool agency. They want me to start as soon as possible. I hope that, once I've delivered on this job, as you know I will, that I can appeal to your more amenable nature and you'll let me go. There's no need for me to serve a full three months. I can hand over to one of the team. Gary, he's pretty good at this sort of thing. Or Mike. He could do it too. In fact, Mike would be a perfect fit, it seems to me that the Head of Comms at the Shetland Tourism Board likes to flirt and he's always up for that.'

'You have a contract, Leigh. You have an obligation.'

Leigh paused, then turned to face her dead on. 'We had a contract, Serena. The one we agreed when we married.'

'That's entirely different.'

'Is it?'

Serena adjusted her posture. She was trying to match him, but he could see it in her face. She was going to fold, he just had to keep up the pressure. Even though it was making him really uncomfortable, and this was the last time he was ever going to be so bloody confrontational with her.

'You know it is.'

Her right eye flinched with the tick she got when she was nervous. 'I was going to offer you a pay rise, actually. To stay. You could do with the money. I know how bad you are with all of that and Christ knows how much worse it's got now I'm not there to keep on top of it all for you.' She stepped towards him. Eye still twitching. 'You need me in your life, Leigh. However much you think you can walk away; you need someone in your life who can keep you in check. Keep you organised. Keep you focussed on the task in hand. You'd be crazy to leave. I won't let you do that to yourself.' She paused. Then went to reach for a button on her blouse which they both knew was probably her most desperate measure yet.

Leigh stepped back, shaking his head. 'Unbelievable.' He went to his door, opening it wide. 'I will stay until Friday, Serena. Then I'm going, whether you pay for my flight or I do. You will have all the work you need, when you need it, and they will love what I have designed for them because however much you like to tell me that I'm nothing without you, it's not true. I'm a grown man, who's pretty great at what he does. And you are not going to push me around anymore.'

Serena stared. She went to say something. And for the first time since they'd first met that night in a bar, when Leigh should have trusted his instinct instead of his ego, she stopped herself, fixed her eyes on the door and left.

He slammed the door behind her. And high fived an imaginary onlooker.

Then sat down at his laptop and brought up the *Sheffield Gazette* web page.

45

Doris handed Isla a steaming mug; her first hot chocolate of the summer. Untraditional as it was at this time of year, Lord knew she needed a bit of comfort, and this stuff smelled of actual nectar . . . Isla to take a deep breath in.

'It's called a Velvetiser,' said Doris. 'Ged bought it for me as a little present and, at first, I was disappointed, it wasn't really the kind of gadget I had in mind for us but then I tried it and . . . well. Go on.'

Isla took another sniff, then sipped at it. 'Oh. My. God.'

'I don't think I've ever had anything so silky in my life. And you should have seen some of the undergarments I had in my twenties.'

'How? How does it make it this perfect?'

'I can't answer that. Though I suspect the little splash of Bailey's helped.'

'Bailey's! Doris, I'm supposed to be working.'

'Yes, yes. But it's board games day, isn't it. And so long as nobody gets the Twister out again, I think we'll all be fine.'

Isla sank down into Doris's chair, her hands clasped round the white, porcelain mug filled with seventy per cent cocoa deliciousness. She took another sip and gazed out the window.

Doris tidied her skirt, removing some imaginary fluff from it. 'It's so hard to see you like this,' she said, avoiding Isla's gaze.

'Like what?' Isla could feel Doris playing her. Not in a mean way, but in the way that people who care about you manage to somehow upset the emotional applecart. The one that, in this case, Isla had been clinging on to for dear life.

'Well, like your duck's been knocked off.' Isla tried to look puzzled. 'Your light's been extinguished. You're flat, Isla. You're not your usual bubbly self.'

'Oh, I see.'

'No man, or men, should ever make you feel like this.'

'I know, and they don't. They haven't.'

Doris gave Isla a look that said she didn't believe her.

'OK, maybe. But it's not just that. My housemates, Sophie and Jay. They're moving out.'

'Oh.'

'We were a team. Like a little family. Us against the landlord and the world. And he's not a bad landlord, but he's still a landlord. So, until I get new housemates all the bills will be my responsibility and that's a worry.'

'Your old housemates can't just move out and leave you high and dry.'

'No. They can't. But they also can't start a new life in their new place if they're flat broke from trying to keep me afloat. I'm a grown woman!'

Doris relented.

'What if I don't like them?'

Doris was losing track.

'The new housemates! What if I end up sharing a house with awful, horrible people.'

'Hey, you never know. It might be the love of your life about to walk through your front door.'

'I think I'm done with all that, don't you?'

'I think you're done with the Ruperts of this world. I never did like him. Shifty looking. Prudence said as much herself.'

'Prudence sang his praises! Said he was a nice young man – and I quote – if she'd been fifty years younger!'

'Yes, because she thought you'd bring out the best in him. The whole family think he needs a good woman to stop his wandering ways. She'd not actually seen him in years, that's why he kept having to re-introduce himself to her. Anyway, he'd worked out that she was living where you worked and he decided it was high time he visited his old favourite Aunt Prudence.'

'I can't believe it. That's . . . no, surely not.'

'She swears. He's a wrong 'un. I think she feels pretty bad about it actually. Knows you deserve way better than him.' Doris paused, then added, 'He once shoved his sister's face right into a chocolate gateau.'

'Bet it wasn't a frozen one from Iceland.'

'I suspect not. Prudence says they are awfully well off. She's not from the money side, however well to do she looks. That's how she's ended up here.'

'Hey! Here's lovely.'

'Well, yes, it is. But, if I had an international hotel chain in my family, I'd be looking for a bit more than an en suite room in a care home up Nether Edge, wouldn't you?'

'I mean . . . Is it really an international hotel chain?'

'Parkers! Yes.'

'Wow. I didn't draw the connection.'

'Prudence says he swoops in, buys out struggling hotels and wraps them all up in the chain. Honestly, that woman is sharp as a tack. She knows full well that they could afford to put her somewhere nice if they wanted to. And room eleven too!'

'There's nothing wrong with room eleven, Doris.'

'You try telling Irene, Wilfred and Cynthia that.'

Isla laughed, unsettled.

'Besides, Rupert was handsome, wasn't he? And you needed someone to put a smile on your face. I thought maybe the two of you could have a bit of fun.'

'I wasn't looking for fun.'

'I know, love. I do.' Doris patted Isla's hand. 'I never imagined I'd find happiness again. After George. I thought that was it, it was done. I'd been lucky to love so fully, so completely, that I couldn't imagine ever feeling anything for anyone ever again.'

'You're not about to tell me that you're in love with Ged, are you?'

'Oh, heavens. No. But there was someone, after my George. I fell hook, line and sinker. I couldn't believe I was getting another go at it.'

'And? What happened?'

'What happened?' Doris studied Isla, carefully. 'I got in the way of myself. I second guessed and I tried too hard. I was, what must I have been, sixty-two? So, you know, compared to now, still young. I had both original knees and good hips. But I think I was so worried about the idea of losing someone again that I couldn't quite let go. I don't know, maybe I didn't trust him fully. Maybe I didn't trust myself. Maybe I just couldn't quite believe I deserved to be loved in the way that I think he loved me.'

Isla swallowed. There was a sadness in Doris's eyes that she'd never seen before.

'Don't get in the way of yourself, Isla. Not now, not ever. I can't say, maybe that Leigh fella wasn't for you in the end, though I'm surprised. I know you look around and see all your friends happy, in love, trying for babies, settling down. And I know you feel like it's maybe not going to happen for you.'

'Doris—'

'But what if it did, if you just took that leap of faith?'

'I will, Doris. If the chance comes again, I'll take a leap of faith. Like all the other leaps of faith I've taken in my life. I'm not afraid to leap, I promise.'

Doris raised her eyebrows and finished her hot chocolate.

'I'd better get on. If I don't track down where the candlestick went from the Cluedo set, we might have an actual murder on our hands.'

'Check Sylvia's room. Kleptomaniac that one.'

'Doris!'

Doris turned to face the window. No further questions.

'I'll wash this and bring it back later, OK?' said Isla about the mug. 'Thanks, it was delicious. I am definitely putting a Velvetiser on my Christmas list.'

Isla wandered down the hallway. She'd always been up for taking a leap of faith, hadn't she? She laid herself bare on dates. Literally in Leigh's case. She hadn't held back or second guessed herself. Had she?

She rinsed the mug out, squeezing soapy water and letting it overflow as she gazed out the window. What if she had got in the way of herself?

But she'd heard Serena's voice; she was still in love with Leigh.

46

Isla had managed to avoid Jay and Sophie while doing her laundry, though she wondered if maybe they were avoiding her a little bit too. It's not that she didn't want to see them, just that they kept nipping off to Ikea, and not just for the meatballs. She also didn't begrudge them a mooch around flatpack showrooms with a delicious and cheap pork-based snack in the middle, it's just that it was all becoming very real. They'd bought a pack of tealights. Together. Joint ownership of tealights could only mean one thing: they wanted an ambience in their new place that was cosy and homely, far homelier than the home they currently shared with her. Isla tried to convince herself she definitely preferred the fairly harsh strip light of their shared kitchen but couldn't help but remember how nice the ambient lighting in Rafters had been.

She stared at the pile of odd socks she'd pulled from the washing line, then shoved them in a bag with all the other odd socks that she'd one day try and match up; when she was bored, which would probably happen sooner than she cared to think about because she had well and truly leaned into that feeling of not wanting to do anything or see anyone or go anywhere, other than work. And as Bill had called her into a meeting on Friday afternoon, she wasn't sure she wanted to go there either. How long before she found herself zoning out in front of the telly, comfort-eating biscuits, and staying awake way later than her drooping eyes would like? A dangerous kind of bored. The kind that nothing and nobody could shift. Something really exciting could happen and she'd likely look up and say, meh.

She'd be like a sloth.

A biscuit-eating sloth.

A biscuit-eating, hibernating, jobless sloth.

Her laptop sprang into life with a FaceTime. The photo of her mum and dad that came up anytime they called hovered on the screen. They'd be back in four weeks. And it couldn't come soon enough.

'Hey!'

'Isla, your mum's found a comfy chair on Facebook marketplace, she wondered if you could pop to Broomhill to pick it up for us?'

'Aren't you supposed to be travelling light if you're renting? What you going to do with it when you head off again? And I don't have a car, Dad.' She glanced around her bedsit. 'Or anywhere to store it until you get here.'

'We'll sell it. Or you can have it. I've got to watch my sciatica, love. That needs decent support.' He lowered his voice. 'Your mum likes to think she's patient and caring about it but if I start complaining she'll have no truck for it. I love your mother, Isla, but she'd have made a terrible nurse.'

Isla smiled, nostalgically. 'I do remember her inability to cope when I got poorly.'

'Do you remember that time you had measles? They were all over. On your eyes! She took one look at you, dosed you up on Calpol and dragged you down the shops. I tried not to blame her for the fact that you were basically bed bound for four days afterwards, but I'm sure a weekly shop down Tesco's is no place for a youngster with a highly contagious disease. Now, I forgot you didn't have a car. I wonder if I could get Tony from the squash club to help?'

Isla tucked her legs up inside her T-shirt, head resting on her hand as her dad talked.

'He owes me a favour. And he's got one of them Citroen Berlingos. You could get a comfy chair in a Citroen Berlingo, couldn't you?'

'I think that's their advertising tagline, isn't it?' Isla smirked to herself.

'Is it?' Her dad asked, innocently.

'Peter? Have you told her?' Isla's mum appeared over her dad's shoulder.

'Give me chance, wo—'

'Don't you dare call me woman! Do you know, your father, sometimes . . . ' she tutted and shook her head, then took the phone off him. 'Isla, have you seen the paper?'

Her tone was impatient. Isla wasn't sure what she'd done to deserve it. Though it probably had nothing to do with her and everything to do with her dad's sciatica and the comfy chair. She was taking a risk though when she said, 'Which one?'

'Isla, don't play the fool, it doesn't suit you.'

Isla groaned. Her mum was taking no prisoners today. 'No. I've tended to avoid it lately, Mum. For obvious reasons.'

'Well, I was having a look for curtains in the free ads, I know, I heard you, we should be travelling light but I do like to make a home and nobody needs to see your father changing into his pyjamas come 9 p.m. Anyway, that's not the point. So I'm searching through the free ads, there's juicers, there's bed frames, there's the odd mattress – though I can't imagine buying a mattress off a free ad, can you? And just above an ad for one of those ab crunching machines, which I do not approve of, by the way. You know, we're supposed to have a bit of fat on our belly to protect our organs, and our unborn children, should we choose to have them, which of course we don't all have to.'

'Mum.'

'Sorry. So, just above the ab crunch ad, there's an ad that fair took my eye. In fact, I can't believe I almost missed it. Hang on, I'm going to read it to you.'

Isla wondered how long this chat was going to go on for and if she'd have the chance to boil the kettle for some noodles before Jay and/or Sophie came back.

'Desperately Seeking Isla.'

Isla looked up. Her mum raised her eyebrows in the way she used to when Isla was a kid. It meant pay attention.

'Desperately Seeking Isla,' she repeated. 'And another chance. No experience necessary, just an open heart. And a willingness to talk.' She put the paper down with an expression on her face that said, well, would you believe it. 'I mean, it's like a movie.'

'Richard Curtis would love it!' dropped in her dad.

Her mum stared at him for a second. 'Makes me wonder why you weren't ever this romantic?'

He smiled at her, which Isla saw thawed her. 'I make you coffee every morning, so you don't have to get out of bed.' He kissed the top of her head. 'Romance takes a different form after thirty years,' he said, retreating.

Her mum paused for a second, watching him. 'Well, yes, I suppose that is quite lovely.' She raised her voice after him. 'Though sometimes you could fill the mug up to the top.' She turned back to Isla. 'So what do you think?'

'I don't know. What else does it say?'

She ran back down the ad, muttering what had already been said. It says "Meet me here, this Friday". Then there's some coordinates. "For the ultimate cheap date".

'Is it signed?'

'Erm . . . '

'Because how do I know it's for me, if it's not signed.'

'Isla, who else would it be for? Honestly, sometimes I do wonder.'

'There were other people on those cheap dates.'

'Not called Isla,' shouted her dad's voice.

Isla grabbed for her phone and pulled up the *Gazette* website. On the home page, there was a story about how a man's romantic intentions had been scuppered by his pet parrot doing a perfect impression of his . . . ex-wife. Isla clicked on the article. Gawped at it . . . and the picture of Leigh in it. No. Surely not. She looked around the room. Was someone about to jump out with a camera? Was Michael McIntyre in on this?

'Have you found it?' Her mum was trying to peer down the laptop screen to get a better look, as if she'd be able to see what Isla was reading.

'No. Just . . . ' She flicked the website away. 'Do you know what, no. This is ridiculous. It's all very well, all very romantic, but no. I can't. I'm just . . . no.'

Her dad was now back beside her mum. Huddled together in the camper, they looked at each other, then back to Isla, then at each other again. Her dad nodded, her mum got comfy. 'What's going on, love?' she asked.

'Nothing.'

They looked at each other again.

'There! That! That's what's going on.'

Her parents looked confused.

'You two. Christ, he might pour a stingy coffee, but he knows what you're saying without you using words. He knows you're a terrible nurse and you know he's got latent misogynist tendencies.'

'Hey!' protested her dad.

'It's just every now and then,' said her mum, patting his hand. 'You're a product of your generation. Not that that's an excuse per se, it's just . . . look, never mind that. Isla, what are you saying?'

'I'm saying, how can I possibly compete with this?'

'With what?'

She waved her hands in the direction of her mum and dad who sat in perfect mirror of one another, staring at her. 'You two! This show. You love the very bones of each other. You're *in* love with each other.'

'It's tested when she passes wind.'

'Peter! What about a lady's dignity.'

'Are you a feminist or not? You can't have it both ways, Marion.'

'You want to bet?' There was a pause. Marion stared at Peter and made it clear that she was not going to tolerate any more of his nonsense. Then she softened and kissed him on the cheek and his eyes flashed and hers warmed and Isla's point was proven.

'I will never have what you have. I just don't think it's possible anymore. I don't think relationships like yours exist anymore. The world is different, we're all different. And . . .

' She gritted her teeth together to buy herself a moment. 'And why would I want anything less?'

Isla's phone pinged with a message then her heart lurched. 'It's from Leigh.'

'And?'

'What does it say?'

Isla closed her eyes.

'Isla Rose Philipson. What. Does it. Say?'

'Mum. I can't do this.'

'Of course you can,' said her dad, taking the phone from her mum's hand. 'We did not raise a quitter. Now put your big girl pants on and read the blooming message.'

'Dad!'

'Sorry, was that a bit harsh? I don't know what came over me.'

'Your dad's right, come on.'

Isla held up her phone and opened the message. She adjusted her composure and read aloud.

> I am hoping you have seen the ad I took out in the paper. I was trying to make a grand gesture then realised if you were anything like me, you'd have been avoiding the Gazette since things went pear shaped. We stumbled. It was my fault. I should have just told you what was going off. Serena—

'Who's Serena?'

'His ex-wife.'

'Oh, that's right.'

Serena rocked up just before you were due to arrive at mine. Declared her undying love. I didn't know what to do. I didn't want you two to meet cos I know what she's like, she'd have made a scene. So I panicked and sent you that ridiculous message out of the blue. Then, when I told her I wasn't interested and that I was looking for another job, she dragged me away with work as if she thought she could persuade me if we just spent enough time on our own. She couldn't have, there is nothing Serena could say that would make me want to get back together with her. I was stuck in the furthest part of the British Isles with no signal and a parrot that I couldn't get anyone to look after.

'A parrot? Who has a parrot?'
'He does. Apparently.'

You should meet him. He's called Tarquin. An utter git. And then when I eventually got signal, I saw the cheap dates roundup, how they suggested I was getting back together with Serena and I couldn't believe it.

She's flat out denied saying anything to them, but I know what she's like. If she thought she could get in the way, buy herself a bit more time, she'd do whatever it took.

I left her in the Shetland Islands yesterday. She can think and say what she likes, I am done. I'm ready to start my new life and I really want to start that knowing you are by my side.

If you say no now, to this last cheap date, I will totally and utterly respect your choice. But if there is even a glimmer of hope for us, please come and meet me. I've chosen Surprise View, up Hathersage. And I've arranged for Sophie and Jay to give you a lift. I hope you don't mind. Turns out Jay is a mate of Jim's and through six degrees of separation . . . never mind. This is an unfeasibly long message . . . '

Through glassy eyes, Isla laughed.

. . . I hope you'll come meet me. Love, Leigh. X

47

'I can't believe you two have been hatching this little plan.'

Sophie stood back to assess her makeup artistry, having taken over from Isla when it was clear she was too nervous to do it herself. She'd gone in a bit heavy-handed on the eyebrows meaning Sophie had to start again.

'I thought you were avoiding me!' added Isla, phone in hand just in case Leigh messaged.

'As if! Why would I avoid you?'

'Well, cos of moving out.'

Jay fiddled with a mascara wand, immediately having it taken out of his hands by Sophie. 'Yeah, we should have said. We're actually moving out because we've suddenly decided you're really terrible company. We said it was to be together, but in fact we've found a whole load of new housemates and we're going to live life to the fullest. Because we really hate *Downton Abbey*.'

Sophie smacked him on the arm.

'If you hate *Downton Abbey* then basically you hate me, so . . . '

Sophie spun her round to face the mirror. 'There, you look . . . gorgeous. Beautiful. I've tried not to go too heavy on the eye, I know you like the natural look.'

Jay wolf-whistled.

'Bit degrading,' said Sophie with a grin.

'Sorry. But she does look, you do look . . . '

'All right, thank you!' Sophie pushed Jay out of the way. 'Three months and he's already got a roving eye.'

He grabbed her round the waist. 'There is nobody in this world for me except you.'

'Ahhh, that's . . . ahhh. You're so sweet. What did I do to deserve you?'

As Jay and Sophie cooed at one another, Isla stepped towards the mirror. She looked . . . amazing, even if she thought so herself. Hair up, makeup done. She'd chosen a simple outfit, just jeans and a jumper with a long trench coat for when it got chilly. But Sophie had persuaded her to go with some extra jewellery and a pair of heeled boots she'd found in a charity shop up Ecclesall Road.

She looked like a version of Isla she would want to be if she had the time and the energy and the money, even. But . . . maybe that version wasn't who she needed to be tonight, if she was really going to see if this 'thing' with Leigh had any potential whatsoever.

You know, you don't have to make yourself pretty for anybody.

She reached for a facecloth, running it under the little sink in the corner of her room. Wiping her face, she got rid of the lot.

'Hey! What are you doing? We'll be late if I have to do that all over again.'

'No. I don't want you to.'

'What do you mean?'

Isla stared at herself in the mirror. Face clean, fresh, as if she was about to get in bed. She unhooked the earrings and stripped off all the jewellery. She unzipped the boots and reached for her trusty converse trainers. 'I've been on too many dates, trying to be somebody I'm not.'

'OK, it's just . . . I gave you really good cheekbones.'

'And you can again, another day. But today . . . it's just me. If it's not good enough for him, then he's not good enough for me.'

Sophie looked at her proudly.

'Don't look at me like that. I might change my mind.'

'I'm not looking at you like anything. Can we at least Dawn O'Porter your fringe?'

'Go on then.'

'It's going to work out you know,' said Sophie, as that teensy bit of worrying steam rose from Isla's hair. 'Especially after today! If you believed in gods, I'd say they are on your side.'

'I know. I can't believe it. I just saw the worst, I couldn't have imagined it would work out like that.' Isla had taken a large bag with her to work that day, ready to pack up her cupboard after her meeting with Bill. But instead, the meeting had ended with her saying that yes, she would consider being based out of another home if it gave her a bigger office, so long as she was allowed to spend equal time across all three sites. They were consolidating, taking some of the homes out of the group so that they could focus fully on the ones they had, and promoting Isla to Events and Entertainment Manager for all three homes. It was more work, a member of staff that she would have to manage, and probably not as much money for the extra responsibility as she deserved, but compared to what she'd expected, she wasn't going to complain.

Ella had just been made redundant and Poppy couldn't make this year's Christmas gathering because she was going to have to move away with Steve and his new job. It was a blow to them all and Tracy had made them all agree that next year they'd plan it so they could definitely be together. But it had all made Isla think, she'd wasted so much time and energy comparing her life to other people's. As Doris had told her, there was no beauty in perfection. And perfection didn't exist anyway.

Fringe done – and set with a bit of hairspray, because although Isla was keen to be herself she hadn't lost all her faculties – she nodded an approval of herself into the mirror.

'Come on,' said Sophie, offering up an arm. 'Get in the car, let's get you to this cheap date.'

'Are you sure it's OK? I can give you petrol money.'

Jay held the door open to a battered Ford Fiesta he and Sophie had gone halves on. They'd called it Felicity. 'No need. The paper sent some over to pay for fuel. Basically, they've had so many letters asking for an update on what happened between the pair of you that they were happy to pay for this on the understanding they could print one last and final update.'

'What if it fails?' said Isla, now terrified.

'What if it doesn't!' said Sophie, with a nudge.

'You've read too many memes.'

'Come on. Get in!'

The road twisted and snaked through moorland, and the further away from the city they got, the more Isla wondered if she'd made a terrible mistake. 'Have you got any lipstick?' She asked Sophie.

'Nope.'

'Mascara?'

'Nope.'

'Dignity. Have you got any spare dignity? Just in case I lose mine again. Oh, why am I doing this? I don't need to do this.'

'Of course you don't need to. But you know as well as I do, this thing with Leigh wasn't over.'

'What if we realise today that it should have been?'

'Then you'll know. And it can all go away.'

They turned the corner. The Peak District stretched out before them in all its sunsetting glory. And as they pulled into the car park of Surprise View, the door of another car opened. And out climbed Leigh.

Isla's heart flipped.

48

No sooner had Isla closed the car door did Jay drive off. Isla suspected Sophie was furious about a missed opportunity to spy for just a moment, judging by how much she strained to watch them as they disappeared out of view.

Isla looked to the ground, then up at a sky full of pinks, yellows and oranges as far as she could see.

'Pretty incredible, isn't it?' said Leigh, following her gaze.

'Just a bit,' agreed Isla, breathless.

He studied her face. His was warmed by the light, but just as beautiful as that first night they met.

'Hey,' he said.

'Hey.'

'Thank you for coming.'

'Oh, you know me. Owt for a cheap date.'

He held his hand out for hers. His touch felt warm; the palm of her hand fizzed.

'I cheated a bit,' he said, leading her to a picnic table and sitting her down. 'I brought biscuits. I mean, technically, I suppose I bought them. Not just brought them. But I bought them the other day before I realised I was going to invite you here and then I brought them tonight because I thought they'd be a perfect addition to the tea in a flask that the *Gazette* so generously sent.'

'I like biscuits.'

'I remember. Hobnobs.'

They looked at each other then laughed then fell silent and the silence went on a little bit longer than she would have liked.

'And as you can tell, my date chat has really escalated so I hope you've strapped yourself in,' she said.

'I'm strapped in.' He reached out for one of her hands, taking it with both of his. 'You look beautiful,' he said, seeking out eye contact. 'I think I'd forgotten how beautiful you actually are. I mean, I remembered but . . . now you're here.'

'It's the reflection from the sky. Free Instagram filter.'

'It's also your face.'

She dropped his gaze, the intensity a bit much.

'Tea?'

'Absolutely.'

As he poured steaming tea into two small, plastic mugs, she was reminded of what her mum had said about her dad's coffee making.

'Careful not to spill it, sorry, I maybe overfilled it.'

'Hey, you can never overfill a cup of tea. Or coffee for that matter.'

'Noted.'

They sat, side by side, cradling their drinks, looking out at the view. In silence again, she realised she wasn't actually uncomfortable after all. And in fact, there'd not been many dates in her life that Isla could say she was truly happy to sit in total silence and just be, beside the other person, no need to perform. She could feel the warmth of his arm just brushing hers whenever he took a sip of his drink. Their legs weren't quite touching but either one could make the smallest of moves and they would be. A bird of prey hovered above a field before swooping to the ground. A plane left its vapour trail across the sky as it made its way to Manchester Airport. The pinks and oranges and yellows were lazily turning into pinks and purples and a deep royal blue.

'Biscuit, then?' Leigh offered. 'I'm afraid I failed on the Hobnob front . . . '

They were bourbons. The cheap kind. 'It could have been worse.' Leigh cocked his head to one side. 'Garibaldi.'

'Fair.'

She took a biscuit. 'Thanks.' She deconstructed it with precision. So did Leigh. 'How would you eat a Twix?' she asked.

'Biscuit first. Then roll up the caramel,' he said, as if the answer were obvious.

'Controversial. But correct.'

'Snickers?'

'Nuts first.'

Leigh's eyes flickered with mischief.

'And then the nougat. I will not be drawn by your filth.'

He grinned and finished his biscuit. 'I'm sorry.'

'I'll forgive you.'

He took a breath, moved the packet of biscuits away. 'I mean, I'm sorry. About our last date and me bailing out last minute. I should have taken the time to explain.'

'Oh . . . '

'And then there was no signal on the island at all, I promise. I couldn't believe it. Ridiculous. Even your text to me didn't arrive until after we spoke – our call must have pushed it through. And I wanted to call you back, I wanted a chance to explain it all, but it seemed so far-fetched and I didn't want to push it, I didn't want to push you to breaking point. Like, I knew it was all such a mess with Serena, I needed to sort that out. Like, get the work done. And get out of there. And absolutely make sure she knew that we were done, she and I. Totally, totally done.'

Isla looked at him.

'You are . . . ' he paused. 'That is to say . . . The thing is . . . '

'A star.'

'Yes.'

'No, over there. A star. The first one.'

He turned to face west. A single star shone brightly.

'Isn't it mad to think that that star isn't there anymore.'

'Totally mad.'

'I've never really understood it. Like, it kind of blows my tiny mind. That they're all the way up in the sky, not shining anymore. And here we are, billions of lightyears or whatever it is away, drinking tea and eating bourbon creams.'

'I think that you are the kind of woman I could one hundred per cent fall in love with.'

Isla's heart lurched. The star suddenly seemed less mind-blowing.

'And I'm not saying this because I want you to say anything back. In fact, maybe it would be better if you didn't, but I just need you to know that I am all in. For whatever this is. I think you're incredible. And so beautiful.' He paused, studying her face and, if her now racing heart were to be believed, her entire being. 'Literally everything about you. You're funny and beautiful and so smart and have I mentioned that you're beautiful.'

'No, no, I . . . ' she tried to regain control of herself. 'I don't think you did mention it.'

He looked at her, taking her face in his hands. 'I really, really want to kiss you.'

'Well, if you don't, frankly, I'll be furious.'

Their lips touched, lightly at first; both caught up in an urgency to be connected, yet desperate not to rush it. Suspended between the absolute need to be one and the momentary nervousness of what-could-this-be, what began as a tentative reconnection, ended with the pair entirely wrapped up in each other and the moment until they'd kissed for so long that Isla couldn't see straight.

'Crikey.'

'God, I missed you.'

'Mhm.'

They both held their breath before Leigh eventually said, 'More tea?'

'Yeah. I think that's probably a very good idea.'

'Before we get carried away . . . '

' . . . yeah . . . '

He poured more tea. Offered up more biscuits. He placed his hand around her waist, pulling her into him as Isla lay her head on his shoulder. They stared out at the sky, more stars appearing the longer they looked.

Isla made a decision. 'I've had some really shitty dates. And I've been with some really shitty men. And even this last three weeks, since you and I . . . I went on a couple of dates with this guy who I then realised was a total creep.'

'Rebound dates?'

She flashed him a warning grin.

'Too soon?' he joked.

'Sometimes I'm a bit insecure. And sometimes I jump to conclusions. And sometimes I switch my phone off or block people's numbers because I decide that they must be terrible because that's pretty much what I've always known.'

'I get that.'

'But . . . '

'But?'

'Someone once told me I shouldn't be afraid to fall in love.'

'They are very wise.'

'And so, if you're in. If you're willing to take this, me, just as I am – and this is the face you'd be waking up to because I did not put any makeup on—'

'Yeah, I was going to mention that.'

She nudged him, grinning. 'Then, I'm in. Even if you are a terrible tease.'

He pulled her hand to his chest and placed his other hand over it. 'I'm in.'

49

The Cheap Dates Club: Newsflash!

So whose eagle eyes spotted the ad 'Desperately Seeking Isla'? It turns out we were a bit too quick to judge Leigh, who was not in fact ghosting us or rekindling an old flame. Turns out you can't believe everything you read, or are told on the quiet by someone with an agenda. We are sorry for the confusion, Leigh! Instead Leigh finally returned from an enforced period of technological disconnect in order to lavish a display of his feelings on our Isla, in a date perfectly befitting their time together so far.

'He prepared a picnic, well, biscuits. And we watched the sun go down.'

'She was utterly bewitching. It got dark before we knew it!'

We can't tell you how happy we all were in our little office here up in Sheffield, to realise that our matchmakers were right all along. The experiment has seen success!

And so, as the Cheap Dates Club comes to an end (for now . . .) we're delighted to conclude that sometimes, the very best dates, are also the cheapest.

#TCDCIslaAndLeigh #HappilyEverAfter

Acknowledgements

I wrote and illustrated a book called *The Owl at Home* when I was 6. If you'd told me then, that by 2023 I'd be writing a rom-com for HarperNorth I'd have asked: *Who are they? Do I have a hover board?*, and, *Can I have another bag of Space Invaders?* Crisp mad I was, and ignorant as hell. Though in my defence, HarperNorth didn't exist in 1983 and even if they had, I've read *The Owl at Home* and not only is it not a rom-com, the plotline is flawed and the characters are one dimensional.

I'm *reeeeally* hoping that none of the above applies to *The Cheap Dates Club* which, I have to tell you, has been an absolute dream to write from start to finish. I have legit loved every minute of it. Even the bit where I couldn't work out how to merge multiple Word documents without losing all the tracked changes, and also the bit where I stared at my laptop screen wondering how to start my acknowledgements.

Which leads me to my acknowledgements.

I am a firm believer that writing a book takes a team. And not just because it makes me feel a bit better about the fact that I don't know if I could ever do it totally alone. Editors are curious, magical creatures who remember things you've said hundreds and thousands of words ago and write brilliant notes like, *have you thought about…* before inserting something genius that you wish you'd thought of yourself. So to Daisy, the magical creature in this particular process, I offer you the hugest thanks. You have embraced me writing a book that I honestly thought I'd never get to write. One in which I have been able to really lean into writing something that I hope will make readers laugh as much as it has done me, at my desk, like a saddo. One in which I've been able to champion my home city, a place that I love. One I've been able to get to the end of writing and not have an existential crisis about, or look at job ads for bus drivers. Which I'm no longer able to do anyway since I got three points on my license. Huge, huge thanks, Daisy. (Not for the points, they were entirely my fault and not at all related to the book.)

Thanks also to the rest of the HarperNorth team who have, I think, created something brilliant in HarperNorth, championing writers from the north, writers writing about the north, writers living in the north, just… the north! Special mention to Taslima, Megan, Alice, and Genevieve. Plus a doffed cap to the copy editing wizadry of Laura G.

A few extra thanks: some of the friends I made at Chatsworth Farm Shop, where I was a seasonal staff member when I started writing the book. Yes, if you recognise your name, it's because I stole it from you. All other details about those particular characters are entirely made up, natch.

Thanks to writing buddy Barbara Copperthwaite who champions me even when I'm being a real whinge bag. Thanks to swim buddies Ian, Rachel and the Mini Biddies, Jo, and the Morning People. You all know who you are, thanks for tolerating my career highs and lows to varying degrees. Thanks also for the cold-water swims – I'm a cold-water swimmer you know. We just can't help ourselves from telling people. Cold water rocks.

Thanks to Cathy Rentzenbrink and Laura Giles for also being excellent champions at a time I really needed it. I hope you can see the confidence instilled, on the pages in this book.

And finally, to Him indoors, the kids, and Henry the dog, sorry I am so intolerable when writing a book. Makes no sense when I love it so much, and yet, we are where we are. Thanks for always being supportive of it, even when it means that sometimes we eat more beans on toast than is advisable for anyone's constitution. I love you.

And finally, to anyone that reads the book, and extra specially if you make it through to the end of these acknowledgements, thank you most of all. It hasn't escaped my notice that you're reading a book about love in a cost-of-living crisis, in a cost-of-living crisis. Without readers like you, writers like me wouldn't get to do this job and honestly, it's my absolute favourite!

Thank you!

Harper North

would like to thank the following staff and contributors for their involvement in making this book a reality:

Fionnuala Barrett
Samuel Birkett
Peter Borcsok
Ciara Briggs
Sarah Burke
Alan Cracknell
Andrew Davis
Jonathan de Peyer
Anna Derkacz
Tom Dunstan
Kate Elton
Sarah Emsley
Laura Gerrard
Simon Gerratt
Monica Green
Natassa Hadjinicolaou
Mayada Ibrahim
Megan Jones
Jean-Marie Kelly
Taslima Khatun
Sammy Luton
Rachel McCarron
Molly McNevin
Alice Murphy-Pyle
Adam Murray
Genevieve Pegg
Agnes Rigou
Florence Shepherd
Eleanor Slater
Emma Sullivan
Katrina Troy
Daisy Watt